CRITICAL ACCLAIM FOR REGINALD HILL,
WINNER OF THE CARTIER DIAMOND
DAGGER AWARD FROM THE CRIME WRITERS'
ASSOCIATION, AND THE DALZIEL/PASCOE
MYSTERY SERIES

"Hill's polished, sophisticated novels are
intelligently written and permeated with his sly and
delightful sense of humor. More than most other
mystery novels, Hill's Dalziel-Pascoe novels are
enjoyable as much for their characters as for their
complicated, suspenseful mystery plots."
—*The Christian Science Monitor*

"The British author's faultless writing, ironic wit
and—above all—recognizably human characters defy
limiting his police stories to the mystery category."
—*Publishers Weekly*

"Hill blends civility and madness in a most
agreeable way."
—*New York*

"Mr. Hill refines his own talent to the highest levels
of mystery fiction."
—*Dallas Morning News*

"Reginald Hill stakes a strong claim as our finest
living male crime writer. . . . The tales of his mid-
Yorkshire police force are now so out in front that
he need not bother looking over his shoulder."
—*The Sunday Telegraph* (London)

Books by Reginald Hill

REGINALD HILL

Asking

for

the

Moon

A DALZIEL/PASCOE MYSTERY

A Dell Book

Published by
Dell Publishing
a division of
Random House, Inc.
1540 Broadway
New York, New York 10036

ISBN: 0-440-22583-3

Reprinted by arrangement with Foul Play Press, a division of W. W. Norton & Company, Inc.

Printed in the United States of America

Published simultaneously in Canada

May 1998

10   9   8   7   6   5   4   3

WCD

TO YOU
DEAR READERS
without whom the writing would be in vain
and
TO YOU
STILL DEARER PURCHASERS
without whom the eating would be infrequent
THIS BOOK IS DEDICATED
in
appreciation
of
your loyalty
in
anticipation
of
your longevity
in admiration
of
your taste
NON SCRIBIT, CUIUS CARMINA NEMO
LEGIT

CONTENTS

THE LAST NATIONAL
SERVICE MAN

'I'M LATE, I'M LATE, for a very important date,' sang Detective Constable Peter Pascoe.

In moments of stress his mind still trawled through the movies in search of a proper reaction.

'It's an immature tic you may grow out of when you've had enough Significant Experience of your own,' an irritated girlfriend had once forecast. 'Ring me when it happens.'

He hadn't rung yet. Surely his move to Mid Yorkshire where they sold Significant Experience by the bucketful would work the cure? But a fortnight into his new job, when he woke to discover he'd slept through his alarm, the section house boiler had failed, and there were three buttons missing from his only clean shirt, he'd immediately dropped into a Kenneth Williams panic routine straight out of *Carry on Constable*.

Sod's Law was confirmed when he got to the station. No time to grab a bite in the canteen, of course; hardly time to grab the essential file from the CID room: then the phone had rung just as he was passing through the door. Not another soul in sight, so like a fool, he'd answered it.

It had been some snout urgently requiring the DCI and not about to push something useful towards a mere DC. Five minutes getting that sorted. Then the Riley reluctant to start; every light at red: traffic crawling at sub-perambulator speeds (did they have different limits up here?); one side of every road dug up (water, or burial of the dead—which had finally arrived?).

And now, in the courts' car park, not a space in sight except one marked RECORDER.

Sod it, thought Pascoe. Little high-pitched instrument played by some geezer in a ruff couldn't need all that much room.

He gunned the Riley in, and was out and running up the steps before the Cerberic attendant could bark more than the first syllable of 'Hey-up!'

Why did the natives need this ritual exordium before they communicated? he wondered. Not properly a greeting, a command or even an exclamation, it was entirely redundant in the vocabulary of a civilized man.

He burst through the swing doors, and thought, 'Hey-up!' as he spotted a familiar face. Well, not really familiar. He'd known it for only two weeks and not even a lifetime could make it familiar. But unforgettable certainly. Straight out of Hammer Films make-up. They'd broken the mould before they made this one, ho ho.

'Sergeant Wield,' he gasped.

'Constable Pascoe,' said Wield. 'Now we've got that out of the way, you're lost.'

'You mean I'm late,' said Pascoe. 'Sorry but—'

'Nay lad. Mr Jorrocks, the magistrate is late, which means you'll not be called for another half-hour. What *you* are is lost. Magistrates' court is in the other wing. This is where the big boys play.'

With that face it was impossible to tell whether you were being bollocked or invited to share a joke. And what was Wield doing here anyway? Checking up? If so he was in the wrong place too . . .

Wield answered the question as if it had been asked.

'Our own big boy's here today,' he said. 'Come back all the way from Wales to give evidence. I need a word.'

'Mr Dalziel, you mean? Oh yes. I heard he was visiting.'

Pascoe knew the name shouldn't be pronounced the way it looked but hadn't quite got the vocalization right. This time, perhaps because of the Welsh connection, it came out as *Dai Zeal.*

Wield's mouth spasmed in what might have been a smile.

'*Dee Ell,*' he said carefully. 'You've not met him yet, have you?'

Detective Constable Pascoe's transfer from South Midlands to Mid-Yorkshire CID had taken place while Detective Chief Inspector Dalziel was in Wales as part of a team investigating allegations of misconduct against certain senior officers. The Fat Man had been pissed off at being turned into what he called 'a bog-brush'. Wield suspected he was going to be even more enraged to discover that the CID boss, Superintendent 'Zombie' Quinn, had taken advantage of his absence to approve the newcomer's transfer.

Trouble was, Pascoe was everything Dalziel disliked: graduate, well spoken, originating south of Sheffield. Wield still had to make his mind up about the lad, but leastways he shouldn't be tossed to a ravening Dalziel without some warning. Not even a bubonic rat deserved that.

'No, but I've heard about him,' said Pascoe neutrally, unaware that Wield's finely tuned ear was well up to detecting the note of prejudgemental disapproval in his voice.

'Come along and see him in action,' said the sergeant. 'You can spare a few minutes.'

'What's the case?' asked Pascoe as they climbed the stairs.

'Sexual assault,' said Wield. 'DCI was leading a drugs raid. Kicked a door open and found what was allegedly a rape in progress.'

'Allegedly?'

'House was a knocking-shop, woman's got three convictions for tomming. Accused's got Martineau defending him. He hates Mr Dalziel's guts.'

That's a lot of hating, thought Pascoe as he tiptoed into the court and had his first glimpse of the bulky figure wedged in the witness box.

Flesh there was in plenty, but more Sydney Greenstreet than Fatty Arbuckle. This was all-in wrestler running to seed rather than middle-aged guzzler running to flab. And if any notion of the comic book fat man remained, it stopped when you moved up from the body to that great granite head which looked like it could carve its way through pack-ice on a polar expedition.

A lemon-lipped barrister with scarcely enough flesh

on him to make one of Dalziel's arms was asking questions in a voice which did not anticipate co-operation or trust. 'So you, Chief Inspector, were the first person through the door?'

'Yes, sir.'

His voice like a ship's cannon booming down a fjord.

'Where you found the defendant and Miss X on the bed, sexually coupled?'

'Yes, sir.'

'Now please think carefully before you answer the next question. Did you *immediately* form the opinion that the defendant was using duress?'

Dalziel thought carefully.

He said, 'No, sir. I did not.'

'Really?' said Martineau, surprise mingling with triumph. 'And why not?'

'Well, I don't expect he had time to put one on, sir.'

When order was restored the judge fixed a stern gaze on Dalziel and said, 'I don't know whether your hearing or your taste is defective, Chief Inspector, but what Mr Martineau wishes to ascertain is whether you *immediately* formed the opinion that sex was taking place against Miss X's will, or was it her subsequent behaviour and allegations which brought up this possibility?'

'Oh aye. I'm with you. It were immediate, m'lud.'

'I see. Perhaps you can explain why.'

'Well, first off, he had his right hand round her throat like he was keeping her quiet by strangling her, and his left hand were holding both her wrists above her head so she couldn't hit him . . .'

Martineau's body and voice shot up together.

'My lord! These assumptions . . .'

'Yes, yes. Mr Dalziel, just describe what you saw without giving us the benefit of your inferences, please.'

'Yes, sir. Sorry. Main thing was, soon as I saw the defendant's face, I said to myself, hello—'

Martineau was now soprano with indignation.

'My lord, witness cannot be allowed to imply—'

'Thank you, Mr Martineau,' interrupted the judge. 'I'm grateful as always for your assistance in points of law, but I'm sure that an officer of Mr Dalziel's standing was not about to say anything contrary to the rules of evidence.'

'Nay, sir!' said Dalziel all injured innocence. 'Tha knows I'd never mention a man's record in court, no matter how rotten it were. All I was going to say was, I said to myself, spotty little scrote like that, I bet he'd have to use force to get his own mother to kiss him goodnight!'

Under cover of the renewed laughter, Wield drew Pascoe out of the court.

'I don't believe it!' exclaimed the younger man as they went back downstairs. 'He's turning the whole thing into music hall. Is he for real?'

'Weren't impressed then?' said Wield.

'Impressed? I was horrified! It's bad enough that poor woman having to go through the trauma of a trial without some insensitive clown playing it for laughs.'

'I did tell you the raid were in a knocking-shop and she's got convictions—'

'And that means she's fair game, does it?' interrupted Pascoe indignantly. 'I thought everyone was entitled to equal protection under the law. Excuse me. I'd better get off to my case.'

Wield watched him stride away. Nice mover, head

held high, good shoulders, slim body, long legs. Lead us not into temptation. Not that there was much chance of that, not in the force. They might be marching for gay rights in San Francisco, but here in Mid Yorkshire, gay was still what poets felt when they saw a bunch of head-tossing daffs. There was even a holiday company in the High Street called Gay Days Ltd. Caused a lot of misunderstanding with tourists from the louche south!

Any road, he couldn't see Constable Pascoe being around long enough to break any hearts. Zombie (which was what Dalziel had christened Detective Superintendent Quinn after catching him enjoying a post-prandial snooze in his office) might propose but everyone knew that in the end Fat Andy disposed.

'Penny for 'em,' said Dalziel who despite his bulk could come up on you like Umslopagaas.

'You'd want change, sir,' said Wield. 'Mr Martineau didn't keep you long.'

'Mebbe it was something I said. I saw you earwigging. Brought a friend, did you?'

Even under forensic assault the Fat Man didn't miss much.

'DC Pascoe. Transfer from South Midlands. Highly recommended, top promotion grades, good on the ground, graduate entry . . .'

'Wash your mouth out, Wieldy! Christ, moment I turn me back, Zombie's trawling the boneyards for the living dead. Where's he at now?'

'Committal proceedings. His first day, stopped two guys on suss by the auction mart. Found they had some weaners in their pick-up and no proof of ownership.'

'Keen bugger. Sounds straightforward. Let's see what kind of a fist Wonderboy makes of it.'

They found 'Wonderboy' under heavy attack from a sharp little solicitor called 'Bomber' Harris.

'So tell us, Detective Constable, what was your reason for being at the back of the market pens?'

'Just passing, sir.'

'Just passing? Along a cul-de-sac whose only function is that of service road to the remoter storage pens of the auction mart?'

'Well, I'm new to the area and I was finding my way about—'

'So, you were lost. And while in this state of uncertainty, you came upon my clients whose driving aroused your suspicions. How so?'

'They were reversing—'

'Out of a narrow cul-de-sac? Sounds reasonable so far. Go on.'

'They looked as if they wanted to get away very quickly.'

'Ah yes. The famous quick getaway. In reverse. And this made you block their path and examine their truck.'

'Yes, sir. That's when I found the piglets.'

'Weaners I believe is the cant term. How many were there?'

'Eight, sir.'

'You counted them?'

'Well, not exactly. They were quite lively and moving around . . .'

'So how can you be sure there were eight?'

'Because,' said Pascoe with an infant teacher's clarity, 'that was how many Mr Partridge said had been stolen.'

Dalziel groaned and ground his teeth.

Bomber Harris smiled.

'Yes, we have heard Mr Partridge's evidence that

on the day in question he had eight weaners stolen from the auction mart. Also that he has since recovered seven. My clients, who should know, state that they had only six in their pick-up. Why incidentally did you fail to make an accurate count, constable?'

'Well, they got away, sir. The defendants let down the tailboard—'

'At your request? To facilitate your inspection.'

'Yes, sir. And the piglets, the weaners, got out and ran off. But they were recovered later—'

'Really? My clients will be glad to hear it, concerned as they are that their compliance with your instructions should have resulted in such a loss of property.'

'I mean that seven were later rounded up which Mr Partridge identified—'

'You will insist on dragging Mr Partridge into this. There is as yet nothing to prove a connection between the eight which he allegedly lost, the seven which he was fortunate enough to recover, and the six which my clients claim are still missing. As things stand, it seems to me what we have here is a serious allegation of crime unsupported by any *corpus delicti* whatsoever.'

'Perhaps, Mr Harris,' said the magistrate who aspired to judicial wit, 'we should say *corpi* as there were six or seven, or even eight, of them.'

'Indeed, sir. *Corpi*. Very good.'

'*Corpora*,' said Pascoe.

'I'm sorry?' said Harris, histrionically puzzled.

'The plural of *corpus* is *corpora*,' explained Pascoe.

And Bomber Harris smiled and said, 'I'm sure we are both grateful to your classical scholarship, Constable Pascoe.'

'Let's get out of here,' growled Dalziel. 'Before I honk my ring!'

Outside, he said, 'Are we stuck with it, Wieldy, or can we flush the useless turd back down south?'

'Fair do's, sir, he may have settled in by the time you finish in Wales. Still much to do, sir?'

'Too bloody much. It's like the wild bloody west out there. Buggers waiting to ambush you behind every slag heap. Some lovely rugby, but. Going to a match tonight. Only schoolboys, but they've got this fly half who's going to give those tossers down at Twickers a few headaches in the near future, always supposing he survives the GBH his compatriots dish out.'

'Oh good,' said Wield with the false enthusiasm of one who found it hard to understand why society found aggression between men so praiseworthy and affection between men so deplorable. 'Then you'll be heading straight back?'

Dalziel was viewing him with great suspicion.

'You're a bit keen to be shut of me,' he said. 'Come to think of it, what the hell are you doing hanging around here anyway?'

'The Super thought I should have a word, sir.'

'Zombie? What else has the useless sod been doing? Hiring the Dagenham Girls Choir as dog handlers?'

'No, sir. Just worried about you, that's all. He thought you should know that Tankie Trotter's on the loose.'

'Tankie Trotter? You don't mean he's made it at last? Wonders'll never cease.'

'Yes, sir. He were returned to the Wyfies' regimental depot at Leeds for discharge at the weekend. From the sound of it, if he'd been serving a civil sentence, he'd likely have been transferred straight to a nut house. But the army are only too glad to have got rid of him at last.'

'Can't blame 'em. Must be an embarrassment still having a National Service Man on the books after all this time. So why're you telling me this, Wieldy?'

'Seems Tankie had a sort of hate list scratched on his cell wall. Didn't matter how often they made him whitewash it over, it always came back. One name was his old platoon commander's. He's a major now, serving out in Hong Kong. Took his family with him, fortunately.'

'Fortunately?'

'He's got a house out near Burley. It were torched night before last. Empty, thank God. Another name was the RSM when Tankie got called up. He retired last year. He's got a flat in Horsforth. Second floor. Someone picked him out of bed last night and tossed him out of the window. He's in intensive care.'

'And what's all this got to do with me, as if I can't guess,' said Dalziel.

'The third name, in fact the one that was always top of the list, is yours, sir.'

'Well, well,' said Dalziel. 'Nice to know that some folk really mean it when they say they'll never forget. Restores your faith in human nature. So you're the errand boy, are you, Wieldy? Sent to see me safely off the premises so if Tankie trashes me, it won't leave a mess on Zombie's doorstep. You'd think the idle bugger could have shown me enough professional courtesy to come along himself. Then I could have had the pleasure of hitting him over the head with that college kid and getting rid of two useless lumps together!'

'Yes, sir, that would really have shown him the meaning of professional courtesy,' agreed Wield. 'So

are you going to go quietly? Seriously, I doubt if
Tankie knows where Wales is, and we should have felt
his collar by the time you get back.'

'Kind of trail he's leaving, what with flames and
folk flying through the air, he shouldn't be difficult to
find. You've tried his sister?'

'Yes, I went round to see Judith myself. Only she
weren't there. Taking a little break. Touring in the
West Country. What do you think, sir?'

'Anyone else I'd have said, wise move,' said Dalziel
frowning. 'But them two have got a lot of common
baggage to haul, and I don't just mean being twins.
Still, things being the way they are, that might be even
more reason for her to hide. Any road it's down to
you, Wieldy. I'll just get a cup of tea and a wad and
I'll be on my way.'

'You'll get better value in a transport caff, sir.'

Dalziel shook his head and said wonderingly,
'You're turning into a right hard bastard, Wieldy. But
I'll not hang around where I'm not wanted. See you in
a week or two. Cheers.'

That wasn't so hard, thought Wield as he watched
the Fat Man head out to the car park. Mebbe he was
learning sense at last. Or mebbe he was heading down
to the station to throw Zombie out of the window!
Still, what a mere sergeant could do, a mere sergeant
had done.

He glanced down the long corridor which led to
the magistrates' wing. Distantly he saw Peter Pascoe
approaching.

'Lost again?' he said when the youngster joined
him.

'No, Sarge. My car's parked out front.'

'So how'd it go?'

'No problem,' said Pascoe. 'Harris is still droning

on, but the beak would have to be brain dead not to commit those two jokers on the evidence. I've left word there's no objection to bail, so no need for me to stay, especially as I'm due at a briefing in ten minutes. See you!'

He was off through the doors at a graceful trot.

Didn't notice me and Fat Andy then, thought Wield. Or perhaps he really didn't think he had a problem. One thing was sure. Bomber Harris would have noticed his exit. Worth keeping an eye on the sly sod. He set off down the corridor.

Pascoe meanwhile, with a quick glance around to make sure the attendant was nowhere in sight, ran down the steps to the Riley. As he got in he could hear the car in the next bay making a meal of getting started. It was a big Rover, facing outwards so it wasn't till he reversed past it that he became aware of the driver. It was Detective Chief Inspector Dalziel.

There was a man sitting beside him, a big man with a Yul Brynner haircut and a blue chin. This didn't mean he couldn't be the Chief Constable, and as Dalziel had probably spotted him anyway, it seemed politic to stop.

He got out and approached smiling. Dalziel ignored him and tried the engine again. It roared impotently.

He tapped on the driver's window. Dalziel's head turned. His leathery lips formed two inaudible words. If Pascoe had not known it to be impossible, he would have guessed the words to be 'Fuck off'.

He tapped again. The man with the polished head spoke. Dalziel slowly wound down the window. His gaze met Pascoe's with a force that almost straightened him up. And the lips were moving again, still inaudibly but this time unmistakably.

'Fuck off!'

'Sorry, sir,' said Pascoe. 'Just thought you were having a spot of bother . . .'

'He one of yours, Dalziel?' growled the man in the passenger seat.

The DCI's expression seemed to suggest the idea gave great pain. Piqued by this response, and also encouraged by the passenger's tone in his suspicion that he might be brass, Pascoe said brightly, 'Detective Constable Pascoe, sir.'

'Right. Out! Jildi! Move your fat arse!'

Peter Pascoe had become aware very soon after joining the police that the rules of civilized social intercourse no longer applied. But did Chief Constables really speak to Chief Inspectors like this?

Perhaps he'd made a mistake. In fact as the Fat Man slid out of the car and the bald man followed him via the same door, the pointers to error began to mount up.

No reason perhaps why a Chief Constable should not be fluent in the patois. But surely no Chief Constable would wear khaki trousers, heavy black boots, and a sweat-stained green shirt whose rolled up sleeves revealed the word MUM tattooed on a brawny forearm, the letters wreathed in roses and all enclosed in a ragged fillet of black?

It occurred to him that he was concentrating so much on the specific gravity of the milk, he was ignoring the trout.

One of the man's outsize hands was gripping the back of Dalziel's jacket while the other was forcing the sawn off barrel of a shotgun against the Fat Man's spine.

'Try anything and his arse says goodbye to his belly,' snarled the man. 'Back in your car!'

Pascoe looked helplessly at Dalziel and said, 'Sir?'

The Fat Man rolled his eyes and said, 'You got yourself into this, lad. You'll have to find your own way out.'

This was new country for Pascoe, in every sense. Certainly he had no Significant Experience to call on. Lots of movies, but the cop in his situation had always had a bull-horn in his hand and a posse of armed policemen at his back. Hadn't he once read a chapter in a textbook about hostage situations?

He looked from the fat man to the bald. It occurred to him that, going by expression alone, their heads were interchangeable. It also occurred to him that it must have been a very boring textbook and he'd probably gone out for a pint and a curry halfway through that chapter.

He got into the Riley and waited.

The bald man pushed Dalziel into the rear seat and slid in beside him. It was a tight squeeze. The gun barrel must have ploughed a furrow in the Fat Man's flesh as it was dragged round from his spine to his belly.

'Go go go!' commanded the bald man.

Pascoe set the car in motion. Not a soul in sight. Where the hell was that blasted attendant when you wanted him? Or Sergeant Wield? Why hadn't he come out of the courthouse? Probably sitting in there somewhere all comfortable with a pot of tea and a fag.

At the exit he said, 'Which way?'

'Left. And drive steady. We pick up a cop car, they'll be picking up little pieces.'

Cop car? What cop car? thought Pascoe as he drove through the town. More chance of seeing a uniform on a nudist beach. And now Sod's Law which had made his journey to the courts seem like a funeral procession was casually flicking every light to green as he approached and letting the light traffic flow with careless ease.

Except for the occasional direction from the bald man, no one spoke. What had happened to all Dalziel's little jokes? thought Pascoe sneeringly. All right for a courtroom where there was nothing but a woman's reputation to worry over. Stick a shotgun in his gut and the case was altered.

Behind him Andy Dalziel was thinking, why the fuck couldn't it have been Wield who'd come out and heard him hammering his deliberately flooded engine? One glimpse of that shaven head and he'd have been off like a lintie to get the car park sown up tighter than a nun's knickers. Outcome still uncertain, but at least Trotter would have had the alternative spelt out loud and clear. Now they were on their way God knows where to face God knows what, and it could be God knows when before anyone got on their trail, or even knew there was a trail to get on!

He paused, fair minded as ever, to give God a chance to share some of His knowledge. All he got was an echo of his own words to Pascoe . . . you'll have to find your own way out.

So be it. He put all recriminations on the back burner and turned his mind to the problem in hand.

First things first. Useless wanker this unweaned college kid might be, but he deserved to know the score.

'So tell me, Tankie,' he said conversationally. 'What fettle? They treat you all right in the glass-house?'

'Belt up, Dalziel!' said Trotter, digging the barrel

so far into the belly flesh it almost covered the trigger guard.

'Nay, lad. Tha's got something better in mind for me than splattering my guts all over this nice upholstery. Any road, it's only polite to introduce you properly to Constable Pascoe. He's new round here and likely he's not heard of one of our most famous sons. That right, Pascoe? You've not heard of Tommy Trotter?'

'Sorry, sir. No, I haven't.'

'Thought not. You might have a certificate or whatever it is you get in them colleges, but your education's been sadly neglected. Right, Tankie?'

Trotter said unemotionally, 'You think you can jerk my string, Dalziel, best think again. I've been needled by experts. I cut loose, it's 'cos I want to cut loose.'

'I believe it, Tankie. So, Constable Pascoe, what we have here is Thomas Trotter, known to all his friends as Tankie, mebbe because of the way he's built, mebbe because of the way he drinks, I'm not sure. What I am sure of is, Tankie's a real star. Unique. With a bit of luck, we'll never see his like again. You see, lad, Tankie's the Last National Service Man.'

He voiced the phrase with a tremulous awe which gave it capital letters if not inverted commas.

Trotter snarled, 'Shitface, you trying to be cute? That was a derestriction sign. Speed it up to fifty. Left at the next roundabout.'

Shocked to be thus addressed, and impressed by the speed with which the man had spotted his attempt to draw attention by slow driving on the open road, Pascoe obeyed.

In the rear-view mirror his gaze met Dalziel's. Was there a message in those stony eyes?

Brightly Pascoe said, 'Last National Service Man? I don't understand . . .'

'Aye, you'll be too young. Stopped in 1960 or thereabouts. It meant every bugger were conscripted into the forces for two years.'

'Yes, sir, I know that. And I know that every time there's any trouble with rockers or hippies, the Cheltenham set start baying to bring it back.'

'Aye, bit of backbone, taste of discipline, teach 'em a bit of respect,' said Dalziel.

Might have guessed you'd go along with it, thought Pascoe.

'Load of bollocks, but,' continued Dalziel, almost causing Pascoe to drive onto the verge with surprise. 'Only thing National Service did for most lads was turn 'em bad or drive 'em mad. In some cases, both together, eh, Tankie?'

'Why don't you shut your gob?' suggested Trotter, digging the gun barrel even deeper into the Fat Man's side.

'Nay, lad, I'm just bringing the constable up to date,' protested Dalziel apparently impervious to either the pain or the danger. 'He ought to know it's not your fault. You're just a victim. You see, Pascoe, Tankie and me are old friends. He were one of the last to be called up only he didn't want to go. Not without reason, either, only when the Queen offers you her shilling, she don't pay much heed to reason. And me, well, I got the job of going and picking him up and making sure he were handed over safe and sound to our colleagues in the military. Full time employment for a while, weren't it, Tankie? Number of times you took off and headed back home! It were regimental punishment at first, which were OK. Then you broke that MP sergeant's nose, and that got you into the glasshouse. Now the thing about glasshouse time, Pascoe, is, it don't count towards your two years' National Service. So if you've got a year left to do when you go down for a year, you'll still have a year to do when you come out. Got me?'

'I think I can just about grasp the concept, sir,' said Pascoe with heavy irony.

Dalziel smiled elephantinely.

'Good. I'll make a note of that, Constable,' he said softly. And despite all the more immediate and apparently greater dangers, Pascoe felt a shiver go down his spine.

Dalziel resumed.

'So you can see Tankie's problem. The more he hated the army, the wilder he got. But the wilder he got, the longer he had to serve. And the longer he had to serve, the more he hated the army. Had to laugh, some of the tricks he got up to. Burning down the officers' mess! Chucking a grenade under the CO's caravan on an exercise! But they've not got a great sense of humour, the military brass. And that's how Tankie became the Last National Service Man. Right, Tankie?'

'Wrong, you fat bastard,' said Trotter dispassionately. 'It's you who's going to be the Last National Service Man. Next left. No! That one there, you stupid cunt!'

Pascoe had almost overshot the narrow entry into an overgrown lane, once metalled but now potholed and greened by the irresistible pressure of weeds and grass. And hope that his sudden braking and turn might have drawn attention was vain. Sod's Law had made sure the road ahead and behind was empty. He bumped down the lane for fifty yards till progress was blocked by a five-barred gate. Assuming not even

Tankie Trotter would expect him to crash through it, he brought the Riley to a halt.

'Out and open it,' said Trotter. 'Try anything funny and you'll hear the air hissing out of this bag o' wind.'

Pascoe got out and took a deep breath of air. It tasted good.

Run you stupid sod, Dalziel urged mentally. *Run!*

Whatever Trotter's threat, his instinctive reaction would likely be to take a potshot at the fleeing man. And if the gun barrel stopped drilling into his gut for even a second . . .

But the prancing academic prat was opening the gate! And now he was getting back into the car. What the hell did they teach them at these sodding colleges. If they went in for mutual masturbation, they'd likely need diagrams!

They passed through.

'Right. Stop. Out and close it,' growled Trotter.

Second chance! Mebbe the lad weren't as daft as he looked. Mebbe he'd worked out he'd have a better chance of escaping when he was behind the car rather than in front of it. Dalziel tensed himself to grab for the barrel the moment he felt it move away from his gut. But the bugger was now shutting the gate, taking real care like he was worried about breaking the Countryside Code! And as he got back in the car, he said insouciantly, 'Lovely day out there.'

Dalziel closed his eyes in pain. Who the hell does he think he is? Captain fucking Oates?

'Drive on,' ordered Trotter.

As the car moved forward Pascoe said, 'You were telling me about Mr. Trotter's career, sir.'

Aye, and I'm looking forward to telling you about yours, lad, thought Dalziel savagely.

He said, 'Not much more to tell. Spent so much

time serving time, it soon worked out he were the only conscript left in Her Majesty's Army. Last bloody National Service Man. The Wyfies were almost proud of him!'

'The Wyfies?'

'The West Yorkshire Fusiliers.'

'Good Lord, I think they were the lot my great-grandfather served in.'

'You one of them army bastards? I might have known,' snarled Trotter.

'Hold on,' protested Pascoe. 'He got killed in the Great War, that's all the army connection I've got.'

'What the hell were he doing in the Wyfies?' demanded Dalziel accusingly. 'Got lost when he went to sign on, did he?'

'No, sir, I'm sorry to say he was a Yorkshireman. But we try to keep it quiet,' retorted Pascoe.

This near blasphemous insubordination momentarily caused Dalziel to forget the shotgun, but as he leaned forward to administer a just rebuke, Trotter screwed it in another quarter inch. This time Dalziel let out a gasp of pain as he subsided. And as his wrath faded, the thought came into his mind that probably both the insolence and the insouciance came from the same source. The boy was scared out of his tiny mind.

He found the thought quite comforting. Last thing a man up shit creek needs is a red-blooded hero willing to use his dick as a paddle.

And Pascoe thought: sitting there like Heckmond-wyke's answer to Buddha, is he really as unfazed as he looks? Or is his brain so atrophied, he's simply incapable of appreciating the situation? What the blazes has he done to make this madman hate him so much? One thing's for certain: whatever it was, this isn't the time to bring it up!

Dalziel said, 'Likely you're wondering, constable, how come after so many years of going steady, me and Tankie finally fell out.'

Oh God, thought Pascoe. Completely brain dead!

'No, sir,' he said brightly. 'I wasn't wondering that.'

'And you call yourself a detective! Motive, lad, that's the key. Once you've got a hold on that, the rest'll not be long in coming, as the bishop said to the actress.'

'Stop here,' said Trotter.

The lane had widened into a small overgrown paddock in front of a cottage which was more Gothic than picturesque. True, round the door there were roses rambling and honey-suckles suckling, but they looked more carnivorous than vegetarian, as if their ambition were to devour the house, which indeed slumped sideways like a stricken deer, only supported by a roofless barn on the left-hand side.

'Blow the horn!' ordered Trotter.

Pascoe blew the horn.

The cottage door opened and a woman came out, rubbing floured hands on a flowered apron. It was a scene so rustically domestic that Pascoe thought: it's a wind-up. Wield and the rest of the CID boys are waiting inside with a birthday cake for Fat Andy. But he didn't really believe it, even before the woman stepped back inside and re-emerged with an under-and-over shotgun in her hands.

'Out,' ordered Trotter. 'Shoot the boy if he tries anything.'

The woman nodded as if she'd been told her guests took sugar in their tea.

'Hello, Jude,' said Dalziel. 'Heard you'd gone off for a trip. Nice place you found. Bet it costs more for a week than a fortnight. This boy you may have to shoot is Detective Constable Pascoe. This here's Judith, Tankie's sister. Twins, would you credit it? She got the beauty, he got the brawn. What happened to the brains, God alone knows, and He's not telling us, is he, Jude?'

A smile touched the woman's lips, acting like a tiny light to reveal the true beauty of her features. But her eyes confirmed her twinship. They were the same unyielding grey discs as her brother's.

She said, 'Some things are beyond working out with brains, Mr Dalziel. You just swim with the tide.'

'Just what I keep telling these folk with degrees,' said Dalziel.

'Inside,' said Tankie.

Pascoe moved in first with the woman in close attendance. Dalziel came behind, the gun barrel still drilling into his spine.

The cottage was almost as decrepit inside as out, but some effort had been made to render it inhabitable and there was a good smell of baking coming from the kitchen.

'Scones,' said Dalziel expertly. 'I could murder a home-baked scone with fresh butter and some strawberry jam.'

Wish he'd stop harping on about killing, thought Pascoe.

They were herded past the kitchen into a stone-flagged, windowless room which must have been built as a dairy. Whatever the state of the rest of the building, this was solid, constructed of great granite blocks thick enough to keep out any warmth from the sun. It was lit by a solitary bulb dangling from the ceiling. It contained a narrow metal-framed bed covered by a thin flock mattress. By the bed stood a rusting metal locker, open to reveal various items of clothing.

'Inspection in ten minutes,' said Trotter stepping back and slamming the door.

Pascoe grabbed the handle and rattled it like they always did in the movies. But he'd heard the key turn in the lock, and the woodwork looked disturbingly solid.

He turned to find Dalziel had taken his trousers off.

'Sir, what are you doing?' he asked, not certain he wished to know the answer.

'Like Judith said, you just swim with the tide. Even if you're a shark,' said Dalziel, removing his shirt. 'I were telling you how Tankie and me fell out, weren't I? Simple misunderstanding. God, I'd forgotten how this stuff itched!'

He'd taken a khaki shirt from the locker and was putting it on. As he buttoned it up, he continued talking.

'Four years back Tankie were getting close to discharge. Then some silly twat of a sergeant spoke to him insensitively. Naturally Tankie nutted him. Then he helped himself to a Champ and took off home. That's where I found him, waving an axe and demanding to know where his mam and Judith was. I told him his mam had taken badly and was down at the infirmary and I said if he gave me the axe, I'd make sure he got in to see her. He saw sense and gave me the axe and I drove him down the infirmary. Only when he got out of the car, the MPs were waiting for him. He seemed to think it were my fault. I still think I could have sorted things out and got him in to see his mam, only by the time I could make myself heard, Tankie had cracked one bugger's head open, broken another's arm and was marking time on a corporal's goolies. There weren't much scope for reasonable debate after that. They dragged him off, and a couple of hours later, his mam died. Christ, these are a bit tight. Long time since anyone thought I was thinner than I am!'

He'd pulled on a pair of grey denim fatigue trousers and was having difficulty fastening them up. Next he squeezed his feet into one of the two pairs of boots in the bottom of the locker. The laces tied, he now began to lay all the remaining clothes on the bed and fold them into neat geometric shapes. Pascoe recalled seeing Sean Connery do this in *The Hill*.

'You're getting ready for a kit inspection,' he said incredulously. 'This is what Trotter meant when he said *you* were going to be the Last National Service Man.'

'Glad they taught you to think at yon kindergarten,' said Dalziel. 'Pity they didn't teach you to think fast.'

'They taught me to think logically,' said Pascoe grimly. 'And logic tells me we should be looking for ways of getting out of here, not wasting time going along with this madman's fantasies.'

'And that's your very best thought, is it?' sneered Dalziel. 'You listen to me, sunshine. Time for you to have great thoughts was back there at the gate when you were out of the car and Tankie were in it. But you missed your chance, and you're in the army now, and you're not paid to think!'

'Now hold on,' said Pascoe. 'Of course I thought of making a run for it back there. But I believed him when he said he would blow you away. What I did manage to do though was drop my wallet with my warrant card in it by the gate. If someone finds it and hands it in . . .'

He hadn't expected fulsome praise for his ingenuity but he was taken aback by Dalziel's expression, as if he'd chewed on a chocolate drop and found it was a sheep dottle.

'All right,' he said defensively. 'At least I tried something which still seems better to me than just going along with Trotter.'

'You reckon?' said Dalziel. 'What do you want me to say? That you're not so green as you're cabbage looking? Consider it said. But you'd be well advised to stop being clever and think of nowt but survival. Your own personal survival.'

'It's kind of you to be so concerned about me, sir,' said Pascoe only half satirically. 'But I get the impression it's you Tankie's really after.'

'Right. And that's why I'll play along with the little game he's got planned. What I don't want is you trying any Boy's Own stuff. Don't lose sleep being grateful. Way I see it is, Tankie's not killed anyone yet. Last thing I want is him finding out how easy it is. Now sit down out of the way and let me get this lot sorted.'

Pascoe squatted on the floor near the door, his back against the wall, and uneasily contemplated his new role as the buffer zone between Dalziel and death.

Suddenly the Fat Man who'd been arranging the items on the bed with a housewifely deftness, snapped to attention, chin high, arms rigid, thumbs pointing straight down the side seams of his trousers. He even managed to hoist part of the bulge of his belly to swell the overhang of his chest.

Pascoe had heard nothing, but now the door flew open sending him scrambling out of its path. Trotter strode in and snapped to a halt inches in front of the Fat Man. He was holding the sawn-off under his arm, like a sergeant major's stick, with his finger on the trigger and the barrel levelled at Dalziel's chest.

But his back was to Pascoe, and for half a second he weighed up the odds of flinging himself onto Trotter's shoulders.

Then he saw the full shotgun barrel sticking through the doorway and met the still, grey eyes of Judith Trotter fixed unblinkingly on his face.

Trotter was speaking in a low impassioned voice.

'You are disgusting,' he breathed. 'You are the most disgusting fucking object it's been my misfortune to see since I joined this man's army. WHAT ARE YOU?'

'Disgusting, sir!' bellowed Dalziel.

'And what's this?' asked Trotter turning his attention to the bed.

'My kit, sir!'

'Kit? This milo heap of rubbish? I've seen cleaner looking gear in a Port Said bazaar. In fact, I've seen cleaner cat crap. And you've actually put it on your bed! You've got to sleep on this bed, soldier. This is unhygienic! UNHYFUCKINGGIENIC!'

He stooped, took the mattress in his left hand and threw it against the wall, spilling all the kit onto the floor.

'That's better. Probably saved your life there, soldier. Now when I come back in here in half an hour's time, I want to see this place looking so neat and fucking tidy you could invite Her Gracious Majesty the Queen Mother, God bless her, to sit down and take tea with you!'

'Sir!' shouted Dalziel.

Trotter stepped back and glanced down at Pascoe

who wondered if he was meant to snap to attention too. Sod that!

'You dropped this,' said Trotter tossing Pascoe's wallet onto the floor.

'Oh yes. Thanks,' said Pascoe, trying to conceal his dismay.

'Photo in there. You in a robe and funny hat.'

'Graduation ceremony. When I got my degree. That means—'

'I know what it fucking means! I could've gone to college!'

Pascoe nodded, aiming at something between *Sorry you missed out* and *It's not all it's cracked up to be,* and trying to hide *And I'm to be Queen of the May*!

'Old girl with you, that your mam?'

'Grandmother.'

'Where's your mam then?'

Over Trotter's shoulder, Dalziel mouthed, 'Dead.'

'Dead,' said Pascoe.

Trotter nodded and said, 'This great-grandfather of yours in the Wyfies, squaddie was he? Or an officer?'

Dalziel's huge lips formed the word, 'Captain.'

Thinking, this could be a mistake, Pascoe said, 'I'm not sure but I think he was a captain.'

'So you've got a degree, and your great-granddad was an officer, and you've still got to jump when this bag of dogshit says Jump!'

'Life does funny things to you,' said Pascoe.

'Don't I know it. What do you reckon to his boots?'

Pascoe glanced at Dalziel's boots.

'They're OK?' he said.

'OK?' echoed Trotter incredulously.

'Well, a bit dull, maybe.' Something in Trotter's expression showed him he was on the right track and warming to the role he went on, 'In fact I think they're pretty filthy.'

'Pretty filthy,' said Trotter savouring the words. 'Why don't you tell him?'

'Yes. Certainly. Look, you, er, Dalziel'—it came out Dyeel—'why are your boots so, er, filthy?'

'Don't have any polish,' said the Fat Man. 'Aagh!'

The groan was pumped out of him by a sudden jab of the sawn-off shotgun into his belly causing the landslide of his newly promoted chest.

'What do you do when you're addressed by an officer?' screamed Trotter. 'What do you say?'

'I salute, sir!' shouted Dalziel saluting. 'And I say sir, sir! Please, sir, I don't have any polish, sir!'

'That's better. And you watch it, soldier. I catch you not addressing this officer correctly and you'll start to wish you hadn't been born.' To Pascoe he said, 'This one needs watching, sir. Perhaps you could keep an eye on him, make sure he gets to work on them boots.'

'But if he doesn't have any polish . . .' objected Pascoe weakly.

'He can spit, can't he?' said Trotter. 'Ought to be able to. Full of piss and wind, I'm sure he's got some spit to spare. Next inspection in thirty minutes if that suits you, sir.'

'Er yes. Er, fine. Er . . . carry on.'

He had a vague recollection from *The Bridge on the River Kwai* that that's the sort of thing they said. It seemed to work. Trotter crashed in a thunderous salute, span on his heel and marched out. The door closed behind him and the key rattled in the lock.

'Not bad,' said Dalziel, sitting on the bed. 'Though you'll need to work on it a bit.'

'Work on what?' demanded Pascoe.

'Being an officer. You're lucky, lad. He's decided to treat you as a genuine buckshee, not just surplus to requirements. You're on the team, but you'd best play to the rules else you might get dropped, from a great height.'

The Fat Man had taken off his boots and was examining them with pursed lips.

'Candle, a metal spoon and some blacking and I'd have these bright enough to get a kiltie done for indecent exposure.'

Pascoe worked this out, then asked, 'You've been in the army, have you, sir?'

'Aye, I've done the state a bit of service,' said Dalziel, spitting on the boot. He wrapped a huge khaki handkerchief (his own, not part of Trotter's issue) round his index finger and began polishing the toecap in with tiny circular movements.

'And which way did it send you? Mad or bad?' enquired Pascoe.

Dalziel stopped polishing and regarded him almost sympathetically.

'Don't give up, lad,' he said.

'I'm sorry?'

'Only reason a sprog like you reckons he can get cocky with someone like me is you don't hold much hope we're ever going to get out of this. My advice is, until you're dying and I'm dead, stay polite and call me sir. Except when Tankie's around that is. Then I'll call you sir and you can call me what you like, short of vulgar abuse. Vulgar abuse is for warrant officers and NCOs.'

The fat oaf isn't joking, realized Pascoe. Curiously it was almost comforting.

He said, 'What did Trotter mean, he could have gone to university?'

'Now that's a good question. More you know about a man, the more you open up opportunity.'

'For negotiation, you mean?'

'For kicking his bollocks into his brain-pan,' growled Dalziel. 'I've been trying to fill you in on the background ever since you let yourself get dragged into this. One thing you've got to grasp about Tankie is, he's no deadhead. He were a bright lad. Passed eleven plus, went to the grammar, got "O" levels, and it were right enough, he could've stayed on for his "A's" and mebbe gone to college, but that would've meant going away, leaving his sister and his mam alone wi' his father. Now he were a real bruiser, Thomas. Tankie were named for him, but he'd never answer to Tommie so that's why he got Tankie. He grew into it when he got on in his teens, but he were nowt alongside Thomas. Made me feel like a ballet dancer, he did!'

Pascoe had a brief vision of Dalziel in a tutu. It was like a snip from *Fantasia*.

'Glad to see you can still smile, lad,' said the Fat Man. 'Lose your sense of humour, and what you got left? Your job, maybe. But what's a job to a man wi' a degree?'

'This Thomas, am I right in assuming Tankie didn't get on with him?' said Pascoe.

'Am I right in assuming . . .' mocked Dalziel. 'I bet you're a whizz in an interrogation, lad! Yes, you're bloody right! He were a violent sod were Thomas, and he made no distinction of friend, foe or family.'

'Wasn't anything done about him?' demanded Pascoe indignantly.

'Oh we kept him straight in the pubs and streets,' said Dalziel. 'But in them days, what a man got up to in his own house was his own business, short of breaking bones, and not even then sometimes. There was some as said there was more than just beatings went on when the kids were young.'

'Incest, you mean?' said Pascoe horror-struck. 'And you say nothing was done?'

'You need complaint, you need proof,' said Dalziel grimly. 'One of these days it's all going to start coming out, things that go on behind closed curtains. My old boss, Wally Tallantire, used to say, "An Englishman's home is his knocking-shop, Andy." That's why the church and the Tories rabbit on about the family. Keeps it under wraps.'

This cold view of society chilled Pascoe to the marrow. He said, 'If you thought something like that was going on . . .'

'I didn't, 'cos apart from a few D and Ds, Thomas didn't really bother us. It weren't till Tankie got his call-up papers the family came to my notice. Came as a shock to Tankie. Everyone knew National Service were coming to an end and the clever buggers were finding six new ways of getting deferred before breakfast every sodding morning. Tankie just said he weren't going. That's when I came in the picture. I arrested him, told him not to be stupid and if he didn't let himself be handed over to the army he'd end up in a civvy jail for the duration, and while you could get home from the army, you didn't get leave from prison—though the way things are going, they'll soon be sending the buggers off to Majorca for a few days in the summer!'

Avoiding the temptation of an excursion into the interesting territory of penal philosophy, Pascoe said, 'Not the best advice you ever gave by the sound of it. Sir.'

'Aye, you're right there,' admitted Dalziel. 'The

army took him, and once they'd got him, well, as long as he kept on breaking their rules, they were going to keep locking him up in their prisons.'

'But he gave them cause, didn't he?' said Pascoe, surprised by the sympathetic tone of Dalziel's voice.

'Oh aye. He weren't a tearaway, but he had a talent for violence. Not surprising, if you think about it. Kids learn from the way they're brought up, even if it's the wrong way. He hated his dad for being violent, but that was the only way he ever saw for getting the things you wanted from life.'

Pascoe knew sociologists who'd needed a whole lecture to make much the same point. Get Dalziel on campus and maybe they could have got through the degree course in a fortnight! Mind you, he doubted if they made mortarboards to fit heads like that.

'You keep on grinning, your face'll stay like that,' said Dalziel warningly. 'People may stop asking you to funerals.'

All the time he talked, his forefinger kept up its tiny circles on the toe of the boot. Occasionally he examined his progress and administered further salivary unction.

'Did Tankie try to stand up to his father, then?' asked Pascoe.

'Oh aye. But it were no contest. Might be different now he's broadened out and learnt a few dirty tricks. But back then, it took me all my strength to sort the bugger out.'

'You had a fight with him?' cried Pascoe.

'Aye, well, after the first couple of times Tankie bunked off from the barracks and headed home, I started getting some idea of the lie of the land. So I thought mebbe I could set the lad's mind at rest by having a quiet word with Thomas. By God. I'd not want many quiet words like that!'

'What happened?'

'I didn't want to talk in public—this were unofficial, fewer folk who saw us the better. So I waited for him in the ginnel that runs from back of their house to the main road. I spoke him fair. I said, "Thomas, tha's got to stop beating thy wife. If tha wants exercise, there's plenty nearer thy own weight as'll be only too pleased to give it thee." And he said, "Name one." And I hit him.'

Puzzled by this apparent *non sequitur,* or perhaps even *ignoratio elenchi,* Pascoe said, 'You hit him? Why?'

'I reckoned if I'd said, "Me for one," he'd have hit me. So it seemed daft to waste time on the courtesies. Big mistake I made was giving him a fair blow on the chin. It knocked him back but it was a long way off knocking him out. Well, after that, he kicked me to one end of the ginnel and I kicked him all the way back. In the end it settled nowt. Don't know if thumping ever does, but you certainly don't get a man to see things your way by fighting a draw with him.'

Pascoe thought, John Wayne did in *The Quiet Man,* but this is the real Wild West up here.

He said, 'If you were going to these extremes to try and help Tankie's family, how come he hates you so much he's threatening to kill you?'

'I never told Tankie owt o' this!' said Dalziel indignantly. 'I weren't doing it to make some doolally kid love me. I just wanted to stop the stupid sod giving me grief by heading back here every two minutes. Also Thomas were overdue a good kicking. Like I say, a lot of good it did. Thomas still ruled his house like Godzilla on a bad day. And Tankie kept on heading for home and walking right over any poor sod who got in his way. My fault for being polite.'

Oh God, thought Pascoe. What have I done coming to this dreadful place? And if I get out of here, can it be undone? All the lies he'd told when he applied for transfer, could they be untold? Or would he have to think of a whole new set in order to move onward? Carry on like this and he'd end up on Orkney!

Dalziel was putting his boots on. Finished, he started restoring all the kit which Trotter had strewn over the floor to the bed.

'Best get yourself ready,' advised the Fat Man. 'Tankie said thirty minutes and that's what it'll be.'

'But what do I do?' appealed Pascoe desperately.

'Let's see,' said Dalziel eyeing him speculatively. 'There's all kinds of officers. Brisk efficient adjutant . . . mebbe not . . . Grizzled old warhorse . . . definitely not! Languid . . . aye, that's it. Languid and a bit poncey . . . has trouble wi' his "r's," calls other ranks other wanks, and probably means it. That's you, lad. Call him Mr Trotter like he was an RSM and treat me like I don't exist. Stand by, he's here.'

His ears were definitely sharper than Pascoe's who once again had to move smartly out of the way of the door.

'Prisoner, 'SHUN!' screamed Trotter.

Dalziel snapped to attention.

'You horrid idle man! You paraplegic or what? Stan' atease! 'SHUN! Stan' atease! 'SHUN!'

Trotter enjoyed himself making Dalziel move from one position to another till the sweat beaded his huge brow. Pascoe didn't much mind the sight till it occurred to him that Dalziel dead of a heart attack might not bode well for his own future. He had a vision of himself digging a grave under the close supervision of the Trotter twins, and when he'd finally excavated a hole large enough for that gross body, hearing the instruction, 'Keep digging.'

He said as languidly as he could manage, 'Ready when you are, Mr Trotter.'

Trotter's head came round and those mad grey eyes focused on this intruder. For a second Pascoe thought the game was over and the man had decided he was after all merely surplus to requirements rather than a genuine buckshee, whatever that was.

Then Trotter stiffened, threw up a salute and said, 'Sir! Prisoner ready for inspection, sir!'

Slowly Pascoe advanced and with an expression of distaste not difficult to simulate he ran his eyes over the Fat Man's frame. Now what was it officers said as they went round the cookhouse? Oh yes.

'Any complaints, my man?'

Who was it who, asked the same question shortly after call-up in 1940, replied, 'Not one in the world, darling. Everything's perfectly ducky'? He couldn't recall. He doubted if the Fat Man was about to make the same answer.

'Nosir!' bellowed Dalziel.

Pascoe found that, despite the underlying menace of the situation, he quite enjoyed this new relationship. He said, 'Good. Mr Trotter, has this man been shown the right way to lay out his kit or have regulations changed to permit a certain amount of idiosyncratic choice?'

Trotter said, 'No, sir. Regulations same as always. You hear what the officer says, you horrible little man?'

He stopped, picked up the mattress and shook the kit to the floor again.

'Next time get it right or you'll wish you had never been born!'

He wheeled towards Pascoe and said, 'Next inspection in twenty minutes, sir?'

The intervals were getting shorter. Must be something he could do to slow the trend. What would happen if he simply used his putative authority to say, no, make it an hour?

He looked into the mad grey eyes and thought, to hell with that! He'd probably cashier me. With his shotgun!

He looked away and saw the Fat Man's lips forming a word. F . . . something. He wasn't swearing at him again surely! No. It was *food*.

He said, 'Carry on, Mr Trotter.'

It was almost a pleasure to see the expression of fury which passed over Dalziel's face like the shadow of a storm cloud over a fell.

He got the thunderous 'SIR!' and the big salute from Trotter, then just as the man reached the door, Pascoe said, 'Oh, by the way. Has the prisoner had any refreshment?'

Trotter came to a halt at the door and turned. It wasn't a military turn and the look he was giving Pascoe wasn't a military look.

Oh hell, I've bounced him out of character, thought Pascoe.

Trying not to let his languid drawl accelerate into a terrified babble, he said, 'Regulations, Mr Trotter. Everything must proceed strictly according to regulations, or where are we, eh?'

Dead, he thought. That's where. Maybe this was the time for the last despairing leap. Hope that one or both of the shotguns jammed. Did shotguns jam? Probably not. All right, hope that the first wound wasn't totally incapacitating. The adrenalin of fury, or hate, or love, could keep a man going even when full of lead. Like Bill Holden in *The Wild Bunch*. Or Gary Cooper at the end of *For Whom the Bell Tolls*. No. Cancel those. They both snuffed it. Think of Shane riding off into the mountains after the big shoot-out, despite having taken one in whatever part of his apparently anaesthetized anatomy he took it in!

He tensed his muscles. All his life should be passing before him now . . . wouldn't take long . . . barely enough of it for a loony 'toon, let alone a full seven reeler.

Trotter too was stiffening up, slowly resuming his military erectness.

He said, 'Yes, sir. You're right, sir. I'll see to it at once. Sir.'

Then he was gone and the door was locked behind him.

Pascoe sat abruptly on the bed. He realized his legs were gently trembling.

Dalziel said, 'Not bad, lad. Do a bit of acting at this college of thine?'

'No,' said Pascoe. 'I was always more interested in films than the theatre. I once auditioned for a part in *An Inspector Calls* but that was only because there was this girl helping with the production . . .'

Relief was making him garrulous. Dalziel was grinning.

'They didn't put bromide in your tea then?' he said. '*An Inspector Calls*, tha says? Good play that. It were written by a Yorkshireman, did you know that?'

'Yes, surprisingly, I did know that,' said Pascoe.

'I'm glad to hear it. And there's a bit of Yorkshire

in you too, is there, with this great-granddad of yours in the Wyfies? That why you transferred up here?'

Pascoe thought, shall I tell him that I have no interest whatsoever in my great-grandfather and that my sole reason for applying for transfer was to get away from a fascist superior whose methods and morality I equally deplored (but whom I am now starting to recall with nostalgic fondness) and whose halitosic daughter fancied me rotten?

He said, 'A man likes to be near his roots, sir.'

Their gazes locked, the younger man's warm with sincerity, the older man's steadfast with understanding.

Then Dalziel said, 'Bollocks. It'll either be trouble with a tart or your boss. Now give us a hand picking up this lot. What the hell were you playing at? All that idiosyncratic crap, encouraging him to fire it on the floor again?'

'I thought, sir,' said Pascoe stooping to pick up the scattered kit, 'that as he was certainly going to do it anyway, I might as well use the certainty to authenticate my own role.'

'By God, lad, if tha thinks as long-winded as tha speaks, I'm surprised you ever got out of nappies. Glad you picked me up on the food, but. I bet the bugger has me doubling to the cookhouse to collect it.'

'Is that why you suggested it, sir? To get a look around, perhaps suss out a way to escape?' asked Pascoe, impressed.

'Don't be bloody daft,' said Dalziel. 'I suggested it 'cos I'm bloody starving!'

I believe he means it! thought Pascoe helplessly. He's just like all of his type and generation. Not without a certain animal cunning and sharpness, but like an animal, incapable of dealing with more than the immediate moment, the short-term crisis. Either something will turn up or it will go away, that's his philosophy. If we're going to get out of this, it's going to need me to take the initiative.

He said, 'I was thinking, sir. The woman, Judith, how far do you think she'll go with her brother's schemes? I wondered if I should try to work on her . . .'

'Show her your dick, you mean, and tell her you love her? She'd shoot it off without a second thought. Very moral lass, Jude. Very faithful. A one man woman and she'll go all the way to protect them as she's given her loyalty to. Man who gets a lass like Jude can count himself lucky.'

Pascoe had finished collecting the kit, and now he watched as Dalziel once more neatly folded it and arranged it on the bed.

He said, 'Do you really think playing this crazy game is going to get us anywhere?'

'Game? Aye, that's what it is, I suppose. That's what the army is, in peacetime any road, and especially in the glasshouse. None of this daft rehabilitation stuff there. They don't want to make good citizens out of you. They want to make good soldiers, and a good soldier is one who does what he's told, no questions asked.'

'So why's Trotter doing this to you?'

'Because it's the worst thing he can think of. Also because he went through it for years and the poor sod reckons he came out on top. And he thinks a few days of what he suffered for years will break me like a pencil point. Which reminds me.'

He stepped onto the bed which groaned under his weight, removed his belt and with the buckle

scratched on the damp granite wall the name TROT-
TER.

'There,' he said stepping down. 'My name kept
Tankie going. Let's see if his can do the same for me.'

'He must have been really fixated on his mother to
hate you so much,' said Pascoe.

'Oh aye. There were another reason, but his mum
would've been enough. Worshipped her like she was
the Virgin Mary. Mebbe that's why he's so bent on
getting himself crucified. You'll have noticed the tat-
too on Tankie's arm? Got that done when he were a
lad. But the black border round it he did himself after
she snuffed it. Used boot blacking and a sharpened
bed spring while he were in the glasshouse. They
thought they might have to cut off the arm, but he
survived. Then while he were convalescing, he hit his
guard with his drip, stole his clothes, jumped out of a
third-storey window and headed home. Only this time
it were my home he headed for. My missus opened
the door and Tankie just walked in.'

'My God, that must have been a terrible shock for
your wife!'

'Aye, might have killed a weaker woman,' said
Dalziel with a faint note of regret. 'But once she realized it were me he'd come to kill, they got on like a
house on fire. They were sitting having a cup of tea
when I walked in. Luckily I'd had some bother with
the car and took the bus home, so he had no warning.
He jumped up and spilt his tea over his lap. Must've
been hot 'cos he didn't half yell! Then I hit him with
the teapot and he stopped yelling.'

'And your wife . . . ?'

'She started yelling. It were her Crown Derby pot. I
said, serve you right for getting the best china out for

a nutter like Tankie, but she didn't see it like that. Why the hell am I telling you all this, Pascoe?'

He turned a coldly speculative gaze on the young DC like a man looking for the watermark in a suspect pound note.

Memo to self, thought Pascoe. This is not a man the details of whose domestic life you want to know.

He said, 'You mentioned another reason Trotter has for hating you.'

'Did I? Not important.'

'Shouldn't I be the judge of that?' insisted Pascoe. 'You keep telling me it's my balls on the block too.'

This sudden descent into the demotic clearly impressed the Fat Man more than any amount of epagogic argument.

He said, 'Mebbe you're right. It's to do with Thomas, Tankie's dad. He died just at the time his mum took ill. I reckon he gave her a punch too many, bust something in her gut. She'd never blow the whistle on him, but he got his comeuppance all the same. Fell into the canal one night coming home pissed. Drowned. Tankie got compassionate for the funeral. Manacled to an MP, naturally. I weren't there, but I heard he spat into the grave.'

'He wasn't on the loose when his father drowned then?'

'Good thinking. No, safely banged up. Inquest brought in accidental death.'

There was an absence of finality in his tone.

Pascoe said, 'You don't think it might have been . . . Judith?'

'You're not just a pretty face then?' said Dalziel. 'Aye, it did cross my mind. But I said, what the hell? No way I could prove it, no way I wanted to prove it!'

'So why should this bother Trotter?'

''Cos I told him I *could* prove it,' said Dalziel gloomily. 'I got to thinking, I didn't much fancy having to look over my shoulder for evermore in case Tankie were coming after me. So before they took him back to the glasshouse, I told him if he ever pulled a stunt like that again, I'd make sure his everloving sister got banged up even longer than he did. I thought, that'll do the trick.'

'Instead of which it just gave him another reason for wanting to sort you out.'

'Worse. I reckon he told Jude. I don't think she'd be risking everything she's got just for love of Tankie. No, she's got her own agenda here, protecting her own interests, her own life.'

'While actually you don't have anything on her at all! Great move, sir. Really clever thinking!'

'Nobody's perfect,' said Dalziel without conviction.

'Joe E. Lewis. *Some Like It Hot,*' said Pascoe.

'What the fuck are you on about?' said Dalziel. 'Stand by! Here we go again.'

Once more he was a second ahead in detecting the key in the door.

This time Trotter didn't enter the room but stood in the doorway. Pascoe saw his eyes take in the name scratched on the wall above the bed. Then he was screaming, '*Prisoner*! Double mark time!'

Dalziel began running on the spot.

'Higher! Get them knees up higher!' yelled Trotter. 'You great bag of lard. We shouldn't be feeding you, we should be fasting you till you start looking like a human being instead of a blubber fucking whale! At the double, forward march. Left wheel! Keep them knees up, d'you hear me? Lef'ri'lef'ri'lef'ri' . . .'

Dalziel went out of the dairy with Trotter in close attendance. Pascoe took a tentative step towards the door, but Judith was there, the gun in her hands as steady as the grey eyes fixed on his face.

He forced himself to take another small step forward.

'Next one takes you off the edge of the world,' she said.

She had a low-pitched voice with a not displeasing huskiness. If she could hold a note, he could imagine her coming over like Bacall in *To Have and Have Not*. (Did Andy Williams *really* dub that?) He put on his Bogart lisp and said, 'Somewhere this has got to stop, you must see that. So it makes sense, the sooner the better.'

The gun barrel moved forward as slightly but as certainly as a Socratic question exposing a flaw in his argument. He gave way before it, retreating both steps he'd advanced and another besides. Bogie wasn't too proud to be scared. Remember *Key Largo*!

'If you kill me . . .' He meant to urge on her the inevitable consequences to herself, her brother, the moral health of the Nation, and the Rule of Law. Instead he heard pathos slipping into bathos as he concluded limply, '. . . I'll be dead.'

Even as he thought, 'Oh God! I didn't really say that, did I?' he saw a reaction. First she smiled . . . that was at the bathos. And then the smile faded and for the first time she blinked as if something other than blank watchfulness was trying to show itself in her eyes. Perhaps that was the pathos getting to her. Perhaps for the first time she was seeing him not just as an adjunct of the gross Dalziel but as a young man with a life still to live, wine still to drink, movies still to see, girls still to . . .

He found he was blinking tears back from his eyes. Well, it had been a hard day so far and he'd had no breakfast. Even as he fought against this weakness which he suspected unfitted him to be a policeman he found himself wondering how his complete breakdown would affect the woman, which perhaps meant he was cut out to be a cop after all.

Before he could test just how meltable she was, he heard the sound of Dalziel's footsteps with their high-pitched *lef'ri'lef'ri'lef* accompaniment. The Fat Man appeared in the cell with a pint mug in one hand and a plate piled with some kind of stew in the other. At Trotter's command he marked time at the foot of the bed. Despite all his efforts at steadiness tea slopped out of the mug at every step and gravy dripped off the edge of the plate.

'Look what you're doing to the officer's meal!' screamed Trotter. 'I've a good mind to make you lick it up, you horrible man. HALT. LEFT TURN. Give the officer his meal and apologize for the mess you've made.'

'SIR!' shouted Dalziel breathlessly. 'Here's your meal, SIR! Sorry about the mess, SIR!'

He didn't look well, thought Pascoe. Or perhaps that greyness round the mouth was his natural colouring. The eyes were lively enough, full of promissory vengeance which came across as all embracing rather than targeted.

Even if I get out of this lot, thought Pascoe, I don't get the feeling I've much of a future in Mid Yorkshire!

He dug deep for his Alec Guinness voice. Because of the thickness in his throat it came out more *Tunes of Glory* than *Bridge on the River Kwai*.

'Carry on, Mr Trotter.'

And the poor fat sod was off again, doubling back down to the kitchen presumably to get his own grub this time.

Pascoe looked speculatively at the woman. The old blankness was back. Impervious she might be to hot tears, but how would she react to hot stew in her face?

Badly, he answered himself. And in these confined quarters there wasn't much chance of ducking out of the spread of two shotgun barrels.

He took a careful sip of his tea, then set it on the floor and examined the stew. There was a spoon half submerged in its rich brownness which gave off a good appetizing smell reminding him he'd missed breakfast. While there was life, there was hunger. He began to eat. It tasted as good as it smelt and he'd almost finished by the time Dalziel returned, clutching another mug and plate.

Trotter noticed his progress and said, 'Sir! Like another helping, sir?'

He almost said yes, then he looked at Dalziel still double marking time, and thought it would mean another trip to the kitchen for the poor sod.

'No, thank you, Mr Trotter,' he said.

'Right, sir. Thank you, sir. Prisoner, HALT! Stan' atease. Next inspection in thirty minutes.'

Then he was gone. Dalziel waited till they heard the key turn in the lock before subsiding slowly onto the bed.

'You OK, sir?' said Pascoe.

The great grey head turned slowly towards him.

'What's up, lad? Worried in case I snuff it and there's nowt between you and Tankie but your fancy degree? Rest quiet. There's nothing wrong with me that a good woman and a bottle of Highland Park wouldn't put right.'

'Glad to hear it, sir. Talking of a good woman, was

Mrs Dalziel expecting you to drop in at home before you went back to Wales? If so . . .'

'Forget it, lad. There is no Mrs Dalziel now.'

'I'm sorry,' said Pascoe. 'Dead?'

'No such sodding luck,' grunted the Fat Man. 'Just divorced. You married?'

'No sir.'

'Good. First thing I've heard in your favour so far. Not engaged or owt like that? Girlfriend filling her bottom drawer?'

'No sir. There was a girl at university . . .'

'Oh aye. The one got you auditioning for *An Inspector Calls*? She still hanging around?'

'No sir. Not the type who hangs around. Not the type who likes her boyfriends joining the police force either.'

'One of them? Then you're well rid of her,' growled Dalziel. 'Ee, that weren't half bad. Wouldn't like to fetch me another helping, would you?'

He'd been demolishing his stew as he talked and now he thrust the plate towards Pascoe who took it and half rose before he remembered.

'Nice to see that being an officer for five minutes hasn't spoilt your manners,' grinned Dalziel.

Angrily Pascoe threw the plate onto the bed. It skidded off the mattress, hit the stone-flagged floor and shattered.

'Clever,' said Dalziel. 'Tha knows who'll get the blame for that?'

'Why the hell aren't we talking about how to get out of here instead of exchanging dull details of our domestic lives?' demanded Pascoe. 'Everyone seems to think you're so bloody marvellous, why don't you do something to prove it?'

'Got a temper, have you?' said Dalziel not disapprovingly. 'All right. Here. Take hold of that.'

He reached down and picked up two long sharp shards of china, one of which he handed to Pascoe.

He went on. 'First chance we get, we jump 'em. You grab the lass, get a hold of her hair, stick that into her throat or her eye, any bit of her you can get at that'll do a lot of damage. Think you can manage that, lad?'

Pascoe looked at the fragment of plate and imagined sinking it into one of those pale grey eyes . . .

'I'm not sure, sir . . .' he said.

'Oh aye? So while I'm doing the business on Tankie, Jude's turning my spine into bonemeal? No thanks. We need another plan. Your turn.'

He tossed the plate shard back onto the floor and looked expectantly at the younger man.

'I don't know,' cried Pascoe. 'I meant something more like escaping . . . this isn't a prison, I mean it wasn't built to keep people in. Surely we can find a way to get out . . . ?'

'Like the Count of Monte Cristo, you mean? Now that were a good movie. Robert Doughnut, weren't it? Only they had to dig for about twenty years, didn't they? About the same amount of time you spent in school, learning fuck all. Tell you what, why don't you take the first shift, lad?'

It wasn't so much the words as the Fat Man's more-in-pain-than-in-anger expression that got to Pascoe.

He said, 'You're forgetting something. It wasn't the tunnel that got him out, it was the old sod dying and being dumped in the sea in a sack. Our only problem is going to be, where will we find a sack big enough?'

He'd gone too far. If Dalziel looked big before,

now he seemed to swell monstrously like the genie let out of the bottle in *The Thief of Baghdad*.

He tried to recall how Sabu had got him back in again. By persuading him he *couldn't* get back in again!

He forced a smile and said, 'You got a temper too, sir? Maybe we're a matching pair.'

For a moment, the Fat Man trembled on the brink of nuclear fission. Then, slowly subsiding, he snarled, 'Man who can believe that should stick to directing traffic.'

His anger must have dulled his hearing for he was still on the bed when the door flew open and Trotter erupted, yelling, 'What the hell's going on here? Who broke that plate? Prisoner giving you trouble, sir?'

Dalziel was back at rigid attention, the genie well back inside.

Pascoe said, 'Accident, Mr Trotter. Prisoner rather emotional. Private interview with officer i.c. As per regulations.'

He was gabbling. He tried to change it to the sternness of reproof, decided that perhaps it wasn't such a good idea and stuck with his gabble.

Happily Trotter wasn't paying him much attention. He stepped back to the doorway, picked up a bucket of hot water his sister had set down there and said, 'Throwing food around the place, are you, Dalziel? You may look like a pig and eat like a pig but you're not going to turn this place into a sty. I want every inch of this tip scrubbed out by the time I get back, understood?'

'SIR!'

Without a glance at Pascoe, Trotter about turned and marched out.

Oh dear, thought Pascoe. Perhaps I'm being written out of the script.

Dalziel was on his knees carefully gathering up the broken pieces of plate tunelessly whistling what might have been a bosh shot at 'Pack Up Your Troubles In Your Old Kitbag' or possibly the scherzo from Beethoven's Fifth. Pascoe looked at the bucket. There was a toothbrush floating in it.

He took it out and said, 'What's this for?'

'Scrubbing the floor,' said Dalziel.

'You're joking!'

'Well, you know what they say. If you can't take a laugh you shouldn't have joined. What's up, lad? You've got that gormless college look on thy face again.'

Pascoe said slowly, 'He had this bucket ready when he came in. As if he knew about the broken plate in advance.'

'Coincidence. Good guesser,' suggested Dalziel.

'Maybe. Or maybe . . .' He stopped voicing the words but mouthed at Dalziel, '. . . he's listening!'

To his amazement Dalziel roared with laughter and applauded.

He's bluffing, thought Pascoe. The old bastard's only pretending he knew all along. How could he . . . oh shit! The wallet. He'd told Dalziel he'd dropped his wallet and a few minutes later Trotter had come in with it. Dalziel had worked it out, this fat, loutish, stupid . . . It was the animal cunning thing, of course. OK, so he'd worked it out, but he didn't have that wider mental scope which might have enabled him to *use* his knowledge. Whereas if he, Peter Pascoe, BA, had realized, he would have . . . what? He tried to think of some way of utilizing the situation.

He looked at Dalziel who was now down on his knees methodically scrubbing the floor with the toothbrush.

Pascoe said, 'Sir . . .'

'Aye?' prompted the Fat Man, but Pascoe was finding speech problematical. Suppose he said . . . ? But if he said . . . ?

Dalziel said, 'Do you reckon the scientists in them vivisectionist places pay much heed to the squeaking of the rats?'

Pascoe whispered, 'You think he's going to kill us then?'

'Speak up, lad. Can't hear you.'

'Do you think he's going to kill us?' shouted Pascoe.

'Depends. He is doolally, even Tankie couldn't deny that. But is he so far gone that killing a man he hates is worth spending the rest of his life banged up for? And if he thinks it is, then he may decide to chuck you in for good measure, that's what you really want to know, isn't it?'

'But why kill me? I've done nothing?'

He knew he sounded plaintive, but if Tankie *were* listening, then perhaps this was a plea for his life and he wasn't going to let embarrassment stand in the way.

'Well,' said Dalziel judiciously, 'he might do it 'cos he thinks you're one of my boys, an extension of me so to speak. If he's not cottoned on how far from the truth that is, let me set him right. I've never seen you in my life afore today, right? You've been transferred into the squad behind my back without my agreement, and having had the pleasure of seeing you in action this last couple of hours, I think I can fairly promise if I do come out of this alive to make it my life's work to get you sent back to whatever kindergarten you escaped from! No offence intended.'

'None taken,' said Pascoe. 'In the same spirit of openness, may I say that I'd rather serve as an underground maintenance man in a sewage works than continue in your employ, sir.'

'Glad we've got all that cleared up,' said Dalziel. 'On the other hand if Tankie thinks that, just because he's topped me, he's got to top you as well to give him a chance of getting away with it, well, he really has flipped it. He's in the frame already. Fingerprints all over my car. He wasn't wearing gloves, was he? And God knows who saw him around the place. Then they'll find this cottage eventually. Lot depends on how clever Jude was. I reckon she'd have to set it up. Probably didn't want to, all she's got to lose. But she owes Tankie, 'cos without him things 'ud've been even worse for her and her mum all them years. And he's her twin. And the bother he got into with the army was mainly because of his family. So, did she find this hole through an ad or go through an agent? Wieldy told me that he were told they'd gone off on a trip. Sooner or later they'll trace t'others. Could take days. Or it could be they've done it already and the army's crawling around the bushes outside.'

Did he really believe that? wondered Pascoe. Of course not, else he wouldn't be saying it. Would he?

'Mind moving your feet?' said the Fat Man. 'I need to scrub under them. By the by, here's a tip. If the tear gas comes in, stick your head in this bucket of water.'

'That will help with the gas?' asked Pascoe.

'Nay, it's just that the sharpshooters have been taught not to blast off at a man with his head in a bucket!'

He bellowed a laugh, and Pascoe thought disgustedly, he's a total clown. Except that the eyes regarding him were shrewd and almost sympathetic.

'No use feeling sorry for yourself, lad,' said Dalziel. 'Like my old ma always used to say, there's plenty worse off than you.'

'Name one.'

'That poor lass Judith for a start,' said Dalziel. 'Tankie's got nowt to lose except his freedom, and to tell truth, I reckon that after all this time, the notion of being free scares the shit out of him. But Judith's got a life to go back to. OK she'd get her knuckles rapped for helping him, but no one's really going to blame her for running scared of a loonie like Tankie and jumping when he says jump! Look at me. I'm jumping aren't I? And I've not got any kids or loved ones he can threaten. We snuff it, but, and Jude can say goodbye to all that. Cleft stick, poor cow. How about you, Sonny Jim? You got anyone who'll miss you, apart from the *Inspector Calls* lass?'

'I told you, she's history,' said Pascoe shortly. 'When I told her I wanted to be a cop, she and her mates started singing that song from *Going My Way* whenever I came into the bar. The one with the line: *or would you rather be a pig?*'

'Bing Crosby,' said the Fat Man. He started to sing in a booming baritone, *'Would you like to swing on a star? Carry moonbeams home in a jar?* Daft bloody words. Daft bloody woman. You're well shut of her. How about family? Is your mam really dead?'

'No, I'm glad to say. Nor my father. And I've got two elder sisters, so there's still an active family unit in existence.'

'Oh aye? Sounds right cosy. I bet you have active family unit reunions at Christmas and birthdays and such,' sneered Dalziel.

The old bastard certainly had a nose for sniffing out trouble, thought Pascoe, feeling a great longing to launch the toe of his shoe at the kneeling man's buttocks.

I'd probably break my leg, he thought.

He said, 'I think my private life is none of your business, just as yours is none of mine. As long as we do the job we're paid for . . .'

Dalziel paused in his scrubbing and looked up at him, the great mouth rounding in big-close-up astonishment.

'*We?*' he said. 'As in you and me? In the same word? Like we were doing the same job? Now listen, sunshine, you'd better get yourself disenchanted. Man who can believe we've got owt in common except two bollocks and a bunghole, and I'm not sure about you, could end up owning a lot of clapped-out used cars.'

'Oh you're right, sir,' said Pascoe angrily. 'I'm so sorry. I'd heard a lot about you and I now see I was wrong not to believe every incredible word. From the moment I heard you this morning allegedly giving evidence on behalf of that poor woman, I knew the last thing I wanted was to be tarred with your brush. Sir!'

'No need to get personal,' said Dalziel looking hurt. 'What were wrong with my evidence anyway?'

'Wrong? You were the main prosecution witness . . .'

'No, lad. That were the woman,' corrected Dalziel gently.

'Yes, and just because she was a prostitute and you felt there was little chance of a conviction, you'd clearly decided the whole thing was a waste of time!'

'Aye, well, you're half right, I'll give you that,' Dalziel replied disconcertingly. 'That's exactly the line yon donkey-pizzle, Martineau, was taking. So I just made sure the jury got a wink and a nod that this weren't no jolly punter willing to pay for a quick bang, but a career sex offender who won't be stopped till it's lopped off!'

'Oh, yes? Easy to say that now,' sneered Pascoe.

'Nay, lad. Easier not to say it at all and I don't know why I bothered,' sighed Dalziel. 'What's a sprog daft enough to correct a magistrate's jokes know about giving evidence?'

Pascoe digested this then exploded, 'So you've been spying on me as well!'

'I went into a public court to see one of my junior officers giving evidence, yes. Bet you thought you were doing all right, too, eh?'

'Yes, as a matter of fact, I did. Damn sight better than you anyway,' said Pascoe who was almost beginning to enjoy the crackling heat of his burning bridges.

'Oh aye? Tell you what. Ten bob says my scrote got sent down, your pair walked free.'

Pascoe did a mental double-take. Against volition, his jaw, as craggily set as Spencer Tracy's in the expectation of moral showdown, dropped. He must have missed something. Otherwise how come he'd moved from career-ending confrontation to settling matters with a friendly bet like two chaps in a pub?

He looked at the Fat Man with growing suspicion. Could it possibly be that this cop, so obviously the archetypical bruiser who got results by kicking down doors and beating out questions in Morse code on a suspect's head, was in fact jerking him around with *words*? No! Reason wouldn't admit it . . . or was it pride that wouldn't admit it? He tried to bring to mind the scene in the court . . . the jury laughing

. . . Martineau furious . . . was that the key . . . ?
Should he have listened more carefully . . . ?

Dalziel straightened up and broke wind.

'Better out than in,' he said. 'So, is it a bet?'

'I'd need odds,' said Pascoe. 'There's two of mine.'

'You cheeky sod. All right. Ten bob to a quid.
How's that?'

'Done,' said Pascoe.

'Grand. And I reckon this is done too.'

He pushed himself to his feet rather creakingly and
massaged his knees. Then he looked at his watch and
said, 'I'll never make it back to Taff-land in time for
the kick-off now. Not to worry. I daresay I'll see a bit
too much of yon little bugger over the next ten years
or so. Here, Tankie's taking his time about the next
inspection, isn't he?'

'I'm not complaining,' said Pascoe.

'Well, you bloody well should be. Officer present,
prisoner ready for inspection, and the RSM absent
from parade? It's not bloody on! Excuse me, SIR!'

And Pascoe, who was getting used to finding himself tumbling in zero gravity every time he began to
feel something like firm ground beneath his feet, was
hardly surprised to be pushed aside as the Fat Man
began to beat a thunderous rhythm on the door accompanied by a raucous bellow of, 'Come on, Tankie,
let's be having you. Plenty of time to sit around playing with yourself when this lot's over. Charley, Charley, get out of bed! Charley, Charley . . .'

Pascoe got well clear of the door but this time instead of being flung violently against the wall, it
swung slowly open. Trotter stood there, the sawn-off
shotgun at the high port. His face was so impassive, it
just needed a cheroot to get him auditioned for a spa-
ghetti western.

He didn't look like he'd come to play at inspections.

'This do you then?' said Dalziel cheerfully, picking up the bucket. 'The floor's so clean you could eat your dinner off it. Shan't be needing this anymore.'

And in an act too suicidal for Pascoe to find an appropriate reaction, the Fat Man hurled the water in Trotter's face.

It wasn't the preliminary to an escape attempt. Dalziel just stood there roaring with laughter. Nor did Trotter react with any explosive show of anger. Instead, the water dripping down his face, he slowly and deliberately brought the gun barrel to bear on Dalziel's chest.

'Nay, Tankie, fair do's,' protested the Fat Man. 'When you chucked your bucket in yon colour sergeant's face, he didn't shoot you, did he? And there were a lot worse than water in it! Mind you, I'm not saying he didn't feel like it, but he kept control.'

'I'm not a bloody colour sergeant,' grated Trotter.

'That's right. And I'm not a squaddy and this ain't the glasshouse. So where does that get us? You want to prove that if I had to put up with what you had to put up with, I'd crack like a Boxing Day wishbone. Well, wish away, lad, but it's not going to come true. Tha's not got the time and tha's not got the talent. So where do we go from here?'

Only one place! Pascoe's fears told him. But fear left just sufficient space for another voice which asked, why is Dalziel doing this? Why the change of tactics? And if there is a game, why the hell couldn't the big, fat, arrogant bastard let me in on it? Because he thinks I'm useless? Because he thinks he's God?

Because, came a tiny voice from somewhere deeper

than reason, because he knew from the start that everything we said was overheard by Trotter.

Could it really be that this Quasimodo, this Incredible Hulk, this Creature From The Black Lagoon had been carefully orchestrating everything he said? Oh, that would be a trick worth knowing, even if it took a lifetime to learn. Did he have a lifetime? He was beginning to hope again. But perhaps it was all just a clutching at straws. His mind was racing through the Fat Man's inconsequential ramblings . . . his bad jokes . . . desperately seeking the small man in the booth who was working the Great Oz's lips . . .

'Tell you what, Tankie,' said Dalziel. 'Why don't you chuck it in? Leave us locked up and take off. I'll not chase you, believe me. Less I see of you in future the better. You can settle down somewhere, forget the past. Jude too. Past's dead and buried. Like your dad. Finished and forgotten, all debts paid. No names, no pack drill. You can both have a future. You wherever you go. And Jude back home with her man and her kiddie . . .'

And at last Pascoe saw it, clear as the hair in Dalziel's nose. All those casual references to Judith's settled life . . . Tankie had known nothing of this! The poor bastard really had believed that during all his time behind bars, his twin had been shut away too in some empathic fastness of the heart and mind, living only for his release, their reunion.

Dalziel had worked this out, guessed that Jude's cooperation wasn't just based on geminate love, or even fear that the Fat Man could tie her in to her father's death, but the much greater fear that if Tankie knew the truth, he might divert some or all of these pent up energies from destruction of Dalziel to destruction of her precious new life.

So why hadn't the Fat Man just spilled the beans straight off?

Because Tankie would probably have killed the messenger! This way, by letting him work it out for himself . . .

It was all a question of timing, of working out when the hints had finally worked. And they had worked. The evidence was there in the woman's face, floating in the shadows over her brother's shoulder. One cheek pale as a winter sky, the other flushed like a summer dawn.

The bastard had hit her. And then Dalziel had summoned him. Why?

So he could learn about the child, of course!

This revelation the Fat Man had kept for now, for face to face, guessing that Jude would keep hidden to the end what she valued most, even in face of—especially in face of!—Tankie's rage. For here was the clincher. A social life, a job, even a fellow, after the first explosion, these could be rationalized away. But a child . . .

Even Tankie would know this meant he was relegated to at least second place forever.

He was looking at her now, seeking confirmation in those eyes which so weirdly mirrored his own.

Pascoe glanced at Dalziel hoping for some sign of how he wanted to play this. Was the idea to take the chance offered by this moment of distraction and jump the Trotters? Or was he relying on the revelation having some softening effect on Tankie, making him realize that any further development of his crazy vengeance plan would not only destroy himself and his sister, but her child too?

He'd have betted on violence, but once again he saw he was wrong. The Fat Man was putting his money on psychology, turning now to the locker and taking his suit out.

'I'll be glad to get back into this,' he said. 'Wearing that stuff's like wiping your bum with sandpaper. Like to avert your eyes, Jude? Or do you reckon, seen one, you've seen 'em all?'

He pushed his fatigue trousers down as he spoke. And Pascoe, watching Trotter's face in profile, saw that for all his jungle cunning, the Fat Man had miscalculated.

Perhaps it was Dalziel's coarseness. Or perhaps it was the confirmation in his sister's expression of all that she'd kept from him, and why she'd kept it, and the difference it must make to their relationship for evermore.

Or perhaps it was simply that if fear of your reputation as a wild beast is the nearest you've had to respect in a waste of years, then a wild beast's response is the only option you ever have.

Reasons didn't matter. Nothing mattered except that he was swinging the gun round to blow the Fat Man away.

As in the climactic shoot-out in *The Wild Bunch*, everything slowed down. Dalziel like a *Carry-On farceur* was immobilized with his trousers round his ankles. Pascoe didn't have time to pick a role. His body was launching itself through the air towards the Last National Service Man leaving his mind some way back, wondering why the hell he should *give* a damn about saving the Fat Man for posterity.

Probably posterity would still have been spared this Grecian gift if Judith hadn't got in on the act.

No doubt about her motives. Where she had imagined her brother's crazy game could lead was never clearly established. Later she claimed that the mental intimidation from her dominant twin, plus the trauma of childhood abuse, not forgetting her fear for her own child, had combined to bring her to this point almost without any conscious thought. Now all she saw was that if the Fat Man were blown away, with him went everything in her life that made any sense of it.

She jumped on her brother's back, flinging both arms round his neck and wrapping her legs around his body in a grip as sexual as a Freudian could have desired as she tried to topple him backwards. He staggered and twisted. The gun wavered away from the overhang of Dalziel's belly, and Pascoe grabbed the barrel and dragged it even further round.

Perhaps Trotter deliberately squeezed the trigger, though later, naturally, he denied it. Perhaps it was a finger-jerk reaction caused by the shock of his sister's assault. Or perhaps Pascoe himself, by pulling on the barrel, literally triggered the explosion.

Whoever or whatever, it went off.

There was no pain, just a sense of some tremendous change in his relation with the universe. Then came a couple of seconds' out-of-body experience, in which he hovered somewhere around the single light bulb, watching Dalziel step out of his trousers, advance three paces across the room and deal Trotter a blow on the temple which felled him like a blasted pylon. As he hit the ground, the whole room dissolved under a tidal wave of white light which bore Peter Pascoe out through the cottage roof and carried him at breakneck speed towards the boundary of the universe.

Later he claimed never to have lost consciousness or even the power of rational thought. For a moment, or a millennium, he even had hopes of passing through a *2001* type stargate and ending up in a nice hotel room. But gradually the white light faded and the speed diminished till finally he was simply tumbling slowly through space.

Far below he spotted the twin orbs of the earth and its circling moon. He recalled in childhood his mother trying to get him to see the man in the latter, but he'd never managed it. Now however he could see his features quite clearly in the broad bright orb, and it came as no surprise how closely they resembled those of Andy Dalziel.

The mouth was opening and shutting as if the Fat Man had something to say. Might even be worth hearing, admitted Pascoe, who was not afraid to learn from experience.

He grabbed a passing star, swung himself into a comfortable position along one of its radials, and settled down to listen.

'Think he'll make it, Wieldy?'

'They say there's no reason why not, sir.'

'Well, he better bloody had.'

'Yes sir. Any particular reason, apart from general humanity, sir?'

'He owes me ten bob, that particular enough for you?'

'Oh yes. What'll you do with him if he does make it?'

'Likely I'll keep him. It'll be a challenge.'

'And if he doesn't want to be kept?'

'Nay, Wieldy, you don't imagine I want anybody working for me who's daft enough to want to work for me, do you? A scared cop is a good cop, as long as it don't stop him thinking. And this bugger kept on thinking.'

'Yes, sir. I think he'll do a lot of that. But I should't bank on him staying scared forever.'

'No? Mebbe not. But there's one bugger who should be running scared for the rest of his life. That's the stupid sod who told Tankie where to find me!'

'Sorry, sir?'

'I asked Tankie when he woke up how come he knew I'd be down at the courts. He said he rang the station and asked to speak to me, and some stupid bastard told him I was away for a while, but I'd be back that morning to give evidence. Can you credit it, Wieldy? No idea who he were speaking to, and this bumbrain gives chapter and verse where I can be found!'

Peter Pascoe, who'd been thinking he might try dropping off his star onto the earth next time it rolled past, decided that maybe he'd give it another couple of whirls.

Andy Dalziel said, 'I could murder a cup of tea, Wieldy. And a bun if you can find one.'

The door opened and shut. The Fat Man leaned over the bed and glowered into Pascoe's pale face.

'Anyone at home?' he asked. 'If there is, here's the deal. It'll be grapes and gruel for a bit, then it'll be hard bloody graft for evermore. 'Cos I'm going to make a man out of you, my son. You're going to be the very last National Service Man. Only it's no soft two-year stint for you. Serve with me and you're in for the bloody duration. I'll badger you, and I'll bully you, and I'll bugger you about something rotten. But I'll not take advantage of you or make a dickhead out of you or fob you off with a load of lies. And when I've driven that college crap out of your head, then we'll find out what you're really made of. You may never amount to much as a cop, but by God, you'll learn to jump when I say jump, and that's something. Aye lad, by the time I'm done, if I tell you to fetch me the moon, you'll take off like a whippet and not come back till you've got it in your gob . . . what's that you say?'

Pascoe's lips had moved. The Fat Man stooped closer to catch the softly breathed words.

'. . . let's not ask for the moon . . . I'd rather swing on a star . . .'

'Eh?' said Dalziel.

The eyes snapped open, the words came loud and clear.

'Bette Davis. *Now Voyager*. Almost.'

And for the first time in his life, Andrew Dalziel wondered if he might be biting off more than even his great cetacean jaws could manage to chew.

In *Pascoe's Ghost* all the chapter headings come from the poetical works of Edgar Allan Poe.

PASCOE'S GHOST

Truth is not always in a well . . .
The depth lies in the valleys where we
seek her, and not upon the mountain
tops where she is found.
THE CHEVALIER C. AUGUSTE DUPIN

I

Oh, the bells, bells, bells!
What a tale their terror tells.

1

THE PHONE RANG.

Swithenbank heard his mother answer it.

'John!' she called. 'It's for you.'

Stuffing the last fragments of toast into his mouth, he rose and went into the hall.

'Hello,' he said.

Everything was quiet. It was like being in church. The morning sun could only manage a dim religious light through the circle of stained glass in the front door and the smell of pine-scented polish was as heavy as incense on the dank autumn air. Could he not have noticed how cold it was here in his childhood? He vowed to bring an electric blanket if he came at Christmas. If he came.

'Hello? Hello!' he said and put the receiver down.

'Mother!' he called.

Mrs Swithenbank appeared at the head of the stairs. Her hair was a deep shade of lavender this month. For a woman in her late fifties, she had a trim elegant figure despite an enormous appetite which she never hesitated to indulge.

'Who was it on the phone?' asked her son.

'Didn't she tell you, dear?'

'She? No, the line was dead.'

'Was it? Oh dear. Perhaps she'll ring again.'

'Didn't *she* give a name?'

'I think so, dear. I always ask who's calling. In case it's Boris or one of the others so I can say you're out. Though I don't really like to lie.'

'It's just the modern equivalent of the butler saying I'm not at home, Mother,' said Swithenbank in exasperation. 'So, what did this woman say?'

'Well, to tell the truth, I didn't really catch it, she had such a funny voice. Very distant somehow. But it wasn't Boris or any of the others. I mean, I know it wasn't Boris, because it was a girl. But it wasn't Stella or Ursula either, or I'd have said.'

'Oh Mother!'

'It sounded a very odd name,' she said defensively. 'Una something, I think. I'm sorry I missed it, but after all, dear, I'm not your secretary. I'm sure she'll ring again.'

The phone rang.

Swithenbank snatched it up.

'Wearton two-seven-nine,' he said.

'John, dear fellow! Caught you at last. How are you?'

'Hello, Boris,' said Swithenbank, scowling at his mother's retreating back. 'I'm fine. I was going to call before I went back.'

'I would be devastated if you didn't. In fact that's why I'm ringing really. I'm having a few of the locals round for drinks tomorrow, Saturday, about seven-thirty. I thought I'd ask our old gang to hang on for a bite of supper afterwards. You know, Stella and Geoff, Ursula and Peter.'

'I know who the old gang are,' said Swithenbank acidly.

'We're all dying to see you again. It's been six months at least since you were last in Wearton. Just before Father died, wasn't it?'

'Yes. I'm sorry I couldn't make it to the funeral, Boris.'

'Don't worry. We all understand. It's been difficult for you.' The voice dropped a sympathetic semi-tone. 'No word yet? On Kate, I mean.'

'No,' said Swithenbank shortly.

'It must be awful for you. Awful. It's a year now, isn't it?'

'That's right. A year.'

'Twelve months, and nothing. Awful. Cheer up, though. I suppose no news is good news.'

'I can't imagine why you should suppose that,' said Swithenbank.

'I'm sorry. What I meant was . . . look, do try to get along tomorrow night, won't you?'

'I can't promise, Boris. I'll give you a ring later if I may.'

'Fine. Good. Excellent. 'Bye!'

Swithenbank was smiling as he put down the phone. He went into the kitchen where his mother was washing the dishes.

'That girl on the phone. The name couldn't have been Ulalume, could it?'

'Ulalume? Yes, that sounds very like it, though it doesn't sound very *likely*, does it? By the way, I'm going into town when I've finished these. I'll probably have lunch there.'

'Mother,' said Swithenbank wearily. 'You've been going into town and having lunch there on Fridays for the last twenty years at least. Everyone in Wearton expects it. I expect it. I can only hope that you may be visiting the hairdresser, too. But I cannot be surprised.'

'I'm not trying to surprise you, dear,' said his mother mildly.

Fifteen minutes later he heard her call goodbye as she passed the open sitting-room door. Almost simultaneously the phone rang.

By the time he got into the entrance hall his mother had picked up the receiver.

'It's that girl again, dear,' she said. 'I must dash or I'll miss my bus. 'Bye!'

He did not touch the phone till he heard the front door close behind her.

'Hello? Hello?' he said.

For twenty seconds or more there was no reply then as from a great distance a thin infinitely melancholy voice said, 'Ulalume . . . Ulalume,' stretching the words out like a street-vendor's cry.

'For God's sake, stop fooling around!' commanded Swithenbank, his voice authoritative and controlled. But the control disappeared when a voice behind him said, 'Mr John Swithenbank?'

He spun round. Standing in the open doorway was a man, tall, slim beneath a short fawn raincoat, early thirties, rather a long nose, mop of brown hair falling over his brow and shadowing the light blue, watchful eyes.

'Who the hell are you?' demanded Swithenbank.

'I met a lady on the drive—she said just to walk in. Something about the bell not working.'

He reached out of the door and pressed the bell-push. A deafening chime echoed round the hall. He looked embarrassed.

'I'm sorry,' he said. 'I'm interrupting your call. I'll wait outside, shall I, till you're finished.'

'It is finished, said Swithenbank, replacing the receiver firmly. 'What do you want with me, Mr . . . ?'

'Inspector. Detective-Inspector Pascoe,' said the man. 'Could I speak with you, Mr Swithenbank? It's about your wife.'

'You'd better come in,' said Swithenbank. 'Hang your coat up if you think it's going to be worth it.'

Pascoe wiped his feet, removed his coat, and carefully hung it up on the old-fashioned hall-stand which loomed like a multiple gallows behind the door.

2

Boris Kingsley replaced the phone on the bedside table. He was sitting on the edge of the bed and the mattress sagged beneath his weight. He was naked and he contemplated his bulging belly with the helpless bewilderment of a weak king confronting a peasants' revolt.

'When did you last see your little Willie?' asked Ursula Davenport, snuggling against his back and peering over his shoulder.

He dug his elbow into one of her bountiful breasts.

'About the same time you saw your little Umbilicus,' he said.

'Will he come?'

'What?'

'Johnny, I mean.'

'Why do you call him Johnny? No one else calls him Johnny. You always try to suggest a special relationship.'

'We had once. At least, I thought so.'

'But Kate put paid to that,' said Kingsley spitefully. 'Funny, I often think that both you and Stella got married on the rebound.'

'Stella?' She raised her eyebrows.

'Your sister-in-law, dear. There are depths beneath that unyielding surface.'

'I'm glad to hear it. I wasn't conscious of a rebound,' she said evenly. 'Unless it was from Stella moving into the bungalow. I could hardly stay on, could I?'

'I wish you'd stayed and the bungalow had moved,' grumbled Kingsley, walking across to the window and peering out.

The lawn had that tousled unkempt look even the best kept grass gets on a dank October morning. He had the sense of peering down at a wild moorland from some craggy height. Away to the right ran an avenue of trees, while straight ahead was a tangle of neglected shrubbery which reinforced the impression of desolation till he raised his eyes a little and the cheerful red-brick of the Rawlinson bungalow some three hundred yards away re-established the scale of things.

'Pa should never have sold your father that land,' said Kingsley with irritation. 'It ruins the view.'

'I dare say Stella will think the same about little Willie if she's out in the garden,' said Ursula.

'She should be so lucky,' said Kingsley. 'How do you think your brother is since his accident?'

'You are an evil-minded bastard sometimes, Boris,' she said.

'And you're the vicar's wife,' he mocked. 'Is it sermon on the mount time?'

She rolled off the bed as he approached.

'I think it's time to go home and have breakfast.'

'Stay here,' he suggested. 'When's Peter due back from his concert?'

'Not till this afternoon.'

'Well then.'

'But old mother Warnock is due here in half an hour.'

'She'll devil us some kidneys. You can say you dropped in to invite me to address the Mothers' Union.'

'Boris, dear, she'd stand up and denounce us before the first hymn next Sunday morning. No, I'll have a quick shower and be off.'

She left the room before he could attempt to restrain her by force or persuasion.

He did not appear too frustrated by her evasion but strolled round the room getting dressed. Unhappy at the selection of trousers in the large mahogany wardrobe which occupied half a wall opposite his bed, he took a key from a chest of drawers and unlocked a smaller oak wardrobe in the corner by the window. Here were hanging the heavier twills which the chill of the morning invited.

Here also hung a woman's dress in white muslin with blue ribbons to gather it gently in beneath the bosom. On the shelf above was a wide-brimmed floppy hat in white linen trimmed with blue roses. He touched it lovingly, then caressed the soft material of the dress with his open hand.

When he turned from re-locking the wardrobe Ursula was standing dripping wet in the bedroom doorway.

'I couldn't find a towel,' she said.

'I'll come and rub you dry,' he answered, smiling.

3

Geoffrey Rawlinson let his binoculars rest on his chest, stood up, collapsed the seat of his shooting-stick and, leaning heavily on it so that he drilled a trail of holes across the lawn, he limped back to the bungalow.

He heard the phone being replaced as he negotiated the high step into the kitchen, and a moment later his wife came into the room, snapping on the light so that he blinked as it came bouncing at him off chrome, tile and Formica. The changes Stella had made in the kitchen never ceased to amaze him. It was, he claimed, more automated than the War Room in the Pentagon. But even in high summer it still needed artificial light till the sun was high in the sky.

'Children off to school?' he asked.

'Yes. Please, Geoff, how many times do I have to ask you? Don't dig up the floor tiles with that thing!'

'Sorry,' said Rawlinson. He leaned the shooting-stick against the waste-disposal unit and took up his heavy blackthorn walking stick which was hooked over the rack of the dishwasher. It had a thick rubber ferrule which squeaked against the floor as he walked towards his wife.

'Who were you phoning?' he asked.

'The butcher,' she said. 'Is *she* still over there?'

'I've been looking at the birds,' he answered in tones of gentle reproach. 'That pair of whitethroats is still here. It's really incredibly late for them. I think one of them may have been injured and the other's waited for it. Touching, don't you think?'

His wife regarded him without speaking. Her face had all the individual features of great beauty, but there was something too symmetrical, too inexpressive about them, as though they had been put on canvas by a painter of great technique but no talent.

Rawlinson sighed.

'I don't know. Just because you saw her walking down the old drive last night doesn't mean she was going to be down with Boris.'

'Don't be a fool,' she snapped. 'Peter's away singing, isn't he? And why else should she be skulking around out there on a nasty damp evening?'

'You were,' he observed quietly.

'I was in my own garden,' she said sharply. 'If she wanted to visit Wear End, she could easily drive round by the road. After all, she does have her own car, which is more than we can afford.'

'It's her own money,' said Rawlinson.

'It's the money you had to pay her for half of your own house,' retorted Stella.

'We've been over all this before,' he said. 'I had to buy her out. And there was something left over from Father's will to pay for all this modernization.'

He gestured at the kitchen.

'While she lets her husband freeze in that draughty old rectory and spends all her money on cars and clothes!'

'She has to live there too.'

'Not when Peter's away she doesn't.'

'Oh, for God's sake,' he snapped. 'She's my sister, so leave it alone.'

'And Peter's your cousin. And you're my husband. But what difference does that make to anything?' she yelled after him as he stumped out of the kitchen.

An hour later she took him a cup of coffee in his study.

The light was on above his draughtsman's drawing-board but he was sitting at his desk with his bird-watching journal. The writing was on the left-hand page. On the other he had sketched with a few deft strokes of a felt-tipped pen a pair of white-throats in a sycamore tree. In the background loomed the bulk of Wear End House with its windows all shuttered.

She put the coffee down by the drawing.

'Are we going to Boris's tomorrow night?'

'I suppose so.'

'Will John be there?'

'He's got the face for it.'

'What do you mean?'

'Oh, leave it alone, Stella!'

'I think he deserves all our sympathy and support.'

'Last time you said it was the biggest stroke of luck he'd had!'

'I still think that!' she snapped. 'But the difference between thinking and saying is called civilized behaviour.'

'OK. OK. Let's drop it,' he answered moodily. 'I must try to get some work done or we'll have nothing to put down the waste-disposal unit.'

At the door she paused and said, 'I don't mean to nag, Geoff, but things . . .'

'Yes, yes. I know.'

'How's your leg this morning?'

'The same. And better.'

'How can that be?' she asked.

'Nothing changes,' he said, reaching for his coffee, 'but you learn to live with pain.'

4

Arthur Lightfoot leaned on his hoe and watched the young woman in the telephone-box. Her Triumph Spitfire was parked with its nearside wheels on the wedge of carefully tended grass which lay in front of the village war memorial. Lightfoot made no secret of his watching. Generations of his family had lived and laboured in Wearton and there was as little chance of a native turning from the close contemplation of a stranger as there was of the soldier on the memorial dropping his rifle.

Lightfoot was a man whose face had been weathered to a leathery mask beneath an unkempt stack of gingery hair. His deep-sunk eyes rarely blinked and his mouth gave little sign of being fitted for human speech. To age him between thirty and fifty would have been difficult.

What nature had done for the man, art had done for the woman. She had blonde hair, a good but not over emphatic figure and a face which happily confessed to twenty-five but left you guessing about thirty-five. It had a slightly preoccupied expression as she came out of the phone-box and took a couple of uncertain steps towards the car. Then, as if feeling Lightfoot's gaze upon her, she turned, looked back at him, and strode with sudden determination across the road.

'Excuse me,' she said, then, her eyes caught by a double row of staked dahlias close by the side wall of the old stone cottage, she exclaimed, 'Aren't they lovely! Such colours for a murky day.'

'Frost'll have 'em soon,' said Lightfoot.

'Are they . . . do you sell them?'

Lightfoot made a gesture which took in the full extent of his smallholding.

'I grow what I need,' he said. 'What I don't need, I sell.'

He did not look like a man who needed many dahlias, so the woman said, 'May I buy some?'

'Aye. Come in and take thy pick.'

He held open the rickety gate for her and she walked along the row of blooms pointing to her choices which he cut with a fearsome clasp knife taken from his pocket. When she reached the angle of the cottage she stopped and said, 'I see you had a fire.'

The ground behind the cottage was scorched and blackened and a pile of charred rubbish looking like the remnants of several outbuildings had been shovelled together alongside a wired pen which housed three pigs.

'Aye,' he said.

'Not too much damage, I hope,' she said, looking at the back of the cottage which also bore the mark of great heat. The window-frames looked as if they'd been recently replaced and reglazed.

'Enough. Nought that money won't mend. Are you done choosing?'

'I think so. Perhaps another pink one. They are gorgeous. Is it good soil?'

'Soil's what you make it,' he answered. 'Many a

barrowload of manure and many a barrowload of compost I've poured into this soil. See there!'

He pointed to where a broad pit which seemed to be full of decaying vegetable matter was sending coils of vapour into the dank autumn air.

'Hot as a curate's dreams in there,' he averred, watching her closely.

She glanced at him, amused by the odd expression.

'It doesn't look very appetizing,' she said. 'What's in it?'

'*Everything*,' he said. 'What pigs won't eat yon pit gobbles up. Dustmen get slim pickings from Arthur Lightfoot.'

His sudden enthusiasm made her uneasy and she was glad to hear the rickety gate shut behind her.

'That your car?' asked Lightfoot as she regained the footpath.

'Yes.'

'Ah.'

He didn't offer to say more so she asked, 'Could you tell me the way to a house called The Pines? I've got a vague idea, but I might as well hit it first time.'

'Swithenbank's house?'

'That's right.'

'Them dahlias for Mrs Swithenbank?'

'As a matter of fact, they are.'

'She's not fond of dahlias, Mrs Swithenbank,' said Lightfoot. 'She says they're a wormy sort of flower.'

'I'm sorry for it,' said the woman, irritation in her voice now. 'Can you tell me where the house is or not?'

'Second turn left, second house on the left,' said Lightfoot.

'Thank you.'

When she reached the car, he called after her, 'Hey!'

She laid the flowers on the passenger seat before turning.

'Yes?'

'Mrs Swithenbank doesn't like people parking on her lawn either.'

Angrily she got into the car, bumped off the grass strip in front of the war memorial, and accelerated violently away.

Arthur Lightfoot watched her out of sight. Turning to his wheelbarrow, he tossed in a couple of weeds prior to pushing the barrow towards his compost pit and tipping the contents onto its steaming surface.

'Feeding time,' he said. 'Feeding time.'

II

. . . I wake and sigh
And sleep to dream till day
Of the truth that gold can never buy.

PASCOE RELAXED IN A commodious chintz-covered armchair whose springs emitted distant sighs and clangings like an old ship rolling at its moorings on a still night. He looked, and felt, extremely comfortable, but the watchful eyes were triangulating the man in front of him.

Swithenbank was a slightly built man, almost small, but with an air of control and composure which created a greater sense of *presence* than another six inches might have done. He had black hair obviously carefully tended by a good barber. Sorry, *hair stylist,* corrected Pascoe, whose own hairdresser was very much a barber, still more a butcher according to Ellie, his wife. Ellie would also have used Swithenbank's clothes as the occasion of more unflattering comparisons. Pascoe was smart in an off-the-peg chain store kind of way, while there was something about the other man's thin-knit pale blue roll-collar sweater that proclaimed without the need of a label that it was an exclusive Italian design and cost forty-five pounds.

Show me a poor publisher and I'll show you a fool, as Dr Johnson may have, ought to have, said, thought Pascoe, forcing his attention from the exquisitely cut slacks back to the man's features. Broad forehead, long straight nose, thick but neatly trimmed black moustache, small, very white teeth, which glinted beneath the dark brush as the man made ready to speak.

'Let's not beat about the bush, Inspector,' said Swithenbank.

'What bush would that be?' enquired Pascoe politely.

'You said you were here about Kate, my wife. Have you found her?'

'No,' said Pascoe.

'Thank God!'

'I'm sorry?' said Pascoe.

'I thought you were going to tell me you'd found her body.'

'No. Not yet, sir.'

Swithenbank looked at him sharply.

'Not yet. But you sound as if you expect to.'

'I didn't intend to,' said Pascoe.

Suddenly Swithenbank smiled and the atmosphere became much more relaxed, as if he had operated a switch. A man of considerable charm, thought Pascoe. He didn't trust men of considerable charm very much.

'So we're really at square one, no further forward than twelve months ago. You think Kate's dead though you've got no proof. And I, of course, remain Number One suspect.'

'It's a position we unimaginative policemen always reserve for husbands,' replied Pascoe, content to fall in with the new lightness of manner.

'But my ratiocinative powers tell me there must be more, Inspector. Visits from your colleague, Inspector Dove of the Enfield constabulary, I have come to expect. I think he believes, not without cause, that ultimately the threat of his company could bring a man to confess to anything. But I'm sure it takes more than mere suspicion to get a Yorkshire policeman into motion. Am I beating anywhere nearer the bush, Inspector?'

'The bush is burning, but it is not consumed,' said Pascoe with a smile.

'A Biblical policeman!' exclaimed Swithenbank.

'Just carry on with the still small voice,' said Pascoe, beginning to enjoy the game.

'Now you disappoint me,' said Swithenbank. 'Wasn't it Elijah who got the still small voice? While, of course, Moses it was who talked to the trees.'

'Both agents of the truth,' said Pascoe. 'You were saying?'

'It's my guess, then, that something has stimulated your interest in me. A tip of some kind. Phone calls perhaps? Or anonymous letters? Am I right or am I right?'

'You're right,' said Pascoe. 'That's really very sharp

of you, sir. Yes, there's been a letter. And, oddly enough, it came to us here in Yorkshire.'

'Why "oddly"?'

'It's just that it's a year since your wife disappeared and we've had nothing about you before. Except through official channels, I mean. All the usual post-disappearance "tips" went to your local station at Enfield—or straight to Scotland Yard. We contacted Enfield about this letter, of course.'

'And the omniscient Inspector Dove told you I was presently visiting Wearton!'

'Right,' said Pascoe. 'And as *we* received the letter and you are in *our* area . . . well, here *I* am.'

'And a pleasant change it makes from your cockney cousins,' said Swithenbank. 'If I may say so.'

'Thank you kindly,' said Pascoe. 'And if I may say, you seem somehow less surprised or taken aback by all this than I would have expected.'

'I work as an editor for Colbridge the publishers. A condition of service is not being surprised. By anything! But you are very sharp, Inspector. In a manner of speaking, I've been prepared for your visit. Or at least its first cause.'

'You've had a letter too?' guessed Pascoe. 'Splendid. We must compare notes.'

Swithenbank smiled and shook his head.

'Alas, no letter. Just phone calls. They started in London about a fortnight ago, three direct, a couple which just got as far as my secretary and the woman who cleans my flat. So I decided to come up here.'

'Why? What did they say?'

'Always the same thing. And again this morning, twice. My mother answered the phone. First time the line was dead by the time I got to it. But she heard the message. And the second time, just as you arrived, I heard the voice myself. Exactly the same as before. Just a woman's name, twice repeated. *Ulalume.*'

'Ula . . . ?'

'Ulalume.'

'And the voice was female?' said Pascoe, perplexed.

Swithenbank shrugged and said, 'Probably. It's an eerie wailing kind of tone. Possibly a male falsetto.'

'And when you spoke sternly in reply?'

'Ah. Of course, you came to the door then, didn't you? The line went dead. End of message.'

'Message?' said Pascoe. 'I'm clearly missing something. There's a message here, is there? Just what does Ulalume signify, Mr Swithenbank?'

The other leaned back in his chair, put the tips of his fingers together beneath his chin and recited.

> *'And we passed to the end of the vista*
> *But were stopped by the door of a*
>   *tomb—*
> *By the door of a legended tomb;*
> *And I said—"What is written, sweet*
>   *sister,*
> *On the door of this legended tomb?"*
> *She replied—'Ulalume—Ulalume—*
> *'Tis the vault of thy lost Ulalume!"'*

'Remarkable,' said Pascoe. 'I'm impressed. But not much wiser.'

'It's a poem by Edgar Allan Poe. Ulalume was a nymph, the dead love of the poet who inadvertently returns to the place where he had entombed her a year earlier.

And I cried—"It was surely October
On this very night of last year
That I journeyed—I journeyed down
    here—
That I brought a dread burden down
    here—
Well I know, now, this dim lake of
    Auber,
This misty mid-green of Weir."

I can do you *The Raven* and *Annabel Lee,* too, if
you like.'

'October,' said Pascoe. 'Weir. Wearton. So that's
what brought you up here! What an apt choice of
poem!'

'Had I killed my wife and brought her to Wearton
to bury her last October, it might indeed seem so,'
said Swithenbank coldly.

'Indeed,' said Pascoe, catching the man's style. 'But
that's not quite what I meant. The reference was aptly
chosen in that you understood it instantly. To me it
meant nothing. Just chance?'

Swithenbank shook his head thoughtfully.

'No, not chance. Among other things I do for my
firm, I edit a series called *Masters of Literature.* Slim
volumes, a bit of biography, a bit of lit. crit.; nothing
anyone's going to get a Ph.D. for, but useful to
sixth-formers and the undergrad. in a hurry. I've done
a couple myself, including one on Poe, accompanied
by a selection of his poems and stories.'

'I see,' said Pascoe. 'Would this be generally
known?'

'It didn't make any best-seller list,' said
Swithenbank.

'But people in Wearton could know? Your mother

might do a spot of quiet boasting. My son, the author.'

'I think when I'm away she tries to pretend I'm still at college,' said Swithenbank. 'But yes, some of my old friends would know. The only true test of an old friend is whether he buys your books! Boris Kingsley certainly bought a copy—he asked me to sign it.'

'Boris . . . ?'

'Kingsley. He lives at the Big House, Wear End House, that is.'

'I see,' said Pascoe. 'Any other particular friends?'

Swithenbank laughed, not very mirthfully.

'I gather that friends come a close second to husbands as popular suspects.'

'For anonymous letters, yes,' said Pascoe.

'I'm sure you're wrong, but let me see. Of my own close circle there remain, besides Boris, Geoffrey Rawlinson. His wife, Stella, née Foxley—big farmers locally. Geoff's sister, Ursula. And Ursula's husband who also happens to be their cousin, Peter Davenport, who also happens to be our vicar!'

'I see,' said Pascoe. 'A close circle, this?'

'To the point of inbreeding,' said Swithenbank cheerfully. 'As good local families, we're probably all related somewhere. Except Boris. They've only been here since the end of the last century.'

'So you all grew up together?'

'Oh yes. Except Peter. His branch of the family lived in Leeds, but he used to spend nearly all his holidays here. Surprised us all when he went into Holy Orders.'

'Why?'

'No one you've stolen apples with can seem quite good enough to be a priest, can they?' said Swithenbank.

'So apart from you, all your circle have remained in Wearton?' said Pascoe.

'I suppose so. Except Ursula and Peter, of course. They married while he was still a curate somewhere near Wakefield. When was that?—about eight years ago, yes, I'd married the previous year—of course, I'd been working in London for nearly two years by then . . .'

'So you'd be twenty-three, twenty-four?'

'So I would. The others fell in rapid succession. First Geoff and Stella, then, almost immediately, Ursula and Peter. It wasn't till three years after that that Peter came to Wearton as vicar. Too young for some of the natives but the local connection helped.'

'But Mr. Kingsley didn't marry?'

'No. He looked after his parents up at the Big House. They weren't all that old, but were both in poor health. His mother went about eighteen months ago, his father last spring.'

'And that's the lot? Of your friends, I mean?'

'Yes, I think so. There's Kate's brother, I suppose. Arthur. Arthur Lightfoot. He was several years older and several ages less couth; certainly not one of the charmed circle that made Wearton the Port Said of the north a dozen years ago. But you'd better prick him down on your interview list.'

'Interview list?'

'I presume it's more than idle curiosity that's making you ask these questions, Inspector!' he said acidly.

The doorbell rang. Its chime would not have disgraced a cathedral.

'Your mother?' wondered Pascoe. 'I should like to talk to her.'

'Never gets home till five on Fridays,' said Swithenbank.

The bell rang again. Swithenbank made no move.

'Your mother was mistaken about the bell,' observed Pascoe. 'It seems to be working very well.'

'She hates to be disturbed,' said Swithenbank, 'so she disconnects it. The first thing I do when I come up here is repair it.'

Again the bell.

'You certainly know your business,' said Pascoe admiringly. 'Yes, I'd certainly say it was repaired. It's just the *tone* you miss, not the function, I gather?'

Swithenbank rose.

'It never does to appear too available,' he said, leaving the room.

He pulled the door shut behind him. Pascoe immediately jumped up and moved as quietly to the door as the creaky floorboards would permit, but he needn't have bothered about sound getting out as the woodwork and walls were obviously thick enough to prevent anything less raucous than the bell getting in.

Working on the Dalziel principle that the next best thing to overhearing a conversation is to give the impression you've overheard it, he did not resume his seat but stood close to the doorway, apparently rapt in contemplation of a small oil painting darkened by age almost to indecipherability, until the door opened and he found himself looking at a pretty blonde carrying a large bunch of dahlias.

'Let me take those to the kitchen. Mother will be delighted. They're her favourite. Oh, this is Detective-Inspector Pascoe, my dear. Jean Starkey.'

Swithenbank removed the flowers and left Pascoe and the newcomer shaking hands.

With an expertise that Pascoe admired, the woman assessed the seating available and chose the comfortable armchair. Not liking the look of the cane chair

Swithenbank had occupied, Pascoe perched gingerly on a chaise-longue which was even harder than it appeared.

'Are you an inhabitant of Wearton, too, Miss Starkey?'

She glanced down at her ringless left hand and smiled approval.

'Oh no. Like yourself, just visiting. At least I presume you're just visiting?'

'For the moment, yes.'

'Does that mean you may eventually settle here?' asked the woman, rounding her eyes.

'I think it means the Inspector doesn't consider "visiting" adequately covers his possible return flanked by bloodhounds and armed with warrants,' said Swithenbank.

He came back into the room carrying a huge vase into which the dahlias had been tumbled with no pretence of aesthetic theory.

Placing them on a small table within reach of the big armchair he said, 'Do what you can with these, Jean dear. I've no talent for nature.'

Then, relaxing into the cane chair which seemed to have been made for a man of his size, he continued, 'Mr Pascoe is here about Kate's disappearance. No, there's been no news, but there's been a new outburst of anonymous activity. Phone calls to me and a letter to the police. By the way, Inspector, you never actually told me what was in the letter, did you? It must have been something pretty striking to get you off traffic duty. Could I see it? I might be able to help with the writing.'

'No writing, sir,' said Pascoe. 'Typewriter. Possibly a Remington International, quite old. You wouldn't know anyone who has such a machine?'

He included the woman in his query. She smiled and shook her head.

'But what did it say?' persisted Swithenbank.

'Not much. Let me see. *John Swithenbank knows where the other is.* Yes, that's it.'

Swithenbank and Jean Starkey exchanged puzzled glances.

'I'm sorry, Inspector,' he said. 'It's like Ulalume to you. I don't get it.'

'No, no. I should apologize,' said Pascoe. 'I haven't been entirely open.'

He pulled an envelope out of his inside pocket and from it he took three colour prints which he passed over to Swithenbank. The prints showed from different angles a pendant ear-ring, a single pearl in a gold setting on a thin chain about an inch long.

'Do you recognize that, sir?' asked Pascoe.

Jean Starkey, unable to contain her curiosity, had risen to peer over Swithenbank's shoulder at the photographs. He glanced up at her and she put her hand on his shoulder either for her support or his comfort.

'Kate had a pair like that,' he said. 'But I couldn't be absolutely sure.'

'It matches the specification in your list of clothes and other items which disappeared with your wife.'

'Does it? It's a year ago. If you say it does, then clearly it does. This was with that cryptic note?'

'Not so cryptic after all,' said Jean Starkey.

'No,' said Swithenbank. 'No. I see now why you came hot-foot to Wearton, Inspector. This really does point the finger.'

'But it means nothing!' protested the woman.

He smiled up at her.

'I don't mean at me, dear. I mean at whoever sent

it. If it is Kate's, that is. Could I have a look at the ear-ring itself, Inspector?'

'Eventually,' said Pascoe. 'Just now it's down at our laboratory for examination.'

'Examination? For what?'

Pascoe watched Swithenbank closely as he answered.

'I'm afraid, sir, that there were traces of blood on the fastening bar. As though the ear-ring had been torn from the ear by main force.'

III

*Much I marvelled this ungainly fowl to
hear discourse so plainly.*

'A POEM,' SAID DALZIEL.

'By Edgar Allan Poe,' said Pascoe.

'I didn't know he wrote poems as well.'

'As well as short stories, you mean?'

'As well as pictures,' said Dalziel. 'I've seen a lot of his stuff on the telly. Good for a laugh mainly, but sometimes he can give you a scare.'

Pascoe regarded the gross figure of his boss, Detective-Superintendent Andrew Dalziel (pronounced Dee-ell, unless you wanted your head bitten off) and wondered whether the Fat Man was taking the piss. But he knew better than to ask.

'I've got it here,' he said, proffering a "complete works" borrowed from the local library.

Dalziel put on his reading glasses which sat on his great shapeless nose like a space-probe on Mars.

Carefully he read through the poem, his fleshy lips moving from time to time as he half voiced a passage.

When he had finished he rested the open book on the desk before him and said, 'Now that's something like a poem!'

'You liked it?' said Pascoe, surprised.

'Oh aye. It's got a bit of rhythm, a bit of rhyme, not like this modern stuff that doesn't even have commas.'

'Thank you, Dr. Leavis,' murmured Pascoe, and went on hurriedly, 'But does it do us any good?'

'Depends,' said Dalziel, putting his hand inside his shirt to scratch his left rib cage. 'Was it meant to be general or specific?'

'Sorry?'

'If it's specific, listen.

> *It was down by the dank tarn of Auber*
> *In the ghoul-haunted woodland of Weir.*

You want to find yourself a bit of woodland round a pond and go over it with a couple of dogs and a frogman. What's the country like round there?'

'Like country,' said Pascoe dubiously. 'Wearton's a cluster of houses, pub and a church in a bit of a valley, so I suppose there are plenty of woods and ponds thereabouts. But if it's *that* specific, Swithenbank would hardly have mentioned it to me, would he?'

'Mebbe not. Or mebbe he'd get a kick. Playing with a thick copper.'

'I didn't get that impression,' said Pascoe carefully.

Dalziel laughed, a Force Eight blast.

'More likely with me, eh? But he'd soon spot you're a clever bugger, the way you get apostrophes in the right place. So if he *has* killed his missus and if this Ulalume poem *does* point in the right direction, he'd keep his mouth shut. Right? *Unless* he was bright enough to think we might have got a few calls ourselves.'

'Which we didn't,' said Pascoe. 'Just the letter.'

'And the ear-ring,' said Dalziel. 'Remind me again, lad. How'd we first get mixed up in this business?'

Pascoe opened the thin file he was carrying and glanced at the first sheet of paper in it.

'October twenty-fourth last year,' he said. 'Request for assistance from Enfield—that's where Swithenbank lives. Says he'd reported his wife missing on the fifteenth. They hadn't been able to get any kind of line on her movements after the last time Swithenbank claimed to have seen her. Like him, she comes from Wearton, so would we mind checking in case she'd done the classic thing and bolted for home. We checked. Parents both dead, but her brother Arthur still lives in the village. He's got a bit of a smallholding. He hadn't seen her since her last visit with Swithenbank, two months earlier. Nor had anyone else.'

'Or they weren't saying,' said Dalziel.

'Perhaps. There was no reason to be suspicious at the time. Routine enquiry. That was it as far as we were concerned. A month later Enfield came back at us. Were we *quite* sure there was no trace? They wrapped it up, of course, but that's what it came to. They hadn't been able to get a single line on Mrs Swithenbank and when someone disappears as completely as that, you start to get really suspicious. But if you're wise, you double check before you let your suspicions show too clearly.'

'Who'd done the checking in Wearton?' asked Dalziel.

'We just left it to the local lad first time round,' said Pascoe. 'This time I sent Sergeant Wield down. Same result. All quiet after that till this week when the ear-ring turned up.'

'How've they been earning their pay in Enfield this past year?' asked Dalziel.

'Saving the sum of things from the sound of it,' said Pascoe. 'But in between the bullion robberies and the international dope rings, they managed to lean heavily enough on Swithenbank for him to drum up a tame solicitor to lean back.'

'Any motive?'

Pascoe shrugged.

'The marriage wasn't idyllic, so the gossip went, but no worse than a thousand others. *She* might have been having a bit on the side, her girl-friends guessed, but couldn't or wouldn't point the finger. *He* wasn't averse to the odd close encounter at a party, but again no one was naming names.'

'That's marriage Enfield-style, is it?' said Dalziel, shaking his head. He made *Enfield* sound like *Gomorrah*.

'Give us his tale again,' continued Dalziel.

'Friday, fourteenth October, Swithenbank arrives at his office at the usual time. Nothing out of the ordinary during the morning except that his secretary told Willie Dove, Inspector Dove that is, who was doing the questioning, that he seemed a bit moody that morning.'

'How moody? *I shouldn't have cut off her head like that*—that moody?'

'The secretary just put it down to the fact that his favourite assistant was leaving that day.'

'Favourite? Woman?' said Dalziel eagerly.

'Fellow. No, it wasn't the fact that he was leaving, more why he was leaving that had got to Swithenbank, it seems. This chap was putting it all behind him, going off to somewhere primitive like the Orkneys to live off the earth and be a free man. There's a lot of it about among the monied middle classes.'

'He's not bent, is he, this Swithenbank?' asked Dalziel, reluctant to leave this scent.

'No,' said Pascoe, exasperated. 'It just made him think, that's all. Doesn't it make you think a bit, sir, when you hear someone's had the guts to opt out? It's a normal sociological reaction.'

'Is it, lad? You ever find yourself fancying somewhere primitive, I'll send you to Barnsley. What's all this got to do with anything?'

'I'm trying to tell you. Sir. They had a party for the dear departing at lunch-time. It started in the office and finished on platform five at King's Cross when they put their colleague on his train. Swithenbank was in quite a state by this time.'

'Pissed, you mean?'

'That and telling all who would listen that he was wasting his life, that materialism was going to be the death of Western society, that any man who was brave enough could sever his chains with a single blow . . .'

'What kind of chains did he have in mind?' wondered Dalziel.

'I don't know,' said Pascoe. 'Though I should say from the way he dresses that he's decided to hang on to the chains and go down with the rest of Western society. Anyway, those sober enough to remember anything remembered this outburst because it was so uncharacteristic of him. An intellectual smoothie was how his secretary rated him.'

'A loyal girl, that,' said Dalziel.

'Willie Dove has his ways,' said Pascoe. 'Where was I? Oh yes. From King's Cross they, that is the survivors, walked back to the office, hoping to benefit from the fresh air. It's near Woburn Place, so not too far, and they got back about two-thirty. But Swithenbank didn't go in. Despite all attempts to dissuade him, he headed for his car.'

'His mates didn't think he was fit to drive?' said Dalziel. 'He must have been bad, considering most of these southern sods drive home half pissed every night!'

'Possibly,' said Pascoe, as if accepting a serious academic argument. 'The thing was, it wasn't home that Swithenbank was making for, but Nottingham.'

'Nottingham? He really must've been drunk!'

'I'm sorry,' said Pascoe. 'Didn't I say? He was due up in Nottingham that evening for a conference with one of his authors. He'd taken an overnight bag to the office with him and planned a gentle drive north at his leisure that afternoon. But as we've seen, events had overtaken him. So far, his story's been confirmable. After this, there's only Swithenbank's word for what happened, and most of that he claims to have forgotten! He says he'd only driven about half a mile when he came to the conclusion he must be out of his mind! He says he didn't really make a conscious decision, but somehow instead of heading for the MI, he found himself on the way home to Enfield. He can't recollect much about the drive, or getting into the flat, but he's pretty certain his wife wasn't there.'

'If she was, he'd be the last person she'd be expecting to see,' said Dalziel. 'Think about that!'

'I believe Inspector Dove has thought about it,' said Pascoe patiently. 'All Swithenbank does remember positively is waking up some time after five, lying on his bed and feeling rough. He had a shower and a coffee, felt better, tried to ring Nottingham to apologize for his lateness but couldn't get through, wrote his wife a note saying he'd been home, and set off up the MI like the clappers. Like I say, there's no support for any of this. But one of the neighbours definitely saw him arrive back the following afternoon about five p.m. His wife isn't in and Swithenbank gets worried.'

'Why? She never misses *Dr Who,* or what?'

'His note was still there,' said Pascoe reprovingly. 'Untouched. He does nothing for an hour or two, then rings around some likely friends. Nothing. Finally late on Saturday night when she still hasn't returned, he contacts the police. And the wheels go into motion. Routine at first. There's a suitcase and some of his wife's clothes missing. So they check the possibilities. Friends, relatives, etc.—that's where we first came in. Her passport's still at home. A month later she's made no drawing upon her bank account. So now Willie Dove moves in hard.'

'Started digging up the garden and chipping at the garage floor, did he?' said Dalziel.

'He probably would have done except that they lived in a flat and he parked his car in the street,' said Pascoe. 'But he found nothing.'

'So what's he think?'

'He thinks Swithenbank's a clever bugger and has got the body safely stashed. He's kept on at him ever since, but nothing.'

'So why's he think Swithenbank's the man?'

'Intuition, I suppose.'

Dalziel snorted in disgust.

'*Intuition!* Evidence plus an admission, that's what makes detective work. I hope I never hear you using that word, Peter!'

Pascoe smiled weakly and said, 'He's not making a big thing out of it. He just feels in his bones that some time between leaving the party and getting to Nottingham, Swithenbank did the deed and disposed of the body.'

'What's wrong with the night before?' asked Dalziel. 'Put her in the boot. That'd explain his bit of depression that morning.'

'So it would,' said Pascoe. 'Except . . .'

'All right, clever bugger,' growled Dalziel. 'What's up?'

'Except, she went to the hairdresser's on Friday morning. Last reported sighting,' said Pascoe.

Dalziel was silent for a while.

'I ought to thump hell out of you twice a day,' he said finally. 'I take it because you've said nowt much about it that this Nottingham visit was confirmed.'

'Yes,' said Pascoe. 'Jake Starr, some science fiction writer. He was doing a bit on Jules Verne for Swithenbank's *Masters of Literature* series. He confirmed Swithenbank arrived a lot later than arranged, about eight p.m. They worked—and ate—till the early hours. Got up late the next morning. Swithenbank left after lunch. We know he was back in Enfield by five.'

Dalziel pondered.

'All we've got really is a cockney cop's feeling that he did it. Right?'

'And the phone calls. And the letter and ear-ring.'

Dalziel dismissed these with a two-fingered wave of his left hand.

'This lass who turned up today. His fancy piece, you reckon?'

'Could be,' said Pascoe cautiously.

'Perhaps she's the other lass in the poem, that Psyche.'

'I think Psyche represents the poetic soul,' said Pascoe.

'Poetic arsehole,' said Dalziel scornfully. 'What's it say?—*so I pacified Psyche and kissed her.* That sounds like flesh and blood to me. Mind you, if she is his fancy woman, it's a funny thing to do, bringing her up to Wearton like that. It's like flaunting it a bit, wouldn't you say?'

Pascoe indicated that he would say. Jean Starkey had been much occupying his mind since he left Wearton that morning. He had made a note of her car number and asked for it to be traced as soon as he got back to the station, but since vehicle licensing had been computerized, this process could now take several hours.

'Well, it all seems bloody thin to me,' said Dalziel, rising from his chair and scratching his left buttock preparatory to departure. 'Some old mate trying to stir things for Swithenbank. Did you check on his old acquaintance in the village?'

'Didn't have a chance this morning,' said Pascoe. 'I had to be back here for a meeting at lunch-time. But I'll go back, I suppose, and have a word. Or send Sergeant Wield.'

'That's it,' approved Dalziel. 'Delegate. You've got plenty to keep you occupied, I hope. *Our* problems. This is nowt but an "assist", after all.'

'If Kate Swithenbank's lying in a hole near Wearton, it's more than an assist!' protested Pascoe.

'If Jack the bloody Ripper's opening the batting for

Yorkshire (and I sometimes think the buggers who are look old enough), it's still someone else's case,' said Dalziel. 'They'll be open in an hour. You can pay for my help with a pint.'

'Dear at half the price,' muttered Pascoe as the Fat Man lumbered from the room.

He spent the next twenty minutes going over his notes on the background to the case. On the left-hand page of his notebook he had made a digest of the facts as he knew them. The right-hand page was reserved for observations and comments and was woefully blank. He managed by an effort of will to break the blankness with a couple of question-marked words, but it was reaching beyond the limits even of that intuition which Dalziel so scorned and he hastily turned the page as though the fat man might be peering over his shoulder.

He was now among the notes on Swithenbank's 'friends' in Wearton. The tedious business of chatting with each of them would have to be done some time. He wondered whether his conscience would permit him to send Sergeant Wield again. Perhaps, if only the woman Jean Starkey hadn't turned up. There was a false note there somehow. It could be, of course, that Swithenbank wasn't expecting her. He was cool enough to carry it off. Perhaps she was a bit on the side who felt it was time to claim a more central position. But there had been nothing in her manner to suggest that her arrival was an act of defiance. Another hyper-cool customer? Like calling to like? John Swithenbank. Jean Starkey. Same initials. Not something you could really comment on in a report, though Dalziel had once told him he could squeeze significance out of a marble tit. Jean Starkey. John

Swithenbank. And . . . and . . . there was something there . . . the marble tit was yielding . . .

'Excuse me, sir.'

'Oh damn!' said Pascoe, roused from his reverie
just on the brink of revelation.

'Sorry, sir,' said Sergeant Wield. 'That car registra-
tion you wanted checked. They've broken all records.
Here you are.'

He placed a sheet of paper on the desk and withdrew.

Pascoe looked down at it, unseeing at first, then
the words hardened into focus.

> Miss Jean Starkey,
> 38A Chubb Court,
> Nottingham.

'Well,' said Pascoe. 'Well.'

The marble was like a wet bath sponge now.

He picked up his telephone and rang the public
library. That done, he asked his exchange to connect
him with Inspector Dove at Enfield.

'Hello, Peter. What's up? Don't say you've cor-
ralled our boy!'

'Not yet,' said Pascoe. 'Look, Willie, that statement
from the writer Swithenbank went to visit, Jake Starr.
Who took it?'

'Hold on. Let's have a look. Here we are. We did
what we did with you lot, relied on Nottingham.
Why? What's up?'

'Do you know if anyone at Nottingham actually
met Jake Starr?'

'Hang about, there's a note here, can't read my
own writing. No, in fact I don't think they did. I remember now. They spoke to his secretary, who said

Starr was on his way to New York. But she remembered Swithenbank arriving and she was there on Saturday morning when he left. She got in touch with her boss who sent a statement confirming this and having Swithenbank in his sights till bedtime. The secretary was around most of the time too. So we didn't ask them to follow it up when this Starr fellow got back. Why?'

'You don't happen to have a note of the secretary's name, do you?'

'Yes. I've got a statement from her here. I'm sorry, Pete, we could have sent you photo-copies of all this stuff but knowing how much your boss hates paper, I thought the brief digest would do. Jean Starkey. Miss Jean Starkey. There we are. Now tell me what this is all about.'

'With pleasure,' said Pascoe. 'I've just been on to our library where they have useful things like a Writers' Who's Who. Jake Starr is a pseudonym. And no prizes for guessing that the real name is Jean Starkey. But there's more. Miss Starkey's a very personable blonde who at this very moment is in Wearton visiting Swithenbank. And it didn't look like business to me!'

Dove whistled.

'That leaves us with a bit of egg on our face, doesn't it?' he said cheerfully. 'Does it get us much further forward, though?'

'Try this,' said Pascoe. 'If somehow Swithenbank did contrive to have his missus in the boot when he drove north that afternoon, with Starkey alibi-ing him, he had all the time in the world to dispose of the body somewhere a long, long way from Enfield. Naturally he'd want somewhere as safe as possible. What if his childhood memories put him in mind of the perfect hiding-place up here?'

'Hidden cave, secret passage, that sort of thing?' said Dove, making it sound like something out of Enid Blyton, much to Pascoe's irritation.

'OK then. Where do *you* think she is?' he asked.

'Stuffed up the chimney in his flat?'

'First place we looked,' laughed Dove. 'Thanks for ringing, Pete. It could be helpful and at least it gives you something better to do than chasing cows out of cornfields. Keep up the good work and let's know when he's planning to come back, then I'll see what a bit of real pressure can do. Anything else I can do for you?'

He can do for *me*! thought Pascoe indignantly. As he flicked through the pages of his notebook, his eye fell on his question-marked words. Never mind what Dalziel said, everyone had one good intuitive guess coming and even Dalziel would reckon this was in a good cause.

He made a mental choice, crossed out one of the words and said in a studiously casual voice, 'Just one thing. Kate Swithenbank's last reported sighting was at the hairdresser's. Did anyone ask what she had done there?'

There was a pause and a rustling of papers.

'It's not here if they did,' said Dove. 'Any particular reason?'

'Just part of the steady plod us yokels go at,' said Pascoe. 'I don't really imagine that you lot have overlooked anything. Else.'

'Get stuffed,' said Dove. 'I'll see if I can find out. Cheers now.'

'Cheers.'

Pascoe sat back in his chair and felt pleased with himself. His social science degree enabled him to regard such phenomena as inter-regional rivalries with academic objectivity. On the other hand you couldn't get away from it, there was something very pleasant about getting one up on those smartalec sods in London. Dalziel would, in his own phrase, be chuffed to buggery.

There was still the problem of tactics. There was no question now of sending Sergeant Wield to Wearton. This was his affair, right to the bitter end. The question was when? And how?

The answer came from the most unexpected source.

His telephone rang and the constable on the exchange said a Mr Swithenbank would like to speak to him.

'Put him on,' commanded Pascoe.

'Inspector, glad to have caught you.'

His voice sounded higher, lighter on the telephone.

'I was just thinking about you, Mr Swithenbank.'

'I'm flattered. And I about you. A thought struck me—you hinted a desire, or rather an intention, of talking about this business with my old acquaintance in the village. Are you still keen?'

'It's on my schedule,' said Pascoe cautiously.

'The thing is, Boris Kingsley is having a little get-together at the Big House tomorrow evening. I was just going to ring him to make it OK to take Miss Starkey along with me. All my old chums will be there. So it occurred to me, if you'd like to take them all in one fell swoop, I'm sure Boris wouldn't mind. He's always had a taste for cheap fiction and a real life detective questioning his guests in the library would be right up his street.'

Pascoe thought about it, felt the silence growing long enough to be significant and decided he didn't mind. After all, Swithenbank mustn't be allowed to think the law was so easily organizable.

'Deep thoughts, Inspector,' said Swithenbank. 'Penny for them.'

'Something about Greeks bearing gifts,' replied Pascoe. 'Yes, I think that might prove very useful, Mr Swithenbank. Thank you.'

'Oh good. Why don't you call here about seven and then you can have a drink and a chat with Mother before we set out.'

'Fine,' said Pascoe. 'Bye.'

'Cheeky bugger,' he said to the replaced telephone. You had to admire the man's nerve, he thought with a smile. Setting him up like Hercule Poirot.

Then his eyes fell on the still open volume of Poe and he pulled it towards him and read:

> *And I cried—'It was surely October*
> *On this very night of last year*
> *That I journeyed—I journeyed down*
>   *here—*
> *That I brought a dread burden down*
>   *here—'*

He glanced at his desk calendar. Tomorrow was Saturday, 14 October.

'Cheeky bugger,' he said again. But there was no humour in his voice this time.

IV

From childhood's hour I have not been
As others were.

1

'*AND SHE CAUGHT HIM by his garment saying, Lie with me.*'

Peter Davenport was so engrossed in what he was writing that he had not heard his wife come into the study and he started violently as she grabbed his cardigan.

Ursula laughed.

'Wrong text, dear?' she said. 'It might produce a livelier sermon than some of your recent efforts.'

'It might,' he agreed, smiling with an effort. 'I'm sorry, my dear, I'm just a bit busy and there might not be time later . . .'

'For what? I should have listened when they told me a counter-tenor was a kind of eunuch.'

She shivered violently and drew her thin silken robe more closely around her.

'You'll catch your death. Here, take my cardigan.'

'*And he left his garment in her hand, and fled, and got him out.* No, you keep it. You must be frozen to the marrow sitting here. God, when are they going to do something about the heating in this place? Or flog it and put us in a nice cosy semi?'

In the summer the big Victorian rectory was a source of delight to Ursula most of the time. Then she could enjoy the role of vicar's wife, enjoy supervising the annual garden party on the huge bumpy lawn, enjoy entertaining various ladies' committees in the cool, airy drawing-room, enjoy discussing with them the recipe for her famous seed cake (purchased at Fortnum and Mason's whenever she went to London), enjoy their resentment of her, their memory of her wild young days, their suspicion that their husbands still lusted after her. And on long warm summer evenings as hostess to more secular groups of friends, she enjoyed throwing open the french windows and leading them into the garden after dinner, walking barefoot across the lawn, laughing and talking and sometimes turning from vicar's wife to essential Eve and back again within the compass of a cloud's passage across the moon or the circumvention of a rhododendron bush.

But when summer's date was done, the draughty old rectory quickly grew chill beyond the reach of its antiquated radiators or the economic flame at the back of its huge open fireplace. She was not altogether joking when she told Boris Kingsley she slept with him for warmth whenever Peter was away at one of his choir concerts, though in truth she had no more real idea of the reason than she had of her reason for marrying her cousin eight years earlier. Perhaps she had needed to show Kate Lightfoot and John Swithenbank that their alliance meant nothing to her. But she lacked the temperament for self-analysis, managing to find even in the worst day something that made the next day seem worth waiting for. She knew there was something wrong between her and her husband, even had a notion of what that something was, but had no solution to offer for the prob-

lem other than to wait and see and enjoy herself as
best she could along the way.

Peter Davenport on the other hand believed he
understood all too well his reasons for marrying Ursula and had long since recognized them as inade-
quate and selfish. But other more pressing matters
had been occupying his mind and his conscience in
recent months. Like Ursula, he had lived from day to
day, but unlike her, he felt an impulsion to definitive,
even desperate action, which he could not resist much
longer.

'I've got nothing to wear tonight,' she averred.

He thought bitterly of the stuffed wardrobes upstairs, then dismissed the uncharitable thought. Ursula had been eager to put her inherited money into
the common pool; he had resisted. He was glad he
had. At least that couldn't be held against him.

'It'll be very informal, surely,' he said.

'Informal doesn't mean scruffy,' she retorted.

'No, it doesn't,' he said. 'Lexicographers the world
over would agree with you. Who's going to be there
anyway?'

'The usual lot,' she said. 'The usual conversations,
the usual tedium.'

'Isn't John going to be there?' he asked.

She looked at him sharply.

'What difference will that make?'

'A breath of fresh air from the great outside world.'

She laughed and said, 'You may be right. I was
talking to Boris earlier. He hinted at a surprise but
wouldn't say what. You know how he loves being
mysterious. Perhaps Kate has come back from the
. . . wherever she's been.'

Davenport put down his pen sharply and stood up.

'Not even Boris would keep back such news just

for effect,' he said sternly. 'Poor John. A whole year now. It must have been hell for him.'

'That depends on what the previous year was like, doesn't it?' said his wife. 'Let's have a drink, shall we? It might warm us up.'

'All right. What time do we have to go?'

'Half seven, something like that,' she said vaguely. 'I thought we'd walk it. Along the old drive.'

'What on earth for?' he protested strongly. 'It looks like rain. And it'll ruin your shoes.'

'I just feel like the exercise. Besides, it's traditional. Vicars and their ladies must have taken that route when summoned to the Big House for a couple of centuries at least.'

'Perhaps. It's not a pleasant walk. At this time of year, I mean.'

He shivered and she regarded him curiously.

'Shouldn't a vicar know how to put ghosts in their places?' she mocked.

'What do you mean?'

'Joke,' she said. 'Though come to think of it, sometimes there does seem a rather excessive amount of noise and movement in the churchyard. Not just foxes and owls, I mean, though some of it's so overgrown it could hide a tiger. You really ought to insist that something's done about it, Peter.'

'Yes, yes. I'll have a word,' he said. 'Let's have that drink.'

He poured the gin with a generous hand and was pouring himself another before his wife had done more than dampen her full red lips on her first.

2

'My name's Pascoe. I'm a police inspector. Could I have a word with you, Mr Lightfoot?'

Arthur Lightfoot viewed him silently, then went back into the cottage as though indifferent whether Pascoe followed or not.

Reckoning that if he waited for invitations round here, he was likely to become a fixture, Pascoe went in, closed the door behind him, pursued Lightfoot into a square, sparsely furnished living-room and sat down.

The room occupied the breadth of the building and Pascoe could see that the uncurtained windows at the back were new and the plaster on the wall had been recently refurbished.

'You had a fire?' he said conversationally.

'What do you want, mister?'

Pascoe sighed. One of the more distressing things about his job was the frequency with which he met Yorkshiremen who made Dalziel sound like something from Castiglione's *Book of the Courtier*.

'It's about your sister, Kate. I've got no news of her, you understand,' he added hastily for fear of creating a false optimism.

He needn't have worried.

'I need no news of our Kate,' said Lightfoot.

'I don't understand. You mean you don't want to hear anything about your sister?'

It was a genuine semantic problem. Lightfoot's face showed a recognizable expression for a moment. It was one of contempt.

'I mean I need no news. She's dead. I need no bobby to come telling me that.'

'Well, if you know that, you know more than I do,' rejoined Pascoe. 'What makes you so sure?'

'A man knows such things.'

Oh God, that awful intuition again. No, not intuition, superstition. This was a medieval peasant who stood before him, but without any feudal inhibitions.

'We can't be sure,' insisted Pascoe gently. 'Not till . . . well, not till we've seen her.'

'I've seen her.'

'*What?*'

'What do you know, mister? Nowt!'

Lightfoot spoke angrily. It was clearly only the gentler responses that were missing from his make-up.

'I've heard her voice in the black of night and I've risen from my bed and I've seen her blown this way and that in the night wind,' proclaimed Lightfoot with terrifying intensity.

Pascoe began to regret that he had sat down as the man loomed over him describing his lunatic visions. Looking for an excuse to get to his feet, he spotted a framed photograph on the mantelpiece.

'Is this your sister, Mr Lightfoot?' he asked, rising and edging past the man. The picture showed a slim girl in a white dress and a wide-brimmed floppy hat from beneath which a pair of disproportionately large eyes looked uncertainly at the photographer. Like a startled rabbit, thought Pascoe unkindly. The background to the picture was a house which could have been The Pines, but identification was not helped by the fact that the print had been torn in half, presumably to remove someone standing alongside the girl.

Lightfoot snatched the frame from his hands, a rudeness perhaps more native than aggressive.

'What do you want?' he demanded once more.

'I'm on my way to see your brother-in-law,' answered Pascoe, deciding that the more direct he was, the quicker he could make his exit. 'There have been some phone calls, and a letter, suggesting that he knows more about your sister's disappearance than he's letting on. We're eager to find the person who's been making these suggestions.'

'So you single me out!' said Lightfoot accusingly.

'No,' said Pascoe. 'I was in Wearton yesterday, and I spoke to Mr Swithenbank then, but I didn't have time to contact anyone else. Later on tonight I'm going to see a variety of people at Wear End, Mr Kingsley's house. I thought I'd drop in on you en route, that's all.'

'You guessed I wouldn't be at t'party then?' said Lightfoot.

Pascoe looked uncomfortable and Lightfoot laughed like a tree cracking in a strong wind.

'Yon bugger wouldn't invite me to suck in the air on his land,' he said.

'Mr Kingsley doesn't care for your company?' said Pascoe redundantly.

'He cares for nowt but his own flesh,' said Lightfoot. 'Like father, like son.'

He replaced the photograph on the mantelpiece with a thump that defied Pascoe to touch it again.

'Is it your brother-in-law that's been torn off the picture?' enquired Pascoe.

'I wanted none of his face around my house,' said Lightfoot.

'Why's that?'

'No reason.'

'Do you not like him either?'

'They're all the same, them lot,' said Lightfoot.

'Kate'd be still living to this day likely if she hadn't got mixed up with them.'

'Surely they were her friends,' protested Pascoe.

'Friends! What need of friends when there's family? Are you done, Mr Detective? There's others have to work late hours besides t'police.'

On the doorstep Pascoe turned and said, 'Have you made any calls to Mr Swithenbank or sent the police a letter, Mr Lightfoot?'

'That's direct,' said Lightfoot. 'I wondered if you'd get round to asking. The answer's no, I haven't. If I knew definite who'd harmed her, I . . .'

'You'd what?'

'I'd know, wouldn't I? Do you question Swithenbank so direct?'

'If the occasion demands,' said Pascoe.

'Then ask him this. What was he doing skulking around the churchyard at midnight night before last? You ask him.'

'All right,' said Pascoe. 'As a matter of interest, what were *you* doing skulking round the churchyard, Mr Lightfoot?'

The door was shut hard in his face. Pascoe whistled with relief as he strolled through the gate and got into his car. There was something frightening about Lightfoot in a primal kind of way. A man who had commerce with ghosts must be frightening! Though a man so certain of his sister's death might have other reasons for his certainty, and that was more frightening still.

Behind him in the comfortless cottage Lightfoot returned to the job which Pascoe's arrival had interrupted. Seated at the kitchen table, he oiled and polished the separated parts of his shotgun till he was satisfied. Then he reassembled it and sat motionless for a long time while outside the light faded, rooks beat their way homeward to the nest-dark trees, a light mist drifted out of the dank fields till a wind began to rise and bore it away and drove the darkness over the land.

Then Lightfoot stood up, put on a black donkey jacket, set his gun in the crook of his arm and went out into the night.

3

Arthur Lightfoot was in many people's minds that night.

Geoffrey Rawlinson as he shaved in preparation for the party at Wear End found himself thinking of Lightfoot. Even in his democratic teens when as a matter of faith such things were not allowed to matter, he had always been conscious of a vague distaste for calling on Kate at her brother's cottage. There was something so brutishly spartan about the place, and in that atmosphere Kate herself, so unnoticing of or uncaring for the near squalor, seemed a different person. By his early twenties, Rawlinson was openly wrestling with the choice he had to make. If he married Kate, he was marrying a Lightfoot. The two major elements of his make-up—the draughtsman's love of order and shape and the naturalist's love of energy and colour—clashed and jarred against each other like boulders in a turbulent sea. His sister looked pityingly at him but refused to speak. It had to be his own choice and he was ashamed of himself for having such a superficially Victorian reason for hesitating.

Then Ursula told him one morning the news she had learnt the previous night and he realized to his amazement that his sense of critical choice had been fallacious.

Now he lived in a framework of meticulous order which he felt both as a scaffolding and a cage.

But even now, even when he regretted the past most passionately, the memory of Arthur, spooning stew into his mouth at the kitchen table with the encrusted sauce bottle and the curded milk bottle on guard before him, made Rawlinson twitch with distaste.

But that memory was just a mental feint to keep his mind from contemplating—as now he did, looking into his own reluctant eyes in the shaving mirror—the events of a year ago, and the pain, mental and physical, he had suffered since that dreadful night.

Stella Rawlinson thought of Arthur, too, and wondered for the thousandth time, with a cold self-analysis which had nothing to do with control, why the humiliation of a fourteen-year-old girl should lay marks on her which persisted throughout womanhood. It was not unusual for a pubescent girl to have a crush on her best friend's elder brother. Nor could it be too unusual that recognition of this should cause dismissive and hurtful amusement. But rarely could this amusement be couched in such terms or such circumstances as to create a hatred stretching beyond maturity.

Only one other person had ever been aware of what she suffered. What were best friends for? But a sharing is as likely to mean a doubling as a halving, she had long ago decided. It was a mistake to be rectified if possible, certainly not one to be repeated. So even with her husband she kept her peace and when he showed signs of wanting to commit the same error of confidence, she turned away.

And Boris Kingsley, too, thought of Arthur as he arranged the chairs and filled the decanters in his library. But he thought of many other things besides as he opened the wardrobes in his bedroom and dressed for his party.

And for a while as his guests arrived he thought of nothing but making them welcome. He didn't like most of them but there are less expensive ways of manifesting dislike than over your own drink in your own house, so he smiled and chatted and poured till a clock chimed and he glanced anxiously at his watch.

Then he smiled again but this time secretively, excused himself, closed the door firmly behind him, and picked up the telephone.

V

The angels, whispering to one another,
Can find, among their burning terms of
  love,
None so devotional as that of 'Mother'.

'YOU'VE MET MY MOTHER?' said Swithenbank.

'Briefly,' said Pascoe. 'How do you do?'

He shook hands with the woman and wondered if he was being conned. Surely this wasn't the woman he had spoken to outside the house the previous day. There had been something distinctive . . . yes, her hair had been a sort of purpley-blue, not the rich auburn of the woman before him.

'You approve my coiffure, Mr Pascoe?' she said and he realized he was staring.

'Very nice,' he said. 'It's very . . . becoming.'

'I changed it at my son's behest,' she said. 'He didn't care for my last colour, did you, John?'

'It seemed inappropriate,' said Swithenbank.

'And this?' said his mother, striking a little pose with her left hand behind her head. 'Is this appropriate?'

'If not to your age, at least to your genus,' he said drily. 'I'll leave you to it, Inspector, and put the finishing touches to my own coiffure. Mother, Mr Pascoe might like a drink.'

'What would we do without our children to teach us manners?' wondered Mrs Swithenbank. 'Scotch, Inspector?'

'Please. Some water. Your daughter-in-law went to the hairdresser's on the day she disappeared.'

It was not quite the way he had intended to open the interview but Mrs Swithenbank was not quite the woman he had expected. She took the transition with the ease of a steeplechaser spotting that the ground fell away on the other side of the hedge.

'Did she now? That would be a year ago today, you mean, Inspector?'

'That's right. Though it was a Friday last year.'

'Yes, I've always found that rather confusing. Though it's nice to have one's birthday shifting around, it's easier to miss. Not that birthdays bother me yet. I had John young, of course. And he looks older than he is. Here's your drink, Mr Pascoe. Do you find me absurd?'

'I don't think so,' said Pascoe gravely.

'Not just a trifle?'

He considered.

'No,' he said. 'Amusing, yes. But not absurd.'

'Good. Neither do I. What did Kate have done at the hairdresser's?'

'Shampoo. Cut. And she bought a wig.'

Dove had phoned through with the information at lunch-time, admitting as cheerfully as ever that perhaps a year earlier they should have been asking questions about a frizzy blonde as well as a straight brunette.

Pascoe was not one to kick a man when he was down but he had no qualms about applying the boot to someone as reluctant to fall as Dove.

'This could knock your Swithenbank fixation into little pieces, Willie,' he had said. 'She could have got to the other end of the country without being noticed.'

'And stopped unnoticed? Bollocks,' Dove had replied. 'All it means is she could have left the flat without being spotted and been picked up somewhere else by Swithenbank, who knocked her off on his way north. Keep at it, Pete. You're doing good. For a provincial!'

'Did your daughter-in-law habitually wear wigs?' he now asked Mrs Swithenbank.

'Never to my knowledge. She had longish straight hair. Reddish brown, a rather unusual colour. She hadn't changed the style much since she was a girl. She wasn't a one for following fashions, not in her clothes either. Always the same kind of dress, whites and creams, soft materials, loose-fitting—she hated constraint of any kind. But she always managed to look right. What colour was the wig, by the way?'

'Platinum blonde.'

'Never,' said Mrs Swithenbank emphatically. 'I can't imagine that . . . unless you mean she could be walking around somewhere *disguised* as a blonde.'

'Any idea why she might do that?' enquired Pascoe.

'She was a strange girl in many ways,' answered the woman slowly. 'There was something about her— a kind of feyness. There were three girls in John's gang, Kate, Ursula Rawlinson and Stella Foxley. Kate was the ugly duckling. The other two . . . I gather you'll be meeting them tonight so perhaps I shouldn't anticipate your reactions . . .'

'A kind thought,' said Pascoe, 'but I'll just be chatting. It's not an identity parade! Please go on.'

'You'd have thought the other two would have walked away with all the boys. Ursula was a big well-made girl, full of life—still is! Stella—well, she was pretty too, but in a rather stiff kind of way. It was strange; before the village drama group folded up, she used to appear in nearly every production and on the stage she really came to life, but off it she's always been . . . no, perhaps the competition she offered was a lot less stiff, but she was still much prettier! And Ursula! As I say, she was the belle. Little Kate Lightfoot with her skinny body and big frightened eyes, she faded away alongside her. Yet . . .'

'Yes?' prompted Pascoe.

'You know how it is when you're young, Mr Pascoe. There's always a lot of chopping and changing of boyfriends and girl-friends in any group. I used to think Ursula called the tune, passing on her discarded beaux to Kate or stealing hers if the fancy took her. But eventually I began to wonder if the reverse weren't true!'

'And what did you decide?'

'Nothing,' said Mrs Swithenbank, sipping her scotch. 'Kate always did things too quietly to give the game away. She moved around like a ghost! And Ursula, though she might behave as if her brains were in her brassiere, had far too much sense to make a fuss.'

'Were you surprised when your son married Kate?' asked Pascoe.

She looked at him reprovingly as though the question were too impudent to be answered, but when Pascoe put on his rueful look, she said, 'John had already been working for Colbridge's in London for two years. He seemed to be breaking links with his Wearton friends, though if he had got engaged to Ursula, I should not have been surprised. In fact I might even have been pleased. She has many good solid qualities. I sometimes think she may have regretted her marriage, too.'

'As your son regretted his?' said Pascoe.

'As I regretted it, Inspector,' she said acidly. 'John has never by word or sign indicated that he had any regrets. And I can't give you any good reason for my own regrets, except perhaps the unhappiness of this past year. I never knew my daughter-in-law well enough to understand her. I tried, but I couldn't get close to her. I even started buying flowers and vegetables from her brother after the marriage, to sort of integrate the families, and *that* required an effort of will, I tell you. Have you met him? He's real Yorkshire peasant stock with something a little sinister besides. His family were all farm labourers, good for nothing, but, God knows how, he bettered himself and runs a smallholding in the village. I stopped going there a couple of months after Kate disappeared. I couldn't bear the way he looked at me.'

She shuddered. Pascoe looked around the room and noticed that the dahlias had been removed.

'But you didn't find Kate frightening, too?' he said.

'Only in the sense that what we don't know frightens us,' she said. 'Perhaps there *is* nothing to know. Perhaps that's the truth of it, that underneath she's just an ordinary dull little girl. Marriage is abrasive, Mr Pascoe. John would find out the truth of her sooner or later.'

'And . . . ?'

'And if what he found bothered him so much that he wanted rid of her, he would ring his solicitor! One of the things I envy your generation is that divorce is there for the asking. Any other reaction is unthinkable!'

'I'm afraid that not everyone would agree with you,' said Pascoe.

This woman was certainly not absurd, he had long decided. And she was only as amusing as she wanted to be. Most important of all, despite the apparent freedom with which she poured out her impressions of her daughter-in-law and others, Pascoe suspected that they were measured with a most exact and knowing eye.

'Meaning what?'

'You took a phone call for your son yesterday morning.'

'Did I?'

'A woman's voice. Don't you remember?'

'The funny name. Is that the one you mean?'

'Yes, that's right,' said Pascoe. 'Ulalume. You didn't recognize the voice?'

'No,' she replied. 'I don't think so, though I am a little deaf, especially on the phone. It's easier when you can observe the lips. I certainly didn't recognize the name.'

'Was there anything distinctive you can recall about the voice?' persisted Pascoe

'Not really. As I say, I'm a little deaf and the line wasn't very good. It sounded terribly distant.'

'What exactly did this woman say?' asked Pascoe.

'Hardly anything, that I can recall,' said the woman. 'I gave our number, she said *John Swithenbank*, I said *who's calling?* She said *Ulalume*, is that right? I said *who?* She didn't say anything else so I went and got John. What does all this signify, Inspector?'

Quickly Pascoe explained, reasoning that if Swithenbank didn't want his mother to know, he shouldn't have left her to be interrogated alone.

'I don't like the sound of this,' she said sharply when he'd finished.

'No?' he said.

'Someone's trying to make trouble. There were one or two nasty calls a year ago when the news first got out. People in the village and round about—old maids with nothing better to do, I usually guessed their names and that made them ring off pretty quickly! But this sounds more organized, as if someone's been thinking about it. Not just an impulse like some old biddy filling the gap between *Crown Court* and *Coronation Street*.'

'That's very astute of you,' complimented Pascoe. 'Any ideas?'

'I can't fathom the precise aim,' said Mrs Swithenbank, 'but I should be surprised if she, or he, were a thousand miles away from you tonight.'

She glanced at her watch and pursed her lips impatiently.

'I hope John isn't going to keep you waiting much longer, Inspector. There's a film I particularly want to see on the television and he promised to have you on the way before it started.'

Taken aback by the sudden change in the objects of her concern, Pascoe downed his untouched drink in one to demonstrate his readiness to be off and said, 'Perhaps it's Miss Starkey who's holding him up.'

'*That* wouldn't surprise me,' she said significantly.

Not quite certain whether she was really underlining the *double entendre,* Pascoe asked if she had known Miss Starkey long.

'I never saw her before in my life. I came home last evening and there she was. I was then consulted about whether she could stay or not, but not in a manner which admitted the possibility of refusal.'

'Despite which, you didn't refuse?' said Pascoe, tongue in cheek.

She glanced at him sharply, then smiled.

'No, I didn't.'

'A business colleague of your son's, perhaps?' said Pascoe casually.

'I'm glad you don't even pretend to believe that!' said the woman. 'No, I imagine she's precisely what she appears to be. His mistress.'

'Here by invitation?' said Pascoe, with doubt bordering on incredulity in his voice.

'No, Inspector. Not by invitation, but certainly by design,' said a new voice.

Jean Starkey was standing by the half-open door, amusedly self-conscious of the dramatic effect of both her timing and her appearance. She wore a scarlet dress of some soft elastic fabric which clung so close that the finest of underwear must have thrown up its contours. None could be seen to break the curving lines of her body and when she moved forward into the room muscle and sinew rippled the scarlet surface like a visual aid in an anatomy class.

Pascoe sighed and she smiled her appreciation.

'Even at court they never go in for more than a year's public mourning,' she said. 'I decided that it was time Wearton became aware of my existence. So here I am.'

'And John?' said Mrs Swithenbank.

'Took me in his stride,' said Jean Starkey. 'He usually leads—don't misunderstand me—but he's not hung up about it. He recognizes a useful initiative when it sticks out before his eyes.'

'You certainly do that,' said Mrs Swithenbank.

'*Mourning*,' said Pascoe. 'That's for the dead, Miss Starkey.'

'Marriages die, too, Inspector,' she replied. 'I don't know where Kate is now, but the point is, if she were to come through that door now, it would make not one jot of difference.'

They all looked at the door, which she had left ajar. Footsteps were heard coming down the stairs. They got nearer, moving without undue haste, and suddenly Pascoe felt tension in the room.

Then the telephone rang.

The door was closed reducing the telephone to a distant vibration of the air. A moment later this, too, was shut off and as Pascoe had already discovered, the walls shut out human speech.

'You need good hearing in this house,' said Pascoe conversationally.

'The Swithenbanks don't miss very much,' said the old woman. 'I do hope you enjoy the party tonight, Miss Starkey. You mustn't mind if John's friends stare a little at first. Remember that while he's been away getting acquainted with the big wide world, they've been stuck here in tiny old Wearton.'

'I'll make allowances,' smiled Jean Starkey.

The door opened and Swithenbank came in. He was wearing cream slacks, a cream jacket and a golden shirt with a huge collar and no tie. Pascoe felt very conscious that his own suit had come from C and A, but sought revenge in telling himself that the other man looked like an advert for the Milk Marketing Board.

'All ready?' enquired Swithenbank. 'We're rather late, I'm afraid. But we can always compensate by coming away early. Good night, Mother. Don't bolt the door if you go to bed, will you?'

'No,' she said. 'Who was on the phone, dear?'

Swithenbank smiled.

'Just a friend,' he said, holding the door open for Jean Starkey and Pascoe.

'Who was it, John?' insisted his mother.

'I told you,' said Swithenbank. 'A friend. The same one as rang yesterday morning, remember? She told me she was lonely and impatient. She said her name was Ulalume.'

VI

And travellers, now, within that valley,
Through red-litten windows see
Vast forms that move fantastically
To a discordant melody.

IT WAS ONLY A short drive to Wear End or the Big
House as Pascoe now found himself thinking of it. It
didn't look that big, he thought as he got out of the
car, but certainly over-large for one man's occupation.
Several windows were lit up and in their light and
that of a rusty ornamental lantern hung in the portico,
his assessing eye picked out signs of decay and ne-
glect—blistered paint, flaking stone, a broken shutter
and a narrow crack which zig-zagged up the façade
till it disappeared in the dark shadow under the pedi-
ment. All the best Gothic decor! sneered Pascoe to
reassure himself of his own indifference to the atmosphere, then felt his hair prickle on his neck as distantly, eerily, somewhere in the darkness a woman's
voice cried, 'John! Oh Johnny!'

Swithenbank stopped in his tracks and all three of
them peered in the direction of the noise. The night
sky was clouded and the darkness made thicker by the
electric glow above their heads. At first all Pascoe
could do was separate the trees from their fractionally
lighter background. There seemed to be a double row
of them running away in symmetry with the sweep of
the drive that had brought them from the roadway.
They swayed and soughed in the slight but chilling
wind and as his night vision improved Pascoe became

aware of another movement. Between the trees something white fluttered and billowed and came towards them with a kind of ponderous bounding gait. Two sounds accompanied it, that breathless female cry of 'John!' and a most unfeminine tread of galloping feet.

Then the oncomer was off grass and onto gravel and with more relief than he would have cared to admit, Pascoe saw it was a woman running with the skirts of her full white satin evening dress kilted up to reveal a pair of muddy wellington boots.

A final spurt took her into Swithenbank's arms with a force that anyone not a gentleman might have staggered under. Dalziel, for instance, thought Pascoe, would probably have stepped aside and let her hit the front door. But the slight figure of Swithenbank bore the brunt without flinching and as Pascoe got a better concept of the new arrival under the lantern light, he observed that it was a brunt worth bearing.

This was most probably that Ursula whose considerable charms Mrs Swithenbank wished had conquered her son, a theory confirmed as the said son now asked with incongruous politeness, 'How are you, Ursula?'

'Johnny! Why have you been hiding from us? I'm so pleased you've come tonight. I can't tell you how disappointed I would have been!'

Over his shoulder her eyes were drinking in Pascoe and Jean Starkey with unconcealed curiosity while behind her another figure came out from between the trees, a tall thin man with a flop of dark hair over pale defeated eyes. He wore a dark overcoat and, like a disingenuous Prince Charming, carried in either hand a silver shoe.

'Hello, John,' he said.

'Hello, Peter. Cured many souls lately?'

'Not many. And you—edited any good poems lately?'

'Not much since Poe,' said Swithenbank.

'Oh, let's get inside where I can see you properly. Has anyone rung? Boris! Boris! Don't let your guests hang about in the cold!'

Ursula opened the front door as she spoke and entered with the familiarity of old acquaintance. The others followed. Davenport, Pascoe noticed, seemed as uninterested in the identity of the newcomers as his wife was curious. She had now seated herself at the foot of a flight of stairs which ran up from the centre of the small but pleasantly proportioned hall. Pulling back her skirt above her knees, she thrust forward what, even accoutred as it was, appeared to be a very elegant leg and said, 'Johnny, dear, help me off with my wellies.'

A fastidious expression skimmed his face, but he obediently seized the proffered boot by heel and toe and began to lever it free.

'Oh, you've started the fun without me, you naughty children, and it's my party, too!'

A balding, portly man, nautical in a brass-buttoned blazer, advanced upon them, his face shining with sweat and *bonhomie*.

'John! How are you? So elusive! I must have spent a fortune trying to ring you. Even tonight, I began to get so worried!'

'We're not the latest, Boris,' replied Swithenbank, glancing at the woman on the stairs.

'Oh, the poor parson and his starving wife, you can always rely on *them* to turn up for supper,' said Kingsley dismissively. 'Ursula, Peter, welcome aboard. Good concert the other night, I hope? And last but not least, these must be . . .'

He shot an interrogative glance at Swithenbank, who said sardonically, 'Surely you can tell which is which.'

Kingsley laughed. He really was doing the jovial host bit, thought Pascoe. A trifle hysterically perhaps?

'Miss Starkey! Jean. Any *dear* friend of *dear* John's is welcome here. And Detective-Inspector Pascoe! Or should I call you mister?'

'As you will,' said Pascoe, who was wondering whether the look of shock on Ursula Davenport's face was caused by the revelation of his job or Starkey's status. Her husband seemed indifferent to both bits of information and Pascoe, seeing him now under the more revealing lights of the hall, began to suspect that he was held very lightly together by drink.

'Ursula, you know your way around, show Jean where to put her things while we go forward and prepare some drinks for you.'

As they went along the hall towards an open door out of which came a hubbub of voices raised to combat James Last on the stereo, Kingsley seized Pascoe by the elbow and slowing him down a little murmured, 'I don't know how you'd like to work, Inspector, but most of these people will be going within the hour. Only those you want to see, or so I believe, that is the Rawlinsons, the Davenports and, of course, myself, will be staying on for a bite of supper. Perhaps you'd like to start by having a couple of drinks and getting a general impression of our local community, leaving the close grilling to later? Less embarrassing, too. I'll just say you're an old chum!'

Pascoe nodded agreement, wondering what it was that made a man he could imagine getting wrathfully indignant if the police tried to breathalyze him so eagerly cooperative.

There were about twenty people in the room, mostly dressed with the relative informality of the age, though none was quite so fashionably casual as Swithenbank. Pascoe observed him as he said his hellos to people before settling quietly against the mantelpiece with a drink, his eyes on the door. A couple approached him, a man with a curious limping gait and a woman wearing the kind of drab black dress in which nineteenth-century governesses hoped to avoid arousing either the envy of their mistress or the lust of their master. Swithenbank greeted her with a non-contact kiss, him with a pre-fifteen-rounds handshake and spoke animatedly, saying in a voice suddenly audible right through the room, 'No, *glad to be back* would hardly be accurate.'

The reason for this sudden clarity was that the end of a James Last track had coincided with an almost total cessation of social chit-chat. Even as Pascoe turned, the hubbub resumed, but cause of the hiatus was there for all to see. Jean and Ursula had made their entrance together. It was neck and neck which was the more eye-catching—Ursula voluptuous in virginal white or Jean outrageous in clinging scarlet. Either alone was worth a man's regard. Together the effect was a golden-days-of-Hollywood dream.

Swithenbank abandoned the limping man and the governess and advanced smiling on Jean.

'Darling,' he said, 'come and meet a few people.'

Ursula came and stood by Pascoe.

'If you don't want people to know you're a policeman,' she said, 'you shouldn't hang around so close to the drink. But pour me a gin as you're here.'

Pascoe obeyed. When he turned from the sideboard, the lame man was talking to Ursula.

'Who is that woman?' he demanded, sounding very angry. 'What the hell is John playing at?'

'Everyone's entitled to friends, dear brother,' she answered.

'You know what I mean, Ursula. It's not decent, not here in Wearton.'

'Because of Kate, you mean? A man's got to make up his own mind what's decent, Geoff. Wouldn't you agree, Mr Pascoe?'

'He might consult the feelings of those close to him,' said Pascoe provocatively, though what exactly he was provoking he did not know. 'It's Mr Rawlinson, isn't it?'

The man turned away without reply and limped back to the woman in black, who hadn't moved from the fireplace.

'His wife?' asked Pascoe.

'That's right. Stella. Not that she twinkles much.'

'What happened to his leg?'

'An accident. He fell out of our belfry.'

'*What?*'

'You heard right. Geoff's a great one for watching birds. He draws them, too, he's got a beautiful touch. Wouldn't you say Geoff's got a beautiful touch, dear?'

Her husband, who was refilling his glass from the gin bottle, shot her a glance of bewilderment, not at her remark, Pascoe judged, but at something much more general. It bothered Pascoe; vicars were paid to be certain, not bewildered.

'Well,' continued Ursula as her husband wandered away, 'Peter, my husband, he's the vicar, gave Geoff permission to go up the tower and make observations,

take pictures, whatever these bird-men do. And one
dark autumn night about a year ago, he fell!'

'Good God! What happened?'

She shrugged, a movement worth watching.

'He couldn't remember a thing. It was a frosty
night and I reckon knowing my brother that he'd be
balancing on a gargoyle or something to get a better
view. And then he slipped, I suppose. Fortunately Peter went out at midnight just to check whether Geoff
wanted coffee or a drink before we went to bed. He
found Geoff unconscious. Luckily he'd missed the
tombstones and landed on grass but he was pretty
badly smashed up.'

'As a matter of interest, when precisely was this,
Mrs Davenport?'

'I told you. A year ago. In fact I'd say, precisely a
year ago. It was a Friday night and it was the weekend
Kate Swithenbank went missing. Not that we knew
about that till later. Is that why you're here, Inspector?'

'Sh! Sh!'

It was Kingsley who had stolen up behind them.

'We can't have everyone knowing the police are in
our midst. Most of these people are respectable
law-abiding tax-evaders and as such deserve to have
their sensibilities protected.'

'Then what *shall* I call you?' said Ursula.

'Try his name,' urged Kingsley. 'I'm Boris. This, as
you've probably gathered, or if you've been bold,
grasped, is Ursula.'

'Peter,' said Pascoe.

'Peter. It's my fate to meet Peters. The rocks on
which I foundered,' said Ursula lightly. 'Where is my
revered husband, by the way?'

'Being all parochial in the corner. Circulate, circulate; you'll have plenty of time, too much perhaps, for close confabulation later.'

From the far side of the room there came a little scream.

'Oh lor,' said Kingsley. 'It'll be the colonel up to his Wimbledon tricks.'

But when he got across there with Pascoe not far behind, it turned out to be the colonel's lady, who claimed to have seen a face at the window.

'It peered at me through the hydrangea bush,' she claimed.

'No need to worry, dear lady,' Kingsley assured her. 'It was probably one of the local peasants, drawn by rumours of wild festivity and your great beauty.'

'There was a man. I think he was carrying a gun,' insisted the woman.

'I shall organize a posse,' promised Kingsley and moved away.

'Silly ass,' said her grey-haired companion, presumably the colonel. 'Soft at the centre. He'll end up like his father. Time we were off, old girl.'

He glowered suddenly at Pascoe to show he resented his eavesdropping. Pascoe smiled embarrassedly and turned away to find himself confronting Peter Davenport, who had obtained a larger glass for his gin.

'What are you after?' he demanded, his light tenor voice scraping falsetto. 'How can the law help? Your law, I mean?'

'What other law is there?' responded Pascoe, thinking to steer the exchange into areas which might sound conventionally theological to those around.

But instead of the hoped-for sermon, Davenport's reply was to laugh shrilly, drawing the attention of everyone in the room and, shaking his head, to say,

'What indeed? What indeed?' before turning abruptly away and making for the bottle-laden sideboard. Geoffrey Rawlinson, his face full of concern, tried to interrupt his progress but was shouldered aside.

Thank God it's not my problem, thought Pascoe as he observed Kingsley join the vicar at the sideboard and talk animatedly to him with his hand resting familiarly on his shoulder.

A few moments later, Kingsley was taking the same liberty with his own person.

'Mr Pascoe, Peter, I wonder if I could ask for your help?'

Pascoe shook his head firmly.

'Not if it involves arresting drunken vicars or chasing gunmen through the shrubbery.'

'No, please. I'm seriously concerned about Peter, the other one I mean. I've never seen him hit the booze like this before, and there are those here quite capable of sending anonymous letters to the bishop.'

'I dare say. But what do you want me to do about it?' asked Pascoe, who was beginning to feel as if he'd strayed on the set of a 1940s British film comedy.

'Just have a word. Something's bothering him and he seems to want to talk to you.'

'He could have fooled me.'

'No, really,' insisted Kingsley. 'If I put you in the library and tell him you'd like a chat, I'm sure he'd go. And it'd be a real favour to the dear chap getting him out of here before he starts falling in the fireplace.'

The library! thought Pascoe. They really are bent on making a little Poirot out of me!

'If you think it would help . . .' he said.

'I'm sure of it.'

Pascoe cast a last look about the room before he left. Swithenbank, his hand resting familiarly on Jean

Starkey's back, just above the swell of her buttocks, was talking animatedly in the centre of a much amused group; Ursula was being serious with Stella Rawlinson, whose husband was standing apart by himself with all the animation of a pillar of salt. The colonel and his lady, hovering to pay their dues to their host, were watching the Reverend Davenport mixing himself a gin and tonic without much tonic. Rather to Pascoe's surprise, their expressions were more regretful than disapproving. *Seen it all too often in the mess,* Pascoe guessed. *Damn shame. Good man. Damn shame.*

Was it? and was he? And did whatever was burning up inside Davenport have anything to do with the Swithenbank case?

The library was a disappointment—an ugly square room with a single wall lined with glass-encased books that looked as if they'd been bought by the yard. In the opposite wall an electric fire had been placed in the fireplace but its dry heat did nothing to dissipate the stale smell of long disuse. Encircling the fireplace were a chesterfield and a pair of upright armchairs in hard red leather. Before the room's solitary window was a large desk with a chair on either side of it. Kingsley gestured ambiguously, saying, 'Please, sit down,' and Pascoe suspected he was being watched with amusement to see whether he would opt for the formal or informal set-up.

'Thank you,' he said, peering through the glass front of one of the bookcases at a series of leather-bound collections of *The Gentleman's Magazine* for the years preceding the First World War.

'Help yourself, do,' said Kingsley, referring, Pascoe hoped, to the decanters and glasses which stood on a pair of small wine tables rather than to the contents of his bookshelves.

'Right,' said Pascoe.

Kingsley left and Pascoe immediately poured himself a large scotch and tried to recall what the hell he was doing here. It all seemed very unreal. Kate Swithenbank, possibly—*probably*—dead somewhere; *that* was the thing to hang on to. Alcoholic vicars with voluptuous wives were probably totally irrelevant. He wasn't sure whether even this Ulalume business meant anything.

He studied a framed map of the West Riding, dated 1786, which hung on one side of the fireplace. It was no more helpful than the O.S. 2½ inch sheet he had examined on Dalziel's suggestion. There were a few patches of woodland around Wearton but the nearest thing to a 'dank tarn' was a small reservoir in open country some three miles to the north.

No, the thing was a mess or at best a confusion. His mind was trying to draw connections which could easily be coincidences, as for example Geoff Rawlinson's accident occurring on the very night Kate *may* have disappeared. Well, at least that gave Rawlinson an alibi, if he needed one. Unless, of course, he had *jumped* from that tower because of something on his conscience. Or perhaps was *pushed* because of something he had seen. *Seen?* Where? In the churchyard, of course. That's what he'd be looking down at—from a vantage point no one would expect to be occupied at midnight. Or perhaps someone had remembered too late that there was a chance it would be occupied, and gone up to check, and . . .

No, he was straining; too much speculation and too little evidence was a bad diet for a policeman. But there was something else about the churchyard. Ar-

thur Lightfoot claimed to have seen Swithenbank
skulking about there—which meant Lightfoot himself
had been skulking about there.

And where else were you likely to find 'the door of
a legended tomb'?

'Rapt in thought, Inspector?'

Unheard, Peter Davenport had entered the room.
He had a full glass in his hand but seemed to have
taken at least temporary control of himself.

'I was just wondering how far the church was from
Wear End. You walked here tonight, didn't you?'

'Yes. We came down the old drive that used to be
the Aubrey-Beesons' private route to church.'

'The who?'

'The old squires of Wearton. They died out in the
nineteenth century and by the time Boris's family
bought the place, the road had been metalled and mo-
tor cars were the new status symbol. It's no use looking at that map, you'll see it much better on here.'

He indicated a picture on the other side of the fireplace in an ornate gilt frame matching that of the
map.

'You know a lot about this,' observed Pascoe as he
approached.

'Local history's easy for parish priests,' said Davenport. 'We've got most of the records.'

He was making a real effort to sound normal as
though eager to postpone an unpleasant moment. But
Pascoe lost interest in the vicar's state of mind as he
looked more closely at the picture before him.

It was entitled *A Prospect of Wear End House 1799*
and as from a fair elevation showed the house and its
estate. The tree-lined drive was clearly marked running up to the churchyard but close by the churchyard

wall a much denser area of woodland was indicated with a small lake in the middle of it.

'These woods, are they still there?' asked Pascoe.

'No. They've all gone. It's a wonder the avenue survived.'

'Why's that?'

'Economics,' said Davenport shortly, as though beginning to feel rather piqued that his reluctance to bare his soul to Pascoe was matched by Pascoe's present indifference to the baring.

'You mean they were sold?'

'Not just them. The Kingsleys had wool money when they came here, but the last two generations, Boris's father and grandfather, were better at spending than making. The estate's nearly all gone. There's a housing development *here,* a new road *there,* the village sports and social club playing fields are *here,* Geoff Rawlinson's bungalow's *there* . . . all Boris is left with is this thin triangle with the old drive running up to the corner *here.'*

His long forefinger, its whiteness stained with nicotine, stubbed viciously at the *Prospect.*

'And the lake?'

'What? That pond? Drained and filled in when the Kingsleys were still spending money on improvements. About the same time as the "library" was refurbished, I expect. There *are* limits to what money can buy, aren't there, Inspector? I mean, you can't buy culture. Or peace of mind.'

The hysterical note was beginning to return to his voice, but Pascoe wasn't done with the *Prospect* yet.

'The old drive—what kind of trees are they?'

'Beech mainly.'

'No cypress?'

'There's a pair of cypress trees by the old lych-gate

at the end of the drive, but they're in the churchyard itself. What's your concern with trees, Inspector? Stop trifling, man! Come out with whatever it is you want to say. It's no secret to me why you're here!'

Now Pascoe gave him his full attention. The problem of why the anonymous phone-caller's geographic references should be a century out of date would have to wait. Perhaps (could it be as easy as this?) it wouldn't be a problem in a few minutes. Whatever it was that was devouring this man would soon be revealed. All he had to do was wait. But he wasn't sure if he would have time. He glanced at his watch. Already he'd heard a couple of cars pulling away from the house. Pretty soon he was likely to be interrupted. So, although his judgement told him to sit quietly opposite this man and wait till he spoke of his own accord, instead he took an aggressive feet-apart stance before the fireplace and said sharply, 'All right. If you don't want to talk about trees, suppose you tell me exactly what did happen in the churchyard last October?'

The man looked at him, a curious mixture of relief and wariness in his eyes.

'Happen? What does happen mean to the dead?'

'The dead? Which dead?' asked Pascoe urgently.

'The churchyard's full of the dead, Inspector. In a way since last October I have been one of them.'

'You can drop that rubbish!' said Pascoe scornfully. 'You're here and now and as alive as me. But who's dead, Davenport? Who *is* dead?'

The vicar held out his glass. Obediently Pascoe slopped it full of gin. The man opened his mouth, was seized by a fit of coughing, drank as though to relieve it, coughed the more, recovered, drank again and made ready to speak.

The door burst open.

'Thank God that's over!' said Boris Kingsley. 'Once one goes, the others soon follow. It's the sheep principle. Mr—Inspector—Pascoe, how would you like us—one by one or all at once?'

VII

There the traveller meets aghast
Sheeted Memories of the Past.

SOME WOMEN CROSS THEIR legs provocatively. Stella Rawlinson crossed hers like a no-entry sign and regarded Pascoe with all the distaste of an assault victim scanning an identity parade.

'It's kind of you to talk to me,' he said with as much conviction as he could manage. His mind was still on the kind of admission or confession Davenport had been about to make before Kingsley's ill-timed entrance. After that the vicar had risen and withdrawn without another word and Pascoe, deciding it would be poor policy at this time to invite the man along to the station to 'help with enquiries', had exercised his only other choice and pretended nothing had happened. He'd get back to Davenport after he had chatted to the others, by which time another half-bottle of booze might have put him in the talkative mood once more.

He had picked Stella Rawlinson first on Kingsley's advice. Evidently when the last of the drinks-only guests had gone, Swithenbank had told the others precisely why it was that Pascoe was here. Pascoe would have liked to have done this himself to observe reactions, but he made no complaint and accepted Kingsley's diagnosis that the only likely non-co-operator was Mrs Rawlinson and it might be well to get her in before her indignation had time to come to a head.

'Can we start by going right back to this time last year?' he said. 'Most people would have a hard time remembering anything after twelve months, but in your case it shouldn't be difficult.'

'What do you mean?' she demanded as if he had accused her of immorality.

'Just that it was the time of your husband's unfortunate accident and I know how an unpleasant experience like that sticks in the mind,' said Pascoe soothingly. 'It must have been a terrible shock to you.'

'I thought you wanted to talk about Kate Swithenbank,' she said.

'You knew her well?' said Pascoe, abandoning charm.

'We grew up together.'

'Close friends?'

'I suppose so.'

'What was she like?'

She looked genuinely puzzled.

'I don't know what you mean.'

'What words describe her?' said Pascoe. 'Plain, simple, open. Devious, reserved. Emotional, hysterical, erratic. Logical, rational, cool. Et cetera.'

'She kept herself to herself. I don't mean she wouldn't go out or was shy, anything like that. But she didn't give much away.'

The woman spoke slowly, feeling for the words. She was either very concerned to be fair or very fearful of being honest.

'I believe she was sexually very attractive as a young girl,' he probed.

'Who said that?' she asked. 'John, was it?'

'You sound as if that would surprise you.'

'No. Why should it? It would be natural, wouldn't it? He married her.'

'In fact it was his mother,' said Pascoe. 'It's interesting when a woman says it. That's why I wondered what your opinion was.'

'Yes,' she said, not bothering to conceal her reluctance. 'She was very attractive. In that way. When she wanted to be. And sometimes when she didn't want to be.'

Pascoe scratched his head in a parody of puzzlement.

'Now you're bewildering me,' he said.

'A bitch on heat's got no control over who comes sniffing around,' she said viciously, then relenting (or at least regretting) almost immediately, she added, 'I'm sorry, I don't mean to be unkind. She was a nice quiet ordinary girl in many ways. We were truly friends. I should be very distressed to think anything had happened to her.'

'Of course. How terrible it must be for all her friends,' said Pascoe fulsomely. 'But if what you say is true, there might be no cause for worry.'

'If what I say . . . ?'

'About her sexuality. Another man, perhaps; a passionate affair. She takes off with him on a sudden impulse. It's possible. If what you say . . .'

'Oh, it's true all right,' she said. 'Right from the start. Ten or eleven. I've seen her. In this room.'

She tailed off. Funny, thought Pascoe. Everybody *wants* to talk, but they all want to feel it's my subtle interrogative techniques that made them talk!

'This room?' He glanced at the *Prospect of Wear End.* 'You used to play in here as children?'

'Oh no. When we visited Boris, this was one room we were never allowed in,' she answered. 'But I was looking for Kate. We'd lost her. I just opened the door and peered in. She was . . .'

'Yes?'

'She was sitting on his knee. Her pants were round her knees.'

Pascoe gave his man-of-the-world chuckle.

'So? Childhood inquisitiveness. A little game of doctors with Boris. It's not unusual.'

'It wasn't Boris. It was his father.'

Pascoe tried to look unimpressed.

'Who is dead, I believe?' he said. 'Just as well. It's a serious offence you're alleging, Mrs Rawlinson. Very serious.'

'I felt sorry for him,' she said vehemently.

'For him?'

'And for Kate, too.' It was relenting time again. 'She couldn't help what she was. Her parents died while she was young. Her brother brought her up. That can't have helped. He's an animal. Worse!'

Dear God! thought Pascoe. Incest is it now?

'I've met Mr Lightfoot. He seems an interesting sort of man. He's very sure his sister's dead.'

She shrugged uninterestedly.

'He says he's seen her ghost,' continued Pascoe.

'He's a stupid ignorant animal,' she said indifferently.

'Perhaps so. But he may be right about his sister. She could very well be dead.'

She laughed scornfully.

'Because some yokel sees ghosts? You must be hard up for clues these days!'

'No,' he said seriously. 'Because what you've been insinuating about the missing woman's morals makes it seem very probable she could provide her husband with a good motive for killing her.'

Her mouth twisted in dismay and for a moment this break in the symmetry of that too well balanced face gave it real beauty.

'No! I've said nothing! I never meant . . . that's quite outrageous!'

She stood up, flushed with what appeared to be genuine anger.

'But what did you imagine we were talking about?' asked Pascoe.

'You're trying to find out who's been suggesting these dreadful things about John.'

'Oh no,' said Pascoe, shaking his head. 'That would be useful, of course. But what we're really trying to discover is whether or not these dreadful things are true!'

Rawlinson looked angry when he came into the room and Pascoe prepared to deal with a bout of uxorious chivalry.

'What have you been saying to Peter?' demanded the limping man. 'He's in a hell of a state.'

'Nothing,' said Pascoe, taken by surprise. 'Why should anything I say disturb him?'

The question seemed to give the man more cause for rumination than seemed proportionate as he subsided into an armchair and Pascoe moved swiftly to the attack.

'Tell me about falling off the church tower,' he invited.

Rawlinson gripped his right knee with both hands

as though the words had triggered off more than the memory of pain.

'Have you ever fallen off anything, Inspector?' he asked in reply.

'Yes, I suppose so. But not so dramatically. A kitchen chair, I recall, when replacing a light bulb.'

'Chair or church, it's all the same,' said Rawlinson. 'One second you're on it, the next you're off. I must have overreached.'

'What precisely were you doing?' asked Pascoe.

'Watching a pair of owls,' said Rawlinson. 'I'm a draughtsman by training, a bird illustrator by inclination. I watch, note, photograph sometimes, and then do a picture. It had never struck me as a dangerous hobby.'

'It's enthusiasm that makes things dangerous,' observed Pascoe sententiously. 'The Reverend Davenport found you, I believe.'

Rawlinson frowned at the name.

'Yes. It was a good job he came when he did. There was a sharp frost and if I'd lain there till morning, I'd probably have died of exposure.'

'And immediately before falling, you remember nothing?'

'I remember arriving at the church, unlocking the door to the tower. Nothing more.'

'How did you get to the church that night?'

'I walked along the old drive, I suppose. I usually did. My bungalow's right alongside.'

'Mr Kingsley didn't mind?'

'Boris?' said Rawlinson in surprise. 'Why should he? I don't think I ever asked him.'

'Technically a trespass then,' smiled Pascoe. 'Do you recall seeing or hearing anything unusual along the drive or in the churchyard that night?'

'Well now,' said Rawlinson slowly. 'I'm not quite certain it was the same night—it's a long time ago—but once I rather thought I heard a crossbill in one of the cypress trees over the lych-gate. Probably I was mistaken.'

He spoke perfectly seriously, but Pascoe did not doubt he was being mocked.

'Your father built the bungalow, you say,' he said abruptly. 'So there's money in the family.'

'A little. He was a jobbing gardener by trade. I earn my own living, if that's what you mean.'

'I'm pleased to hear it,' said Pascoe, faintly sneering. 'Mr Kingsley now, does he also have to find ways to eke out the family fortune?'

If they start being funny, hit 'em hard, was a favourite maxim of Dalziel's.

'I don't see what this has got to do with anonymous letters, Inspector,' said Rawlinson.

'Don't you? Well, I'll explain. I want to get a clear picture of the missing woman. One thing that's starting to emerge is that she came from a very different background from most of the people she called her friends in Wearton. Just *how* different isn't quite clear to me yet.'

Rawlinson looked unconvinced but replied, 'All right, there's no secrets. Me you know about. Boris has some inherited money, but not much. I believe it came as something of a shock to find out just how little when his father died earlier this year. But in addition he's a "company director", whatever that means. You'd better ask him. John you'll know about, too . . .'

'Not his family. What did his father do?'

'He was a solicitor, rather older than Mrs

Swithenbank, I believe. He died ten years ago. The Davenports—well, Ursula's my sister, of course . . .'

'And therefore shared in the family fortune?'

'We split what little there was,' said Rawlinson acidly. 'When I married, I bought out her share of the bungalow. Shortly afterwards she married Peter, who is also one of the family. A cousin. His family live in Leeds. He had delicate health as a child and used to come down here for the good country air nearly every holiday. No real money in the family, and a damn sight less in his job! Now, let me see. Anyone I've missed out?'

'Yes,' said Pascoe. 'Your wife.'

'I thought you'd have quizzed her yourself,' said Rawlinson. 'Stella's from farming stock, one of the biggest farms in the area.'

'Well off?'

'Oh yes. Though show me a farmer who'll admit it!'

Pascoe laughed, though the attempt at lightness came awkwardly from Rawlinson's lips.

'So I'm right to say that Kate Lightfoot was the odd one out? Everyone else had some kind of well-established financial and social background.'

'Village life is surprisingly democratic,' protested Rawlinson. 'We all went to the same schools, no one bought their way out.'

'Democracy works best where there's a deep-implanted pecking order,' observed Pascoe cynically. 'Everybody can be equal as long as we all know our places. What was the Lightfoots' place, do you think? Her father was an agricultural labourer, I believe.'

'That's right. He used to work for Stella's father, in fact. Not that he was much of a worker at the end. He boozed himself to death. The mother took off soon after and there was some talk of putting Kate in care, but she made it clear she wasn't going to leave her brother easily. He was about twenty at the time, working on the farm like his father. Then suddenly he gave up his job and the tied cottage that went with it and bought up a smallholding just on the edge of the village, opposite the war memorial, you might have noticed it as you drove in?'

'No,' said Pascoe. 'The way you said "suddenly" sounded as if you meant "surprisingly".'

'Did it? This was a long time ago. I was only a lad, but in a village you learn early that all business is conducted in public. There was some talk of insurance money from his father's death. But knowing the old man, it didn't seem likely.'

'And what were the other speculations?' asked Pascoe.

Rawlinson looked at Pascoe as if for permission, then poured himself a glass of sherry.

'If you were a farm labourer in those days, you didn't save. The only handy source of a bit of extra income was fiddling your employer. Bags of spuds, petrol for the tractor, that sort of thing. Not that it could come to much, and with a Yorkshire farmer like my father-in-law watching over you, I hardly believe it could come to anything! But Stella, my wife, believes wholeheartedly that Lightfoot's fortunes such as they are were based on robbing her father rotten!'

'So he brought his sister up,' said Pascoe. 'Were they close?'

'You might say so,' said Rawlinson cautiously.

'What would *you* say?'

He shrugged and rubbed his knee again.

'Kate was—is—very much her own person, Mr

Pascoe. I was—am—very fond of her. We went out together for a while—nothing serious, all our gang tried various combinations till we settled as we are. I think I got to know her as well as anyone, but there were points beyond which you were not permitted to go.'

'Physically, you mean?' said Pascoe, acting stupid.

'Physically you went precisely as far as Kate was in the mood for,' replied Rawlinson drily. 'But I mean mentally, emotionally even. She shut you out. It was difficult to guess what she felt about Arthur, even when they were together.'

'And about the rest of you?'

'Friendly tolerance.'

'Even John Swithenbank?'

'No. No,' said Rawlinson, a spasm crossing his face as he rose suddenly to stretch his leg. 'John was different. I'd have said she disliked and despised him with all her heart.'

'I thought as host you'd have saved me for last, Inspector,' said Boris Kingsley in a hurt voice.

'Why? Aren't you ready for me?' asked Pascoe.

Kingsley laughed.

'On the contrary, I'm perfectly rehearsed. *What do I know about the letter and phone calls?* Nothing at all. *What do I know about Kate's disappearance?* Ditto. *Do I think John might have murdered her?* No. *Do I think anyone else here tonight might have murdered her?* Improbable but not impossible. *Who am I not one hundred per cent sure about?* Mind your own business.'

He sat back looking vastly pleased with himself.

'Why were you left on the shelf, Mr Kingsley?' asked Pascoe as if the man hadn't spoken.

'What do you mean?'

'The Wearton Six. Rawlinson gets his Stella, Swithenbank gets his Kate. Symmetry requires that you end up with Ursula, Mrs Davenport. But she opts for an outsider.'

'Hardly an outsider,' protested Kingsley. 'Peter spent most of his hols here. And he's Ursula's cousin. We knew him almost as well as each other.'

'Almost,' said Pascoe. 'Still, you did end up unattached.'

'What the devil's this got to do with anything?' demanded Boris.

'I don't know,' said Pascoe. 'Probably nothing. But if, say, you didn't get married because all your life you'd nursed a passionate but unrequited love for Kate Lightfoot, it might mean much.'

'Who's been talking to you? Has someone been saying something? Who was it? Geoff?' He sounded genuinely angry.

'No,' said Pascoe. 'That wasn't one of the things Mr Rawlinson told me. Where were you a year ago tonight, Mr Kingsley?'

The anger subsided and Kingsley shook his head like a boxer who has walked into a sucker punch and now means to take more care.

'I can't be sure. I'd need more notice of that question.'

'I'd have thought by now everyone here had notice of it,' remarked Pascoe drily. 'It was the weekend Mr Rawlinson fell off the church tower. Remember?'

'Of course. Yes. Dreadful business. I remember wondering . . .'

'What?'

'Mustn't even hint these things, of course, but

Geoff had been behaving rather oddly for some time before. You know, very moody. Self-absorbed.'

He paused invitingly. Pascoe made a note. He distrusted invitations.

'You mean he may have been upset because his affair with Kate was coming to some kind of climax, so when they met on the Friday evening he killed her, hid the body and then tried to commit suicide in a fit of remorse?' he asked with mild interest.

It was a long time since he'd seen a man splutter, but Kingsley spluttered now.

'*Please.* No! Don't say such things!'

'All right,' said Pascoe indifferently. 'What about you? What were you doing that night?'

'I've no idea. I didn't hear about it till next day, so I wasn't directly involved. Probably sitting in front of the television at home.'

'Alone?'

'If that was what I was doing, yes. Surely people who have the alternative of human conversation never watch television, do they, Inspector? It's a kind of mental masturbation, essentially a solitary pursuit.'

He had stopped spluttering. Pascoe yawned widely.

'Where do you think Kate Swithenbank is now?' he asked through the yawn.

Boris rolled his eyes upward and slapped the arm of his chair.

'I do wish you'd stop trying to confuse me with these changes of direction,' he said. 'They're irritating without being effective. Unless, of course, your aim *is* merely to irritate.'

'Do you think she's dead?'

'I've no idea. How should I know?'

'I didn't say *know.* I said *think.* Only one person could really *know.* Except her brother, of course.'

'Why him?' said Kingsley sharply.

'Hadn't you heard? He's seen her ghost.'

Kingsley laughed merrily.

'What a cretin!'

'Why do you dislike him, Mr Kingsley?'

'Who says I dislike him?'

'He says. It hardly seems worth denying. I mean, is there anyone who can really be said to like him? I'm just interested in reasons. Irrational Dr Fell prejudice? Aesthetic repugnance? Or perhaps, like Mrs Rawlinson, you think he cheated your father?'

The reaction was astonishing.

'What the hell do you mean?' demanded Kingsley, his face suddenly twisting in porcine ferocity. 'What've they been saying to you? Come on, Inspector, spit it out. You'd do well to remember this is my house and you'd be wise to watch what you say!'

There seemed to be something contradictory in this simultaneous demand for frankness and caution but Pascoe, who had been completely innocent of subtle intent, was not long in finding a hypothesis to resolve the contradiction.

'Come on, Mr Kingsley,' he said with the weary certainty of one who knows exactly what he is doing. 'I'm a policeman, remember? That means I've a job to do. It also means that I know all about discretion. In any case, there can't be any question of charges, not now. Not either way.'

He held his breath and hoped he was making sense. Kingsley's features gradually resumed a more normal colour and expression.

'You're right,' he said. 'I'm sorry. It's just that it makes me angry, even thinking about it.'

'How long have you known?' enquired Pascoe, still feeling his way.

'I never liked the man,' said Kingsley, 'but it wasn't till after Father died. I was going through his papers. The figures told the story. Then there was a diary . . . well, God, he was wrong, of course. But to suffer like that all those years!'

'This was how Lightfoot bought his smallholding?' pursued Pascoe.

'That's it. And how he's compensated for its inefficient running ever since! You wouldn't think he needs money to look at the man! But he's got expensive habits—drinking, women, too. God, he'd need to pay well to get any half decent woman near him!'

Ignoring the curious scale of values this suggested, Pascoe went the whole hog and said, 'So Arthur Lightfoot steadily blackmailed your father ever since he discovered he'd been interfering with an under-age girl, to wit, his sister Kate.'

Kingsley nodded. It seemed to be some relief to the man to hear someone else say it openly.

'I went to see him, of course, when I realized. I didn't know what I was going to do, but it was going to be bloody extreme!'

'And.'

'And he said nothing. Admitted nothing. Denied nothing. He just sat there cleaning that blasted shotgun of his. I ran out of words! There was nothing to do. I couldn't get him through the law—there was some evidence, but nothing certain enough, and besides even though he was dead, my father had paid for peace and quiet and a good name.'

'So what did you do?'

'Do, Inspector? Do? I did nothing.'

Kingsley was now back in full control.

'I hope one night I may catch him poaching on the bit of land that remains to me. Or that he might catch food poisoning from his own disgusting cooking. Yes, I can only sit and pray for some happy accident.'

'Like his cottage burning down, for instance?'

'Yes, that was a real tonic when I heard about it. A pity our fire service is so efficient.'

'He didn't come to see you afterwards?'

Kingsley regarded him shrewdly.

'Now why on earth should he do that? You're not suggesting I had anything to do with the fire, Inspector?'

'Of course not,' smiled Pascoe. 'But he'd need money for repairs. He doesn't sound as if he'd carry much insurance.'

'You may be right,' said Kingsley indifferently. 'He certainly wouldn't get it here. I only wish he'd had the cheek to try!'

'And now we come to the sixty-four-thousand-dollar question,' said Pascoe.

'And what's that?'

'Did Kate Swithenbank have any idea what her brother was up to all those years?'

There was a long silence.

'And if she did, what then, Inspector?'

'What indeed, Mr Kingsley? Something perhaps that some people might call a motive.'

There was a knock on the door.

Jesus! thought Pascoe. They time their interruptions here better than a French farce!

'Come in,' called Kingsley.

A wizened old head with eyes like a blackbird's thrust itself round the door.

'Can ah see thee about t'supper?' it demanded.

'Just coming, Mrs Warnock,' said Kingsley.

The blackbird's eyes regarded Pascoe unblinkingly for twenty seconds, then the head withdrew.

'Hostly duty calls,' said Kingsley, rising. 'Motive, you say? Hardly for me, though. I mean, I didn't find out about Lightfoot's bit of nastiness till six months after Kate disappeared, did I?'

'So you say, Mr Kingsley,' agreed Pascoe.

'But as for the others, well, I'll leave you to find your own motives there, you're clearly so good at it. Must fly now. Work up an appetite, dear boy. I'll send Ursula in, shall I? *That* should start the juices running!'

'Boris seemed very pleased to get away from you,' said Ursula, rippling into the red leather armchair. 'What were you talking about?'

'I'm not sure,' said Pascoe. 'He was on occasion a trifle obscure. Though he seemed to find no difficulty in accepting that someone in your little group might have been capable of murdering Kate Swithenbank. But he wouldn't say who he had in mind.'

'Me,' said Ursula promptly.

'Really? Why should he think that?'

'He likes playing Noel Coward, does Boris, but in fact he's terribly straightforward and conventional. His wisdom is proverbial in the strict sense. I mean his mind works in maxims. *Hell hath no fury like a woman scorned* has all the ring of eternal truth to Boris.'

'Meaning you have been scorned by . . . ?'

'John Swithenbank, of course. And it's true. I was furious. But only for a time.'

'How long a time?'

'Till the wedding. John so clearly regarded the whole business as farcical and whatever Kate regarded it as just as clearly had nothing to do with all those loving vows they made at the altar. Resentment has to have an object. I seemed to have lost mine on that day.'

'So you don't think the marriage was happy?' said Pascoe.

'What's happy?'

'I don't know *what,* but I know *where.* It's somewhere this side of either running off or committing murder,' said Pascoe.

She didn't seem to feel this required any answer. She was probably right, he thought. He was beginning to see possibilities but the problem was like one of those trick drawings beloved of psychologists—sometimes he saw a rabbit and sometimes he saw a goose. A frightened rabbit that had nothing to do with the missing woman, or a Christmas goose being led to an early slaughter.

'Why do you think he married her?'

'She wanted him to.'

She spoke as if this should have been obvious. Was it an answer? There were women, and men, too, in whom volition and achievement appeared contiguous. This Kate Lightfoot was emerging as a formidable woman.

'And Kate, why should she wish to marry a man she didn't love, perhaps even like?'

Ursula leaned forward and opened her arms and knees to the electric fire. Pascoe shuddered but not from the cold.

'John offered her an escape route from Wearton.'

'Why should she need that?' he asked. 'No one was keeping her prisoner.'

'Strictly speaking, no. But she had no training, no employment. She left school and looked after Arthur's cottage, that was all. She'd been doing it for years, and taking care of the business paperwork, too. She was surprisingly ignorant of the world in many ways. She asked my advice once . . .'

'About what?' interrupted Pascoe.

'Getting away, of course. She wanted to go to London. I told her there were two ways for a country girl to go to London, as a typist or as a tart. Unless, that is, she could find some nice well-heeled fellow and marry him! Next thing she and John were engaged.'

Ursula laughed ruefully and rubbed her hands together, then crossed her arms and rubbed her bare shoulders, making a sound which Pascoe found very disturbing.

'That was, what? Nine, ten years ago?'

'Something of the sort.'

'And since their marriage, what have your relations with her been?'

'Excellent,' she said promptly. 'Why? You don't really think I killed her, do you? I used to see her a couple of times a year in Wearton, and on the odd occasion I saw her in London. She was always the same, me too, I hope. I enjoyed her company and she never had occasion to push me around. No, that's the wrong phrase. There was never anything Kate wanted me to do except be myself, so I never got taken over.'

'And your feelings for Mr Swithenbank?'

'I'm very fond of John,' she said. 'I might have had an affair with him if he'd suggested it, but he never did. And Kate never showed the slightest interest in Peter.'

'What about your brother?' enquired Pascoe. 'Did she ever show any interest there?'

Now her expression turned cold as though the electric fire had been switched off.

'I'm sure you've discovered they were once very close, Inspector,' she said. 'But I'm equally sure you know that Geoff has the perfect alibi for that weekend. He was lying in hospital half dead.'

'Yes. Did you notice anything odd in his behaviour before the accident?'

'Odd? No. Why do you ask?'

'Just that Mr Kingsley said he was rather moody at that time. That's all.'

She laughed.

'Boris! The great psychologist now! It must do dreadful things to your ears, having to admit so much rubbish.'

Pascoe decided the time was ripe for a hard push.

'I think you're being rather unkind to Mr Kingsley,' he said. 'After all, it was he who took care of your husband tonight.'

'What's that mean?' she asked fiercely.

'Nothing, except that he got him out of the way when he started drawing attention to himself. He brought him to talk to me. Mr Kingsley seemed to feel your husband wanted to get something off his chest.'

That was stretching things a bit but Boris was big enough to look after himself.

'He said *what*? Then obviously Boris was talking even more stupidly than he usually does.' She stood up abruptly. 'I'll go and have a word with him and with Peter. That is, if you're finished with me, Inspector?'

There was clearly no way that he was going to get her to stay—the words were a challenge, not a request for permission to leave—so Pascoe shrugged philosophically.

At the door she paused.

'One thing I will tell you about Kate. She was the same in London as she was in Wearton. If she wanted out and I think she did, she wasn't just going to walk off alone into the great unknown. There'd have to be someone to go *with* or go *to*.'

'From what I've heard of her, I agree,' said Pascoe. 'Which means, if she came to Wearton . . .'

'What?'

'Well, the Wearton men seem to be all alive and well and still living in Wearton. So, unless she's locked in an attic somewhere . . .'

The anger left her face.

'Yes, I see that,' she said softly. 'I don't think . . . no, not that.'

The door closed quietly behind her.

Pascoe studied his notes for ten minutes. They were sketchy. He tended to use his book as some men use a pipe—to occupy the hands, permit significant pause and accentuate dramatic gesture. Much of his scrawl meant nothing. But as he jumped from one page to the next, his mind traced a line between the points where his scrawls quavered into sense and a shape began to form. But he still couldn't see if it were a goose or a rabbit.

He was interrupted by a discreet tap on the door.

'Come in, Miss Starkey,' he called.

She entered, smiling and saying, 'Wow, that was clever. Wasn't that clever, John?'

Swithenbank, close behind, agreed.

'I knew he was clever the first time I laid eyes on him,' he said.

'You two seem very pleased with yourselves,' said Pascoe.

'We've been watching their faces after you'd finished with them,' said Swithenbank, 'and they've all looked so wrought up, I've been certain you've got something out of them.'

'And that's what you've come to tell me?'

'No,' said the woman. 'Boris says supper will soon be ready. A trifling foolish banquet which some ancient crone is slowly hauling up from the kitchen. I think he's hoping that between the *hors-d'oeuvre* and the cheese you will reveal all and send the guilty party screaming out of the window into the police net you've doubtless cast around the house.'

'It's no joking matter, Jean,' said Swithenbank, frowning.

She made a mock penitential face but slipped her hand into his and gave it an affectionate squeeze as though to express real apology.

Pascoe sighed and wondered what to do. It was like being a blacksmith surrounded by hot irons. Which should he strike first?

'I think I'd like another word with Mr Davenport before supper,' he said finally.

With a bit of luck the alcoholic reverend would once more be ripe for the confessional. Pascoe was ready to make a fair guess at what he would say, but like all good detectives he basically distrusted deduction. Evidence without admission was of as doubtful efficacy as works without faith. To hypothesize from clues was fine so long as you remembered the basic paradox that the realities of human behaviour went far beyond the limits of human imagination. Intuition was something else, but you kept it well in check if you worked for Dalziel!

Swithenbank said, 'I'll fetch him, shall I? You will be fairly quick, though, else Boris's goodies will get cold.'

Pascoe said, 'As quick as I can, but do start without me.'

Swithenbank left but Jean Starkey hesitated at the door.

'Yes?' said Pascoe, shuffling his notes.

Suddenly he knew what was coming and would have preferred not to receive it at this juncture. But there's no evading a woman determined to make a clean breast of things.

'You know that I'm Jake Starr, don't you?' she said.

He looked up now. 'Clean breast' had been the right image. She was leaning back against the jamb, one knee slightly raised and the foot planted against the woodwork behind her in the traditional street walkers' pose. The red dress seemed to cling more tightly than ever and her nipples, tumescent from the room's coldness or (could it be?) some more personal sensation, were blatant beneath the taut material.

He wondered if she was about to make him an offer he would have to refuse and he wondered why the certainty of his refusal didn't prevent his mouth from going dry and his leg muscles from trembling.

'Yes, I know it,' he managed to reply.

She laughed and came and sat down on the chesterfield, but her approach diminished rather than intensified the sexuality of the moment.

'I told John you'd found out,' she said triumphantly. 'He wouldn't believe me, but I could tell. You were puzzled by me yesterday, but not tonight.'

He realized now, not without disappointment, that he'd been mistaken and no offer for his silence was going to be made. She was grinning at him slyly as if she could read his thoughts and he said coldly, 'You didn't imagine you could get away with it for ever, did you?'

'I didn't imagine I could get away with it at all!'

she replied. 'It's no secret. I mean, you get lists of pseudonyms in half a dozen reference books. I even got mentioned in a colour supplement article last May—don't policemen read the Sunday papers?'

'Not in Enfield it seems. OK, so you fooled us. Why?'

She looked at him closely and shook her head in reproach.

'Nothing sinister,' she said. 'It's just that ever since I started using a male pseudonym, I've found it very useful to pretend to be my own secretary. When people ring who don't know me, it's useful to be able to say Mr Starr's not available, can I take a message? That way I get time to think about offers, check up on things generally; as myself I'm a lousy negotiator, always say yes too quickly, never dream of trying to up the price of a story or an article. As Mr Starr's secretary, I pass on the most devastating messages without turning a hair. So when the police contacted me I automatically responded in the same way. Even when I realized it wasn't about not paying a parking fine, I didn't let on. I was due in New York the following day and I'd no intention of letting a bumbling bobby delay me. So I made a statement as Jake Starr's secretary, rang John to find out what the hell was going on, told him what I'd done, and sent another statement as Jake Starr from America. It all seemed a bit of a laugh, really.'

'A woman goes missing and you're amused?' said Pascoe.

'Hold on! I thought she'd merely taken off with some boyfriend. And I was glad. John had seemed to be hedging his bets a bit, I thought. Always on about his marriage being on the rocks but never getting close to *doing* anything about it. So if she'd made the break, what do you expect from me but a big *whoopee*!'

'And later? When she didn't show up?'

She shrugged expressively.

'We got worried, naturally. I couldn't understand why the police weren't on to the Jake Starr thing, you really have been pretty inefficient, Inspector. But I could see no profit in doing your work for you. John was being given a rough enough time. So I lay low and hoped that Kate would turn up again. Funny that, isn't it? I was delighted to learn she'd gone. Now here I was desperate to have her come back.'

Pascoe nodded approvingly. It was a good story. He had no idea whether he believed it or not, but in the circumstances it was a very good story. He must try some of her books.

'One more thing,' he said. 'Why have you come to Wearton?'

She warmed herself at the fire, reminding him of Ursula. Two women; similar problems? Then she smiled widely and the problems whatever they were seemed defeated.

'I changed my mind about doing the police's job for them,' she said. 'Come with me.'

She rose and took him by the hand like a small child, or a lover, and led him out of the library, across the hall, up the stairs and into a bedroom.

'Am I to go to bed without any supper?' he asked.

She laughed and taking up a nail file from a huge mahogany dressing-table, she approached a small oak wardrobe which didn't match anything else in the room. Sliding the file into the crack between the door and the jamb, she forced it upwards till it met the lug of the lock and made half a dozen sideways twisting movements.

'*Voilà!*' she said triumphantly and opened the door.

'Why did you bother to lock it after you last time?' enquired Pascoe, regarding the scarred woodwork which advertised forced entry like a neon sign.

She looked hurt.

'I didn't want Boris to know I'd been in here,' she said. 'But look inside.'

With a sigh, Pascoe obeyed.

And the sigh turned into a whistle of appreciation as he spotted the white muslin dress with blue ribbons and the floppy white hat trimmed with cotton roses. In his mind's eye he saw again the half-photograph he had examined in Arthur Lightfoot's cottage just a few hours ago.

'You've broken the law, you realize,' he said casually to Jean Starkey, who was standing beside him with the repressed smugness of one who anticipates congratulation.

'*I've* broken the law?' she began indignantly, but stopped as she heard rapid footsteps on the stairs and a man's voice calling, 'Pascoe! Pascoe!'

A moment later Swithenbank appeared at the door, his customary calm surface considerably ruffled.

'Pascoe, you'd better come,' he said urgently. 'It's Peter Davenport. I don't know what the hell's going on but he's been having the most tremendous scene with Ursula and now he's taken off back towards the church. He seems quite hysterical.

'Ursula thinks he's going to kill himself!'

VIII

While from a proud tower in the town
Death looks gigantically down.

THE NIGHT HAD GROWN wilder during the hours since
their arrival. There were flurries of rain in the gusty
wind which tore at the clouds and sent bunches of
stars scurrying across the sky. The ancient beeches
rustled and groaned and swayed like an old Disney
forest, and underfoot the long grass laid an-
kle-twisting traps over the forgotten coach ruts.

Here once through an alley Titanic
Of cypress I roamed with my Soul—

Pascoe found himself jogging to the contrived but
controlled rhythm of Poe's poem. Behind him, im-
peded by the woman's dress and shoes, ran
Swithenbank and Jean Starkey.

Far ahead in the tunnelled darkness he caught an
occasional glimpse of a swaying light as though someone were holding a torch.

At the end of our path a liquescent
And nebulous lustre was born.

And there it was, not the pin-prick of a torch but a
distinct glow hazed through the fine mist of rain. Pascoe paused and the pursuing couple came up with
him.

'Someone's switched the Christmas floodlights on,'

said Swithenbank. 'God, they'll have half the village at the church!'

As though this were a congregation devoutly to be missed, he abandoned the hard-panting woman to Pascoe's care and sprinted ahead. Hard panting became Jean Starkey, Pascoe suspected, and normally he would have accepted the charge gladly, but he wanted to be at the church on time before the voices of reason and discretion had a chance to prevail.

'You OK?' he asked.

A change of note in the heavy breathing and a vague movement of the shadowy head seemed affirmative, so abandoning chivalry and the woman together, he pressed on.

In the darkness of the great outdoors a very few yards can make the difference between good vision and total obscurity. Suddenly what lay ahead swam into close focus—a gateway, a pair of looming evergreens immediately beyond, and fifty yards further on the bulk of the church, its grey stone silvery in the light which flooded its tower.

The wrought metal gate hung open between its two stone posts. Pascoe leapt lightly through onto a neglected weed-snagged gravel path which curved among a forest of mossy and sometimes drunkenly angled tombstones. Leaning against one of these was a figure which might have been taken for an exuberant mason's impression of Grief had it not moved and said, 'Pascoe!'

His recognition of Rawlinson was almost instantaneous but that 'almost' had his skin crawling chillily.

'Give us a hand,' said Rawlinson, groaning as he pushed himself up from the headstone. 'I came out in such a hurry, I forgot my stick and the leg's gone.'

'Look,' said Pascoe. 'Shouldn't you hang on here till I can rustle up a stretcher?'

'For Christ's sake, man! Peter's up that fucking tower! I've got to get there!'

Dalziel would not have let such an opportunity pass, but Pascoe knew he was of more tender and humane stuff than his gross superior.

It was this knowledge that made him regard himself with some surprise and distress as he took half a step backwards from Rawlinson's grasping hand and said coldly, 'Why? Why have you got to get there?'

'Why? Because it's my fault,' the man cried in anguish. 'I was as much to blame. And I said I forgave him, but he knew I didn't. Knowing that, where could he turn for help?'

Pascoe nodded. He felt rather disappointed. The picture was going to show a frightened rabbit after all.

'He didn't find you by accident,' he said. 'He was up on the tower with you. He pushed you.'

'No, no, *that* was an accident,' insisted the distraught man. 'Please help me while there's still time.'

'Come on,' said Pascoe, suddenly full of self-disgust, an emotion which won the wholehearted support of Jean Starkey, who had arrived soon enough to catch the drift of the exchange and who now said to him as she lent her strength to getting Rawlinson upright, 'That was a shitty thing to do.'

'Don't you preach at me, lady,' he snapped back. 'Not you.'

In silence, supporting Rawlinson between them, they made their way to the church.

Here Kingsley came to meet them.

'Thank God you're here,' he said to Pascoe with what sounded like genuine relief. 'He's on top of the tower. He's locked the stair door behind him and he won't speak to anyone.'

'Who put that floodlight on?' demanded Pascoe.

'I did,' said Kingsley rather proudly. 'It's just used at Christmas really but I thought . . .'

'Switch the bloody thing off!' commanded Pascoe, easing Rawlinson against an old rugged cross. 'Leave the outer porch light on. Then see if you can break the tower door open.'

'It's five hundred years old,' said Kingsley, shocked.

'Then with a bit of luck it'll have woodworm,' said Pascoe. 'Hurry!'

A moment later the bright light faded, leaving the tower as a black monolith while those below stood in the gentler glow which spilled out of the church porch.

'Why've you switched it off?' demanded Ursula. She looked wild and distraught, her gown sodden, her make-up smeared like an action painting by the driven rain. All her sexuality had gone, whereas even in the stress of the moment Pascoe had noted under the floodlight the amazing things dampness was doing to Jean Starkey's scarlet dress.

'If he looked down, all he'd be able to see was the glare,' said Pascoe. 'Like being on a stage. We don't want him to feel he's on a stage. I want him to be able to see us—and what he's likely to hit. And I don't want a crowd here either. Now tell me, has he said anything?'

'No, not a word.'

'But he's definitely up there?'

'Yes. We nearly caught up with him. He had to unlock the outer door of the church.'

'Where was the key to the tower?'

'Hanging up in the porch with all the other keys.'

'Is the outer door always locked?'

'It has been since last year, since Geoff's accident. But what's all this got to do with getting Peter down from there?' Ursula demanded angrily.

She was right, thought Pascoe guiltily. He must keep his eye on the rabbit for the moment and forget the goose.

He took the woman by the arm and led her unresisting to where Rawlinson was standing by the cross peering helplessly upwards.

'Listen,' he said. 'I think I know why he's up there, but I'm not sure what'll bring him down. You'd better tell me. Is it just the drink talking? I mean, when the rain and the cold sobers him up, will he come down of his own accord?'

Brother and sister exchanged glances.

'No,' said Ursula. 'Drinking's an escape. The soberer he gets, the worse it'll be.'

'I guessed so,' said Pascoe. 'Then you two had better talk to each other fast. Whatever you know, you've both got to know it, because he's got to know you both know it.'

Ursula managed to raise a wan smile.

'That's a lot of knowing.'

Pascoe regarded her seriously.

'Too much for you?'

She shook her head, then to her brother she said gently, 'Geoff, I'm a good guesser. And I'm Peter's wife.'

Rawlinson rubbed the rain off his face or it may have been tears. Then he began to talk rapidly, in a confessional manner.

'When he used to come and stay with us, we always shared a bed. Some time, it must have been in our early teens, I don't remember, but one summer when he came, well, we'd always played and wrestled before like boys do, only now puberty was well under way and we started exciting ourselves and each other with talk and pictures. For me, I believe for most adolescents if it happens, it was just a sort of marking time. I'd have been terrified to go near a real girl but that was always the image I had in my mind. Later, as I got older and started making dates with girls, I wanted to stop. It would have been earlier but for Peter; but in the end we did stop. We did our college training, settled down to our careers. I got married, John and Kate got married and finally Ursula and Peter married. I was delighted. I liked him, we were close friends, our childhood was far behind us, then last year . . .'

'It was after the harvest supper, wasn't it?' interrupted Ursula with the certainty of revelation.

Rawlinson nodded glumly, unsurprised that she knew.

'Yes. We were clearing up together, alone. I was . . . unhappy. Well, that's my affair. I talked to Peter. He touched me. And what we did seemed natural, innocent almost. Till next day. I was so full of guilt it almost choked me. I couldn't believe it of myself. The only thing to do seemed to be to pretend it hadn't happened. I made sure I was never alone with Peter during the next couple of weeks. He made no sign that anything was between us, and when he told me about the owls in the tower, I didn't think twice about asking if I could go up there at night. The first three nights I was by myself, getting them accustomed to my presence. The fourth, that was the Friday, he came up with a flask of coffee for me. What happened then—well, all you need to know is the falling was pure accident. My own fault. I was stupid. But stupid or not, it did this . . .'

He slapped his damaged leg in anger and frustration.

'We've got to get him down,' he said desperately. 'Yes, I've blamed him for this and he knows it. But I never wished the same on him. Never!'

Pascoe was looking at the woman. She put her arm round her brother's shoulder.

'It's OK, Geoff. It's OK. I know, I know. Or at least I guessed. It's OK.'

'And your husband, have you talked about it with him?' asked Pascoe.

'No, not directly. It's a myth, isn't it, that everything's solved by bringing it out in the open? We have a kind of jokey relationship about sex. It's a delicate balance but we keep it, we keep it.'

She sounded desperate for reassurance.

'Something's upset the balance,' urged Pascoe gently.

'Yes, I know. Three or four months ago something, I don't know what. And tonight. Perhaps it's something to do with you being at Boris's!'

She flashed this at him furiously as though delighted to have found a target.

'My God!' cried Rawlinson, who'd never taken his eyes off the tower. 'He's there!'

Pascoe screwed up his eyes against the now driving rain. The figure leaning over the parapet could have been part of the stonework, some graven saint, so still and indistinct it was.

'Peter! Peter!' screamed Ursula, cupping her hands in an effort to hurl her words skywards. So strong was the wind now that Pascoe doubted if anything but the thin edge of that cry sounded aloft the tower. His training told him he should already have summoned the fire brigade, at least got them on stand-by. But this story could destroy those concerned just as much as the fall could destroy Davenport.

A figure darted from the church porch. It was Swithenbank, excited but controlled.

'We've got the door open,' he said. 'What next?'

Pascoe thought rapidly.

'What's at the top of the stairs?' he demanded of Rawlinson.

'Another door out onto the tower.'

'Does it have a lock?'

'Just a hasp and a padlock.'

'So he can't lock it from above. OK. Mr Rawlinson, can you manage to move forward a bit, get onto the path right beneath Davenport? Ursula, give him a hand.'

Rawlinson clung heavily to his shoulder and limped into position.

'Now stand there the pair of you and bellow at him. He may not be able to hear, but keep on bellowing. I want him to see you two side by side. And I don't want him to be able to jump without risking landing on one of you. If he shifts position, follow him!'

Accompanied by Swithenbank, he dashed into the church porch. Jean Starkey was there, so wet she might as well have been naked. By contrast Stella Rawlinson was relatively dry. She had found time to put on a raincoat and headscarf before coming out, though her patience had not stretched to moving at her lame husband's pace. Pascoe wondered how much she knew and what the knowledge was doing to her. She it was who carried the torch he had spotted in the distance. He took it from her hand without speaking and pushed his way past Kingsley, who was peering through the tower door with all the nervous excitement of a subaltern about to go over the top.

'You come second,' said Pascoe to Swithenbank. 'Keep three steps behind me. If I stop, you stop. No talking. I'll try to go through the door at the top quietly. If I can't, I'll go at a rush. Come quick then, I may need help.'

'What about me?' said Boris eagerly.

'Stay at the bottom,' ordered Pascoe. 'If he gets past us, stop him.'

It was an unlikely contingency, an unnecessary job. But he didn't want Boris's bulk creaking up those wooden stairs and past experience had taught him that the fewer men you had making an arrest in the dark, the less chance there was of ending up with each other.

The original staircase of the tower must have long since rotted away, but this one was quite antiquated enough. It consisted of five steep wooden steps to each narrow landing and when he gripped the banister, the newel post above rocked so alarmingly in its joint that he ignored the rail thereafter and proceeded bent double to test the stairs by eye before weight. The air smelt musty and what little light came through the narrow windows was hardly reinforced by the dim glow of the torch. Soon Pascoe could see neither the floor he had left nor the roof he approached. He remembered a ghost story in which a girl counted three hundred steps going up a tower, but coming down soon found herself far beyond that figure without any sign of the bottom. Perhaps this was the way it ended for him, too. He flashed his torch downward to seek reassurance in the presence of Swithenbank, but the sight of that narrow intense

face with its high forehead, blank eyes and black
moustache brought little comfort. For all he knew this
man was a murderer. It was still very much a possibility. Though his theory that Rawlinson had been
hurled from the tower because of what he had seen
had proved a non-starter, that meant nothing. The
rabbit could co-exist with the goose.

On the other hand, if Swithenbank were a murderer, he had been too successful so far to need to
risk attempting to dispose of a suspicious policeman.
Indeed, if one of Pascoe's other hypotheses proved
true . . .

But speculation was terminated by the sudden
awareness that the next landing was the last. Ahead
was the door leading to the top of the tower.

There was no latch on it, only an empty hasp with
the discarded padlock lying on the floor.

Gently Pascoe pushed at the door. He felt a resistance and for a moment thought that Davenport must
have wedged it shut from without. Then he realized
that it was only the force of the wind which pressed
against him, and as he pushed again that same wind,
as if delighted to get a grip on what had so long resisted it, caught the partly opened door and flung it
wide with a tremendous crash that almost tore its
hinges out of their post.

The dark figure against the furthermost parapet
started and turned.

Pascoe hurled himself forward. The figure placed
one foot on the parapet and thrust itself upwards.
What might have been a shriek from below or merely
a new crescendo of wind cut through the air. Pascoe
sprang to the parapet, gripped one of the castellations
with his left hand and caught Davenport by the jacket

pocket. He felt the material begin to tear but dared not release either handhold to try for a better grip.

Where the hell was Swithenbank?

He heard the steps behind him, glanced back, saw that intense, controlled stare, and for a long ghastly moment wondered how he could have been so wrong about his own safety.

Then with a strength unpromised by his slight frame, Swithenbank caught Davenport by the shoulders and bore him easily backwards.

There was no resistance.

'I wouldn't have jumped,' he said mildly as they thrust him before them through the doorway. Pascoe half believed him but not enough to relax his grip as they clattered down the wooden stairs.

Once in the church porch he released him to Ursula's equally tight clasp and thought ruefully that of them all Davenport probably looked the least distraught, though what emotion it was that twisted Stella's face as she watched her husband talking earnestly to Davenport was hard to say.

'Is he all right?' asked Kingsley anxiously.

'I doubt it,' said Pascoe. 'We'll get him home, call a doctor and get him sedated. After that . . .'

He shrugged.

'Terrible, terrible,' said Kingsley. 'Look, Ursula won't want us all tramping around the rectory. Shall I take the main party back to Wear End to dry out? Oh, and there's the supper! It'll be ruined! And you can come on as soon as decently possible.'

Pascoe sought for some way of saying that, as the matter was not official, a close friend would be more suitable company for the Davenports than an intrusive policeman, but nothing came to mind.

'All right,' he sighed.

And in any case, he was still curious to discover what it was that had sparked off Davenport's extraordinary behaviour.

He found out in the next ten seconds.

'All right everybody,' called Kingsley. 'Here's what we're going to do.'

But nobody was listening. Behind him the big church door, closed against the violent weather, was swinging slowly open.

Into the lighted porch stepped a dark-clad figure in a dripping shapeless cap. In the crook of his arm was a shotgun.

Pascoe saw the glance of hatred that came from Davenport's eyes even before the newcomer spoke.

'Evening, Vicar,' said Arthur Lightfoot. 'Here we are again, then.'

IX

But see, amid the mimic rout
A crawling shape intrude!

'HOW DO, INSPECTOR?' CONTINUED Arthur Lightfoot. 'Have you got him yet?'

'Got who?' asked Pascoe.

'T'chap who killed our Kate,' said Lightfoot.

'Mr Lightfoot, as I've explained, there's no real evidence that your sister's dead.'

'There's the ear-ring,' interrupted Kingsley. Pascoe regarded him curiously and wondered what his game was.

'Come on, Peter. Let's be getting you home. Whatever the rest of this lot think, you're in no fit state for a metaphysical discussion.'

It was Ursula who spoke but when she moved forward with her arm round her husband's waist, Lightfoot made no effort to step aside.

'Do you mind, Arthur!' she said clearly and savagely.

'Just hold on there, missus,' said Lightfoot. 'I asked Mr Detective here a question. No one sets foot out of here without I get an answer.'

'You've had your answer!' said Ursula. 'And in any case, you can't imagine my husband could have anything to do with Kate's disappearance.'

'I know what t'vicar can and can't do as well as any,' said Lightfoot with a note of vicious mockery in his voice. 'And you too, missus, I know what you're capable of. All on you, I know as much about all on you as'd fill a Sunday paper through till Friday.'

He raised his voice as he spoke and there was no mistaking the note of threat.

'There's been notes, has there? And telephone calls, has there? And it's you that's been getting them, brother-in-law?'

'That's right,' said Swithenbank calmly. 'But . . .'

'Who's she? What's she to you?'

The barrel of the gun rose slowly and pointed at Jean Starkey.

'This is Miss Starkey. She's a writer and . . .'

'I can see *what* she is,' said Lightfoot scornfully, his eyes running up and down the soaking clinging red dress. 'I said, what's she to you?'

'A friend.'

'A friend, is it? And our Kate not yet properly buried!'

'What makes you so sure she's dead?' burst out Swithenbank.

Lightfoot looked at him with a baring of the teeth which might have been a smile.

'I've seen her through glass and I've heard her in the night. Oh, she's dead, she's dead, never have doubt of that.'

A spasm of awful grief crossed his face.

'She shouldn't have left, she shouldn't have left,' he keened softly, almost to himself.

'I didn't make her leave,' protested Swithenbank.

'Not *you*, you girt fool! Wearton. Her home. *Me*. It were you as caused all this. Like as not whoever wrote that letter knew the truth. It were you, weren't it? Tell us where she's hid, you owe her that. Tell us where she's hid!'

Now the barrel was pointing straight at Swithenbank's chest.

'I wish I knew, Arthur, believe me,' protested Swithenbank in tones of sweet reasonableness whose only effect was to bring the gun stabbing at his rib-case.

'Liar! I've watched you in this churchyard at dead of night. Is she laid here? Is she? I feel her close!'

Pascoe shivered with more than cold. The animal intensity of this man was terrifying beyond the reach of middle-class neurotics, or even suicidal vicars!

'I don't know!' Swithenbank's voice had the ghost of a tremor now, as though he was just beginning to admit the possibility that the trigger might be pulled.

'Tell him what you were doing here, Mr Swithenbank,' Pascoe suggested. He could see no way to disarm the man without risking a reflexive tightening of that gnarled brown finger.

'I just thought, if Kate did come to Wearton, she

might be here, somewhere, in the churchyard. I
thought perhaps the tomb of the Aubrey-Beesons
. . . we used to play round there as kids . . . once
we went in . . . there was a key at Wear End, Boris
got it . . . but there was another in the bunch of
keys hanging in the porch here, only Peter had started
locking the door, so I couldn't get in.'

He was definitely gabbling now.

'You mean you thought that stupid poem might be
true?' asked Ursula.

'Why not?' Swithenbank demanded.

'Why not indeed?' echoed Pascoe. 'I mean, the
man responsible for the telephone calls ought to know
what precisely they signify, oughtn't he?'

There was a moment of puzzled silence which involved Lightfoot, too, and Pascoe was glad to see that
though the direction of the shotgun remained un-
changed, the man took half a pace backwards and
switched his unblinking gaze to the detective's own
face.

'What on earth can you mean, Inspector?' enquired
Kingsley.

Swithenbank and Jean Starkey exchanged looks.
She smiled fondly at him and nodded encouragingly,
like a mother to a shy child.

'All right,' he said defiantly. 'It's true. There were
no anonymous phone calls.'

'A couple,' corrected the woman. 'I made them to
John's mother and his secretary. Just to provide a couple of independent ears.'

'And I sent the letter and the ear-ring,' said
Swithenbank as though eager to claim his share of the
credit.

'But the blood?' said Ursula.

'Cow's. Probably off the weekend joint,' said Pascoe cheerfully. 'We have very good laboratories.'

'Sod your laboratories,' said Lightfoot in angry bewilderment. 'What's going on?'

'Arthur, listen to me,' said Swithenbank. He spoke urgently, but he was back in full control. 'I'm like you. I believe Kate's dead. A year, no sign, it's too much. The police think so, too. And they think I'm responsible, but I swear I'm not! But they're fixated; result is, my life's permeated with suspicion while the real murderer gets off scot free. They're not even looking for him, just watching me!'

Willie Dove really got to him, thought Pascoe.

'But why this charade?' demanded Rawlinson.

'It was my idea,' said Jean Starkey defiantly. 'I'm a writer. I used my imagination. We wanted something to stir the police out of their stupor and to get the killer worried at the same time.'

'But why up here?' retorted Rawlinson. 'You know how much we loved Kate, John; some of us, that is. Why bring this trouble up here?'

His wife looked at him with disgust, then turned away.

'Because I believe this is where the trouble belongs, Geoff,' said Swithenbank. 'Up here. In Wearton. Where else would Kate come? Where else might there be someone to meet her?'

'She lived with you in London for years!' protested Kingsley.

Swithenbank shook his head.

'I've checked and double-checked the possibilities there. Not many. She liked a quiet kind of life, Kate. Well, you all know that. No, I'm almost certain she came back here. And was not welcome. And got killed for her pains.'

'But who would kill her? And why?'

It was Ursula who spoke, her husband's needs momentarily forgotten.

Swithenbank smiled humourlessly.

'Killing's not so difficult, Ursula dear. We've been pretty close a couple of times tonight, haven't we? You know what Kate was like. Simple, direct, impulsive. Insensitive. If she was sick of me, of our life in London, and wanted to come back to Wearton, she'd just set off. Suppose she has a choice here. Arthur in his cottage or a lover, someone she's been sleeping with on and off for years, perhaps. A man who thinks she takes it as casually as he does, a bit of sensual titillation when the chance offers. A man who doesn't want a scandal, certainly doesn't want a permanent relationship. She goes to him, rather than Arthur. Obvious choice it seems, till this man laughs at her, tells her to go back to London. She wouldn't make a fuss, not Kate. She'd get up quietly and say she was going. But not back to London, no; back to her brother.'

Arthur Lightfoot groaned from the depths of his being. The others regarded him uneasily, except for Swithenbank, who went relentlessly on.

'Angry husbands are one thing, but the prospect of an angry Arthur was quite another. Look at him, for God's sake! And so, one thing leads to another . . .'

'But not to murder!' protested Ursula. 'It makes no sense!'

But her words were subsumed by Lightfoot's groan which had swollen to a cry of rage.

'It's sense to me!' he cried. 'And there's only one here that fits the bill. The stud, him as has covered every mare hereabouts. Like father, like fucking son!'

Oh God. Here we go again, thought Pascoe as the

black barrel rose once more and this time came to a halt against Boris Kingsley's ample belly.

To his surprise, Kingsley showed not the slightest sign of fear.

'Come off it, Lightfoot,' he sneered. 'You're not going to fire that thing. That's not your way. A bit of sneaky poaching of another man's game. Or even dirtier ways of getting your hands on another man's money. That's all you're good for. So put that thing away.'

'Did you kill my sister?' demanded Lightfoot.

'Oh go to hell!'

'And whoever did kill her, she probably asked for it!' hissed Stella Rawlinson with a venom that shocked even Lightfoot into silence for a moment.

'Listen who's talking!' he rejoined eventually. But before he could elaborate Swithenbank said in his most casual voice, 'Yet it's a question which needs answering, Boris.'

Now everyone was quiet. Lightfoot had stepped further into the porch, leaving the door unguarded, but Ursula made no effort to shepherd her husband through it, nor from the expression of rapt attention on his face would he have allowed himself to be removed if she'd tried.

Strange therapy! thought Pascoe.

'What do you mean, John?' asked Kingsley courteously.

Swithenbank was standing under the arch of the doorway up to the tower and the light from the single small bulb that lit the porch scarcely reached him so that his voice came drifting out of the shadows.

'It's an odd place, Wearton, Mr Pascoe,' he said. 'You try to escape it but it comes after you. And I was foolish enough to take one of the oddest pieces of it away with me! Oh, don't be shocked, friends. Even among your outstanding oddities, Kate stood supreme! And when she left me, I knew that sooner or later she'd come back here, as long as she was alive, that is.'

'Or dead.'

Arthur Lightfoot spoke so solemnly that no one dared even by expression to show disbelief.

Swithenbank ignored him.

'You know what I did when Jean and I first started brooding on schemes to start our rabbit?'

'Goose,' muttered Pascoe to himself.

'I wrote down the names of everyone here, you excepted, of course, Inspector. And I started to cross out those who I couldn't bring myself to believe capable of killing Kate. Do you know, I sat for an hour and hadn't crossed out a name!'

'Oh, come on, John,' said Ursula.

'Not even yours, dear,' he said regretfully. 'So I made a league table instead. And do you know, Boris, however I constructed it, you kept on coming out on top!'

'Well, you know me, John,' said Kingsley. 'Always a winner.'

'Shut up!' snapped Lightfoot, prodding him with the gun.

This had gone far enough, thought Pascoe. This lunatic could accidentally fire that thing at any moment.

He coughed gently and was flattered to note that he immediately had everyone's attention. He also had for the first time a full frontal of Lightfoot's shotgun. He reached out, took the barrel fastidiously between thumb and forefinger and moved it aside.

'Mr Lightfoot,' he said quietly. 'If that weapon is pointed once more at anyone here, and most especially at me, I shall arrest you instantly for threatening behaviour. Lower it and break it!'

The man gave him a look full of hatred, but obeyed, and Davenport, as though the action held some personal symbolism for him, suddenly stepped away from Ursula and in best vicarial tones said, 'Please, everybody, hasn't this gone far enough? You're all soaking and it's mainly my fault. I don't want pneumonia on my conscience as well. You're all welcome to dry out at the rectory. Mr Pascoe, I'd like a private word with you later, if it's convenient.'

He was looking at Lightfoot as he spoke these last words and it was the smallholder whose hitherto unblinking gaze shifted first.

Pascoe made an educated guess at what Davenport was going to tell him. He'd lay odds that a year ago Lightfoot, out on a poaching trip perhaps, had witnessed Rawlinson's fall from the tower. He had kept out of sight when the vicar descended—he would hardly want to draw the local bobby's attention to himself—and his curiosity had later been whetted by the discrepancy between what he had seen and the official version. But he'd done nothing about it till the summer when he needed money after the fire. With Kingsley senior's death, his old source had dried up, but a visit to the vicarage, a few dark hints of deep knowledge (he had the perfect manner for it), and he had found a new supply of funds to tap. What precisely he did know hardly mattered. He emanated evil intent like few men Pascoe had met.

He made a mental vow that whatever else came out of this extraordinary evening, Arthur Lightfoot was going to get what was coming to him.

But there were still many other questions to be answered. Obviously Swithenbank had deliberately angled his campaign towards Kingsley, with how much justification was not yet clear. Perhaps he just had a 'feeling'. Like Willie Dove had a feeling! Or perhaps he knew more than he had yet said. There was still the dress to be explained. He suddenly felt very tired.

There had been a general movement to the doorway. Outside the wind still gusted fitfully but for the moment the rain seemed to have stopped. Not that that mattered, Pascoe thought ruefully. He was so damp that nothing short of total immersion could aggravate his condition.

'Hold on a moment. I don't think we're finished here yet!'

It was Jean Starkey and her words were greeted with a groan of exasperation in which Pascoe joined. He guessed what she was going to say, but he judged that the moment for dramatic revelation was past. What had been an atmosphere of high emotion in a Gothic setting had now become one of damp and discomfort in a draughty church porch. The time had come for warmth and whisky, followed by some hard questioning in a police interview room. He wanted to save his knowledge of the woman's dress in Kingsley's bedroom till then.

But the woman insisted.

'Tell us about the dress, Boris. You haven't told us about the dress.'

'What dress?'

'The white muslin dress and the big straw hat. Kate's favourite gear, wasn't it? How does it come about that you've got a woman's dress hidden in a locked wardrobe in your house?'

Now the audience's attention was engaged once more. Kingsley made no effort to deny it but asked indignantly, 'How does it come about you know what I've got locked up in my house!'

'It's true, then?' said Lightfoot, who had been smoulderingly subdued for the past few minutes.

'Why shouldn't it be true?'

Whether because of Pascoe's threat or out of personal preference, Lightfoot didn't try to use his gun this time but jumped forward and seized Kingsley one-handed by the throat, bearing him back against the opened door which lay against the wall. No one seemed inclined to interfere, not even when the enraged assailant started using the fat man's head as a knocker to punctuate his demands, 'Where-is-she? Where-is-she?'

It was constabulary duty time once more. Pascoe stepped forward and said, 'That's enough.'

When Lightfoot showed no sign of agreeing, Pascoe punched him in the kidneys and stepped swiftly back. The blow was a light one and Lightfoot swung round as much in surprise as pain. Kingsley, released, staggered out of the church holding his throat, but he could have suffered no real damage for he was able to scream, 'I'll tell you why I've got the clothes! It's Kate's ghost, you superstitious cretin! Do you really think anything would come back from the grave to an animal like you in that sty of a cottage?'

He even managed a derisive laugh but it stuttered off into a fit of coughing.

'You'd better explain yourself, I think, Mr Kingsley,' said Pascoe, putting himself between the fat man and Lightfoot.

Though the man was genuinely angry, Pascoe could see the quick calculation in his face. He wasn't about to admit anything illegal, but what was illegal about a practical joke?

'He had it coming to him, that bastard,' snarled Kingsley, adding weakly, 'It was just a kind of joke.'

'To convince him that the sister he loved was dead and he was partly responsible? Very amusing,' said Pascoe. 'But hardly a one-man show? You must have had a leading lady.'

He let his eyes run down Kingsley's corpulent figure.

'You mean, it were play-acting?' said Lightfoot, who seemed far more affected by this news than by Pascoe's punch.

'That's right,' said Kingsley with malicious satisfaction. 'If ever a man deserved to be haunted, it was you.'

'Play-acting!'

'But where does the acting end, the truth begin?' said Swithenbank. A trifle melodramatic, thought Pascoe, but a good question nevertheless.

'There's still one theory untested, Inspector. Remember the tomb I mentioned? The resting place of the Aubrey-Beesons, the old squires of Wear?

> And I said—"What is written, sweet
>   sister,
> On the door of this legended tomb?"
> She replied—"Ulalume—Ulalume—
> 'Tis the vault of thy lost Ulalume!"'

He held aloft a large metal ring with several keys which chimed together as he shook it.

'I can't get it out of my mind that perhaps by accident when I chose that poem, I was closer than I knew to the truth. What say you, Boris? I'm going to take a look before I leave this churchyard tonight. Are you coming, Inspector? Anyone for menace?'

There was a note of hysterical bravado in his voice which caused the others to stir and draw closer together. He took a few paces down the path towards the old lych-gate, which itself was not visible, though the wind-swayed arch of cypress trees loomed dark against the grey wash of the sky. Suddenly the wind dropped altogether; the sough and scrape of branches, the rustle of dried leaves among the headstones, the buffets of violent air against the old stones of the tower, all these sounds ceased and were succeeded by a silence so complete that the screech of the lych-gate opening might have been heard had it been twice the distance.

No one moved.

No one spoke.

Out of the dark at the end of the path a figure was emerging with the strange marking-time approach of someone on a film screen. It was a woman, slight of form and light of step, for she came forward with scarcely a sound, her loose white dress floating softly about her.

Swithenbank, a few yards ahead of the rest, was first to speak.

'Who's there?' he called uncertainly. 'Who is that?'

'Hello, John,' returned a soft, distant voice. 'Arthur, is that you?'

Pascoe felt himself shouldered violently aside.

'More play-acting!' bellowed Lightfoot.

The gun came up, the barrel locked and the cartridge exploded all in an instant.

The woman's form swayed and fell without a sound, making such a small heap on the ground that Pascoe would scarcely have been surprised to find nothing there but a white muslin dress.

But the world of physical reality was not to be denied by churchyards and tombs and arches of cypress.

It was a woman who lay there. Swithenbank knelt at her head, horror and amazement on his face. Lightfoot took one fleeting look but needed no more. Pascoe paused for a second to check the pulse, then plunged into the darkness after him, but stopped when he heard the second shot. Some things there was no need to rush towards.

> *Ah! what demon has tempted me here?*
> *Well I know, now, this dim lake of*
> *   Auber—*
> *This misty mid-region of Weir—*
> *Well I know, now, this dank tarn of*
> *   Auber,*
> *This ghoul-haunted woodland of Weir.*

X

> *Thank Heaven! the crisis—*
> *The danger is past.*

'IT WAS LIKE THE last act of *Hamlet Meets Dracula*,' said Pascoe.

Some things were far too serious for anything but flippancy.

'And they're both dead?' repeated Inspector Dove at the other end of the line.

'He died instantly. Well, he would, his head was mostly missing.'

Pascoe remembered his promise that he would see that Lightfoot got what was coming to him.

'He doesn't sound much of a miss,' said Dove cynically.

'He was a blackmailer twice over,' agreed Pascoe. 'Though now he's dead, Davenport won't need to talk and Kingsley's backtracking like mad. There'll be more tight mouths around Wearton than at a lemon-suckers' convention. Not that it matters. My guess is that Stella Rawlinson played the ghost. She hated the Lightfoots, and Kingsley may or may not have been screwing her into the bargain.'

'Into what?'

'Oh, for God's sake!'

Pascoe found that he was sick of the jokes and the lightness. It was eight-thirty in the morning. He had got home at three but been unable to sleep. Dalziel had observed his arrival at the station with nothing more expressive than an upward roll of his eyes, then suggested that even southern pansies should be awake by this time and he might as well put Dove in the picture.

'I'm sorry,' said Dove.

'So am I,' said Pascoe. 'I'm a bit knackered. It's all turned out so badly. This Lightfoot, he seems to have been a nasty bit of work all round. But he loved his sister. God, even that sounds like the cue for a crack!—and it shouldn't have come to this. Not for anyone. He was the only one she asked for in the ambulance. Arthur, Arthur, all the time.'

'And she said nothing else before she died?'

'Not a thing. The only people she'd spoken to were Swithenbank's mother and Kingsley's housekeeper. She must have gone straight to Arthur's cottage when she arrived. We found her stuff there. Arthur was out, of course. She rang Swithenbank. His mother answered. She was flabbergasted naturally, told her about the party, asked where she'd been but got no answer. Kate went up to Wear End, learned from the housekeeper that everyone had taken off towards the church, so she set off after them along the old drive.'

'Where the hell had she been?' asked Dove in exasperation. 'You say you found some things of hers at Lightfoot's. Any clue there?'

'Nothing obvious,' said Pascoe wearily. 'At first glance it looks about the same as that list of things she took when she left Swithenbank last year. But it doesn't matter much now, does it?'

'I suppose not. Well, we were dead wrong about Swithenbank. Thank God I stopped this side of pulling his floorboards up! Still, you can't win 'em all.'

'No,' said Pascoe.

'Cheer up, Pete, for God's sake! You sound like it's all down to you. It was just an "assist", remember? You can't legislate for maniacs!'

'I know. I just feel that if I'd handled things differently . . .'

Dalziel had come into the room with a sheet of paper in his hand and when he heard Pascoe's remark, the eyes rolled again. It was like a lesson with the globes in an eighteenth-century schoolroom.

'Pete, it wasn't your job to find out where she'd gone. That was our job, it's down to us. Like I say, OK, we missed out. I feel bad about it, but not too bad. I mean, Christ, she came back and we still don't know where the hell she's been! It's our fault. How could you be expected to work it out if we couldn't? Can't!'

'Too bloody true!' bellowed Dalziel, who had come close enough to eavesdrop on Dove's resonant voice.

'What's that, Pete? Someone there with you?'

'Mr Dalziel's just come in,' said Pascoe hastily. 'I'll keep in touch.'

'You do that, old son. I'm avid for the next instalment. I used to think it was just a joke about you lot north of Watford having bat-ears and little bushy tails, but now I'm not so sure. Love to Andy-Pandy! Cheerio now!'

Pascoe put down the phone.

'I don't know what he's got to be cheerful about,' said Dalziel malevolently. 'Or what you've got to be miserable about either.'

'Two people dead,' said Pascoe. 'That's what.'

'And that's your fault?'

'Not court-of-law my fault. Not even court-of-enquiry my fault,' said Pascoe. 'It's just that, I don't know, I suppose . . . I was enjoying it! Secretly, deep inside, I was enjoying it. Big house, interviews in the library, chasing up to the churchyard, stopping the vicar from jumping, uncovering all kinds of guilty secrets—you know I was thinking, gleefully almost, wait till I get back and tell them about this! They'll never believe it!'

'I believe it,' said Dalziel. 'And I'd have done much the same in your shoes. You did it right. The only thing you couldn't know was that she was alive. That's what you call a paradox, you philosophers with degrees and O levels, isn't it? If you'd known she was alive, she'd be alive! But you didn't. You couldn't!'

'Someone should have done,' said Pascoe. 'They should have looked harder.'

'Too true,' said Dalziel with grim satisfaction.

'Cases like these, you follow up every line. One line they didn't follow.'

'What?'

Dalziel scratched his backside on the corner of the desk, a frequent preliminary to one of his deductive *tours de force*, which one of his more scurrilous colleagues had categorized as the anal-lytical approach.

'What was Swithenbank doing on the day his missus disappeared?'

'The Friday, you mean?'

'Aye.'

Pascoe opened his notebook at the page on which he'd first started jotting down notes on the Swithenbank case.

'He was at a farewell party at lunch-time.'

'Who for?'

'One of his assistants.'

'Name?'

'I've no idea,' said Pascoe.

'Cunliffe. David Cunliffe,' said Dalziel triumphantly. 'Thought you'd have known that.'

'It wasn't in any of the papers Enfield sent me,' said Pascoe defensively.

'Bloody right it wasn't,' said Dalziel with relish. 'They've a lot to answer for. This fellow was heading for the good life, back to Mother Earth, do-it-yourself, all that crap, right?'

'Yes. Up in the Orkneys, I think.'

'That's right,' said Dalziel. 'One of the little islands. Him, a few natives, a lot of sheep; and his wife.'

'His wife?'

'Oh yes. Only, suppose she wasn't his wife! They don't take kindly to living in sin up there, so it'd be better for community relations to *call* her his wife. But suppose that on that Friday your Kate packed her few things, put on her new blonde wig and set off for the Orkneys!'

Pascoe shook his head to fight back the waves of fatigue, and something else, too.

'Why the wig?' he asked.

'She was meeting her boy-friend at King's Cross, on the train. She had the wit to guess there might be mutual acquaintance there to see him off and she didn't want to be spotted. As it happened, the whole bloody party came along, including hubby, so she was very wise. Imagine, there's Swithenbank shooting all that shit about how he wished he had the guts to up and leave everything, meaning his missus, for a better life, and there she is sitting only a few carriages away, doing just that!'

'Oh Christ,' said Pascoe. 'Is this just hypothesis, or have you checked it out?'

'What do you think I am, bloody Sherlock Holmes?' exploded Dalziel. 'No, there's no way any of us could have worked out any of that. It was up to Dove and his mates, as I'll make bloody clear! What we've got is this. Arrived this morning.'

He handed Pascoe the sheet of paper he had been carrying.

It was a request for assistance from Orkney Police HQ in Kirkwall. They were holding one David Cunliffe on suspicion of murdering his 'wife', whom he now claimed was not his wife but Katherine Swithenbank, formerly of Wearton in the county of Yorkshire, where, he suggested, it was most likely she would return after leaving him.

It was clear the Orkney constabulary had no great faith in his claim. No one had seen her leave the small island on which their croft was situated. No one had spotted her on the ferry from Stromness or on a plane from Kirkwall Airport. Pascoe got a distinct impression that the croft which Cunliffe had so lovingly repaired was now being taken down again, stone by stone, and the land which he had tilled was now being dug over again, spadeful after hard-turned spadeful.

'She was a right little expert at the disappearing trick,' said Dalziel admiringly. 'When she gets fed up she just packs her bag and goes. And no one ever notices!'

'Someone noticed this time,' said Pascoe.

'Belt up! Think on—there's going to be some red faces this morning! Which do you want to do—Enfield or Orkney? Best you do Orkney; Dove'll try to shrug it off, well, the bugger won't shrug *me* off in a hurry!'

He sounded really delighted, as though the whole of the Wearton business had been arranged just so that he could crow over the inefficiency of the effete south.

But before he left the room, he made one more effort to cheer up his dull and defeated-looking inspector, who was sitting with his head bowed over his open notebook.

'I'll say it one last time, Peter,' he said. 'It wasn't your fault. You reckoned she was dead, everyone reckoned she was dead, her brother, her husband, that Enfield lot. You *had* to go ahead as you did. You'd have needed second sight to know where she was hiding herself. I mean, inspired guesses are one thing, but to work out she was in the Orkneys on the basis of what you knew, you'd have needed a miracle. Right?'

'Right,' said Pascoe.

'Good,' said Dalziel. 'Come twelve, you can buy me a pint for being right. Again.'

He went out.

Pascoe closed his eyes and saw again the white-clad woman floating up the path from the lych-gate.

Why had she come back? What had she hoped for?

He shook his head and opened his eyes.

He would never know and he had no intention of trying an inspired guess. Dalziel was right. A detective should have no truck with feelings and intuitions.

He looked at his notebook, which still lay open at the first page of his scribblings on the Swithenbank case, made as he talked to Dove on the telephone two days before.

On the left-hand page there were two words only. One was HAIRDRESSER?

The other lightly scored through was ORKNEY?

He took his pen now and scratched at the word till it was totally obliterated.

Then he closed the book.

DALZIEL'S GHOST

'WELL, THIS IS VERY COSY,' said Detective-Superintendent Dalziel, scratching his buttocks sensuously before the huge log fire.

'It is for some,' said Pascoe, shivering still from the frosty November night.

But Dalziel was right, he thought as he looked round the room. It *was* cosy, probably as cosy as it had been in the three hundred years since it was built. It was doubtful if any previous owner, even the most recent, would have recognized the old living-room of Stanstone Rigg farmhouse. Eliot had done a good job, stripping the beams, opening up the mean little fireplace and replacing the splintered uneven floorboards with smooth dark oak; and Giselle had broken the plain white walls with richly coloured, voluminous curtaining and substituted everywhere the ornaments of art for the detritus of utility.

Outside, though, when night fell, and darkness dissolved the telephone poles, and the mist lay too thick to be pierced by the rare headlight on the distant road, then the former owners peering from their little cube of warmth and light would not have felt much difference.

Not the kind of thoughts a ghost-hunter should have! he told himself reprovingly. Cool calm scepticism was the right state of mind.

And his heart jumped violently as behind him the telephone rang.

Dalziel, now pouring himself a large scotch from the goodly array of bottles on the huge sideboard, made no move towards the phone though he was the nearer. Detective-superintendents save their strength for important things and leave their underlings to deal with trivia.

'Hello,' said Pascoe.

'Peter, you're there!'

'Ellie love,' he answered. 'Sometimes the sharpness of your mind makes me feel unworthy to be married to you.'

'What are you doing?'

'We've just arrived. I'm talking to you. The super's having a drink.'

'Oh God! You did warn the Eliots, didn't you?'

'Not really, dear. I felt the detailed case-history you doubtless gave to Giselle needed no embellishment.'

'I'm not sure this is such a good idea.'

'Me neither. On the contrary. In fact, you may recall that on several occasions in the past three days I've said as much to you, whose not such a good idea it was in the first place.'

'All you're worried about is your dignity!' said Ellie. 'I'm worried about that lovely house. What's he doing now?'

Pascoe looked across the room to where Dalziel had bent his massive bulk so that his balding close-cropped head was on a level with a small figurine of a shepherd chastely dallying with a milkmaid. His broad right hand was on the point of picking it up.

'He's not touching anything,' said Pascoe hastily. 'Was there any other reason you phoned?'

'Other than what?'

'Concern for the Eliots' booze and knick-knacks.'

'Oh, Peter, don't be so half-witted. It seemed a laugh at The Old Mill, but now I don't like you being there with him, and I don't like me being here by myself. Come home and we'll screw till someone cries *Hold! Enough!*'

'You interest me strangely,' said Pascoe. 'What about *him* and the Eliots' house?'

'Oh, sod him and sod the Eliots! Decent people don't have ghosts!' exclaimed Ellie.

'Or if they do, they call in priests, not policemen,' said Pascoe. 'I quite agree. I said as much, remember . . . ?'

'All right, all right. You please yourself, buster. I'm off to bed now with a hot-water bottle and a glass of milk. Clearly I must be in my dotage. Shall I ring you later?'

'Best not,' said Pascoe. 'I don't want to step out of my pentacle after midnight. See you in the morning.'

'Must have taken an electric drill to get through a skirt like that,' said Dalziel, replacing the figurine with a bang. 'No wonder the buggers got stuck into the sheep. Your missus checking up, was she?'

'She just wanted to see how we were getting on,' said Pascoe.

'Probably thinks we've got a couple of milkmaids with us,' said Dalziel, peering out into the night. 'Some hope! I can't even see any sheep. It's like the grave out there.'

He was right, thought Pascoe. When Stanstone Rigg had been a working farm, there must have always been the comforting sense of animal presence, even at night. Horses in the stable, cows in the byre, chickens in the hutch, dogs before the fire. But the Eliots hadn't bought the place because of any deep-rooted love of nature. In fact Giselle Eliot disliked animals so much she wouldn't even have a guard dog, preferring to rely on expensive electronics. Pascoe couldn't understand how George had got her even to consider living out here. It was nearly an hour's run from town in good conditions and Giselle was in no way cut out for country life, either physically or mentally. Slim, vivacious, sexy, she was a star-rocket in Yorkshire's sluggish jet-set. How she and Ellie had become friends, Pascoe couldn't work out either.

But she must have a gift for leaping unbridgeable gaps for George was a pretty unlikely partner, too.

It was George who was responsible for Stanstone Rigg. By profession an accountant, and very much looking the part with his thin face, unblinking gaze, and a mouth that seemed constructed for the passage of bad news, his unlikely hobby was the renovation of old houses. In the past six years he had done two, first a Victorian terrace house in town, then an Edwardian villa in the suburbs. Both had quadrupled (at least) in value, but George claimed this was not the point and Pascoe believed him. Stanstone Rigg Farm was his most ambitious project to date, and it had been a marvellous success, except for its isolation, which was unchangeable.

And its ghost. Which perhaps wasn't.

It was just three days since Pascoe had first heard of it. Dalziel, who repaid hospitality in the proportion of three of Ellie's home-cooked dinners to one meal out had been entertaining the Pascoes at The Old Mill, a newly opened restaurant in town.

'Jesus!' said the fat man when they examined the menu. 'I wish they'd put them prices in French, too. They must give you Brigitte Bardot for afters!'

'Would you like to take us somewhere else?' enquired Ellie sweetly. 'A fish and chip shop, perhaps. Or a Chinese takeaway?'

'No, no,' said Dalziel. 'This is grand. Any road, I'll chalk what I can up to expenses. Keeping an eye on Fletcher.'

'Who?'

'The owner,' said Pascoe. 'I didn't know he was on our list, sir.'

'Well, he is and he isn't,' said Dalziel. 'I got a funny telephone call a couple of weeks back. Suggested I might take a look at him, that's all. He's got his finger in plenty of pies.'

'If I have the salmon to start with,' said Ellie, 'it won't be removed as material evidence before I'm finished, will it?'

Pascoe aimed a kick at her under the table but she had been expecting it and drawn her legs aside.

Four courses later they had all eaten and drunk enough for a kind of mellow truce to have been established between Ellie and the Fat Man.

'Look who's over there,' said Ellie suddenly.

Pascoe looked. It was the Eliots, George

dark-suited and still, Giselle ablaze in clinging orange silk. Another man, middle-aged but still athletically elegant in a military sort of way, was standing by their table. Giselle returned Ellie's wave and spoke to the man, who came across the room and addressed Pascoe.

'Mr and Mrs Eliot wonder if you would care to join them for liqueurs,' he said.

Pascoe looked at Dalziel enquiringly.

'I'm in favour of owt that means some other bugger putting his hand in his pocket,' he said cheerfully.

Giselle greeted them with delight and even George raised a welcoming smile.

'Who was that dishy thing you sent after us?' asked Ellie after Dalziel had been introduced.

'Dishy? Oh, you mean Giles. He *will* be pleased. Giles Fletcher. He owns this place.'

'Oh my! We send the owner on errands, do we?' said Ellie. 'It's great to see you, Giselle. It's been ages. When am I getting the estate agent's tour of the new house? You've promised us first refusal when George finds a new ruin, remember?'

'I couldn't afford the ruin,' objected Pascoe. 'Not even with George doing our income tax.'

'Does a bit of the old tax fiddling, your firm?' enquired Dalziel genially.

'I do a bit of work privately for friends,' said Eliot coldly. 'But in my own time and at home.'

'You'll need to work bloody hard to make a copper rich,' said Dalziel.

'Just keep taking the bribes, dear,' said Ellie sweetly. 'Now when can we move into Stanstone Farm, Giselle?'

Giselle glanced at her husband, whose expression remained a blank.

'Any time you like, darling,' she said. 'To tell you the truth, it can't be soon enough. In fact, we're back in town.'

'Good God!' said Ellie. 'You haven't found another place already, George? That's pretty rapid even for you.'

A waiter appeared with a tray on which were glasses and a selection of liqueur bottles.

'Compliments of Mr Fletcher,' he said.

Dalziel examined the tray with distaste and beckoned the waiter close. For an incredulous moment Pascoe thought he was going to refuse the drinks on the grounds that police officers must be seen to be above all favour.

'From Mr Fletcher, eh?' said Dalziel. 'Well, listen, lad, he wouldn't be best pleased if he knew you'd forgotten the single malt whisky, would he? Run along and fetch it. I'll look after pouring this lot.'

Giselle looked at Dalziel with the round-eyed delight of a child seeing a walrus for the first time.

'Cointreau for me please, Mr Daziel,' she said.

He filled a glass to the brim and passed it to her with a hand steady as a rock.

'Sup up, love,' he said, looking with open admiration down her cleavage. 'Lots more where that comes from.'

Pascoe, sensing that Ellie might be about to ram a pepper-mill up her host's nostrils, said hastily, 'Nothing wrong with the building, I hope, George? Not the beetle or anything like that?'

'I sorted all that out before we moved,' said Eliot. 'No, nothing wrong at all.'

His tone was neutral but Giselle responded as though to an attack.

'It's all right, darling,' she said. 'Everyone's

guessed it's me. But it's not really. It's just that I think we've got a ghost.'

According to Giselle, there were strange scratchings, shadows moving where there should be none, and sometimes as she walked from one room to another 'a sense of emptiness as though for a moment you'd stepped into the space between two stars'.

This poetic turn of phrase silenced everyone except Dalziel, who interrupted his attempts to scratch the sole of his foot with a bent coffee spoon and let out a raucous laugh.

'What's that mean?' demanded Ellie.

'Nowt,' said Dalziel. 'I shouldn't worry, Mrs Eliot. It's likely some randy yokel roaming about trying to get a peep at you. And who's to blame him?'

He underlined his compliment with a leer straight out of the old melodrama. Giselle patted his knee in acknowledgement.

'What do *you* think, George?' asked Ellie.

George admitted the scratchings but denied personal experience of the rest.

'See how long he stays there by himself,' challenged Giselle.

'I didn't buy it to stay there by myself,' said Eliot. 'But I've spent the last couple of nights alone without damage.'

'And you saw or heard nothing?' said Ellie.

'There may have been some scratching. A rat perhaps. It's an old house. But it's only a house. I have to go down to London for a few days tomorrow. When I get back we'll start looking for somewhere else. Sooner or later I'd get the urge anyway.'

'But it's such a shame! After all your work, you deserve to relax for a while,' said Ellie. 'Isn't there anything you can do?'

'Exorcism,' said Pascoe. 'Bell, book and candle.'

'In my experience,' said Dalziel, who had been con-suming the malt whisky at a rate which had caused the waiter to summon his workmates to view the spectacle, 'there's three main causes of ghosts.'

He paused for effect and more alcohol.

'Can't you arrest him, or something?' Ellie hissed at Pascoe.

'One: bad cooking,' the Fat Man continued. 'Two: bad ventilation. Three: bad conscience.'

'George installed air-conditioning himself,' said Pascoe.

'And Giselle's a super cook,' said Ellie.

'Well then,' said Dalziel. 'I'm sure your conscience is as quiet as mine, love. So that leaves your randy yokel. Tell you what. Bugger your priests. What you need is a professional eye checking on things.'

'You mean a psychic investigator?' said Giselle.

'Like hell!' laughed Ellie. 'He means get the village bobby to stroll around the place with his truncheon at the ready.'

'A policeman? But I don't really see what he could do,' said Giselle, leaning towards Dalziel and looking earnestly into his lowered eyes.

'No, hold on a minute,' cried Ellie with bright mal-ice. 'The Superintendent could be right. A formal in-vestigation. But the village flatfoot's no use. You've got the best police brains in the county rubbing your thighs, Giselle. Why not send for them?'

Which was how it started. Dalziel, to Pascoe's amazement, had greeted the suggestion with ponder-ous enthusiasm. Giselle had reacted with a mixture of high spirits and high seriousness, apparently regard-ing the project as both an opportunity for vindication and a lark. George had sat like Switzerland, neutral and dull. Ellie had been smilingly baffled to see her bluff so swiftly called. And Pascoe had kicked her ankle savagely when he heard plans being made for himself and Dalziel to spend the following Friday night waiting for ghosts at Stanstone Farm.

As he told her the next day, had he realized that Dalziel's enthusiasm was going to survive the sober light of morning, he'd have followed up his kick with a karate chop.

Ellie had tried to appear unrepentant.

'You know why it's called Stanstone, do you?' she asked. 'Standing stone. Get it? There must have been a stone circle there at some time. Primitive worship, human sacrifice, that sort of thing. Probably the original stones were used in the building of the house. That'd explain a lot, wouldn't it?'

'No,' said Pascoe coldly. 'That would explain very little. It would certainly not explain why I am about to lose a night's sleep, nor why you who usually threaten me with divorce or assault whenever my rest is disturbed to fight *real* crime should have arranged it.'

But arranged it had been and it was small comfort for Pascoe now to know that Ellie was missing him.

Dalziel seemed determined to enjoy himself, however.

'Let's get our bearings, shall we?' he said. Replenishing his glass, he set out on a tour of the house.

'Well wired up,' he said as his expert eye spotted the discreet evidence of the sophisticated alarm system. 'Must have cost a fortune.'

'It did. I put him in touch with our crime prevention squad and evidently he wanted nothing but the best,' said Pascoe.

'What's he got that's so precious?' wondered Dalziel.

'All this stuff's pretty valuable, I guess,' said Pascoe, making a gesture which took in the pictures and ornaments of the master bedroom in which they were standing. 'But it's really for Giselle's sake. This was her first time out in the sticks and it's a pretty lonely place. Not that it's done much good.'

'Aye,' said Dalziel, opening a drawer and pulling out a fine silk underslip. 'A good-looking woman could get nervous in a place like this.'

'You reckon that's what this is all about, sir?' said Pascoe. 'A slight case of hysteria?'

'Mebbe,' said Dalziel.

They went into the next room, which Eliot had turned into a study. Only the calculating machine on the desk reminded them of the man's profession. The glass-fronted bookcase contained rows of books relating to his hobby in all its aspects from architectural histories to do-it-yourself tracts on concrete mixing. An old grandmother clock stood in a corner, and hanging on the wall opposite the bookcase was a nearly lifesize painting of a pre-Raphaelite maiden being pensive in a grove. She was naked but her long hair and the dappled shadowings of the trees preserved her modesty.

For a fraction of a second it seemed to Pascoe as if the shadows on her flesh shifted as though a breeze had touched the branches above.

'Asking for it,' declared Dalziel.

'What?'

'Rheumatics or rape,' said Dalziel. 'Let's check the kitchen. My belly's empty as a football.'

Giselle, who had driven out during the day to light the fire and make ready for their arrival, had anticipated Dalziel's gut. On the kitchen table lay a pile of sandwiches covered by a sheet of kitchen paper on which she had scribbled an invitation for them to help themselves to whatever they fancied.

Underneath she had written in capitals BE CARE-FUL and underlined it twice.

'Nice thought,' said Dalziel, grabbing a couple of the sandwiches. 'Bring the plate through to the living-room and we'll eat in comfort.'

Back in front of the fire with his glass filled once again, Dalziel relaxed in a deep armchair. Pascoe poured himself a drink and looked out of the window again.

'For God's sake, lad, sit down!' commanded Dalziel. 'You're worse than a bloody spook, creeping around like that.'

'Sorry,' said Pascoe.

'Sup your drink and eat a sandwich. It'll soon be midnight. That's zero hour, isn't it? Right, get your strength up. Keep your nerves down.'

'I'm not nervous!' protested Pascoe.

'No? Don't believe in ghosts, then?'

'Hardly at all,' said Pascoe.

'Quite right. Detective-inspectors with university degrees shouldn't believe in ghosts. But tired old superintendents with less schooling than a pit pony, there's a different matter.'

'Come off it!' said Pascoe. 'You're the biggest unbeliever I know!'

'That may be, that may be,' said Dalziel, sinking lower into his chair. 'But sometimes, lad, sometimes . . .'

His voice sank away. The room was lit only by a dark-shaded table lamp and the glow from the fire threw deep shadows across the large contours of Dalziel's face. It might have been some eighteenth-century Yorkshire farmer sitting there, thought

Pascoe. Shrewd; brutish; in his day a solid ram of a man, but now rotting to ruin through his own excesses and too much rough weather.

In the fireplace a log fell. Pascoe started. The red glow ran up Dalziel's face like a flush of passion up an Easter Island statue.

'I knew a ghost saved a marriage once,' he said ruminatively. 'In a manner of speaking.'

Oh Jesus! thought Pascoe. It's ghost stories round the fire now, is it?

He remained obstinately silent.

'My first case, I suppose you'd call it. Start of a meteoric career.'

'Meteors fall. And burn out,' said Pascoe. 'Sir.'

'You're a sharp bugger, Peter,' said Dalziel admiringly. 'Always the quick answer. I bet you were just the same when you were eighteen. Still at school, eh? Not like me. I was a right Constable Plod I tell you. Untried. Untutored. Hardly knew one end of my truncheon from t'other. When I heard that shriek I just froze.'

'Which shriek?' asked Pascoe resignedly.

On cue there came a piercing wail from the dark outside, quickly cut off. He half rose, caught Dalziel's amused eye, and subsided, reaching for the whisky decanter.

'Easy on that stuff,' admonished Dalziel with all the righteousness of a temperance preacher. 'Enjoy your supper, like yon owl. Where was I? Oh aye. I was on night patrol. None of your Panda-cars in those days. You did it all on foot. And I was standing just inside this little alleyway. It was a dark narrow passage running between Shufflebotham's woolmill on the one side and a little terrace of back-to-backs on the other. It's all gone now, all gone. There's a car park there now. A bloody car park!

'Any road, the thing about this alley was, it were a dead end. There was a kind of buttress sticking out of the mill wall, might have been the chimneystack, I'm not sure, but the back-to-backs had been built flush up against it so there was no way through. No way at all.'

He took another long pull at his scotch to help his memory and began to scratch his armpit noisily.

'Listen!' said Pascoe suddenly.

'What?'

'I thought I heard a noise.'

'What kind of noise?'

'Like fingers scrabbling on rough stone,' said Pascoe.

Dalziel removed his hand slowly from his shirt front and regarded Pascoe malevolently.

'It's stopped now,' said Pascoe. 'What were you saying, sir?'

'I was saying about this shriek,' said Dalziel. 'I just froze to the spot. It came floating out of this dark passage. It was as black as the devil's arsehole up there. The mill wall was completely blank and there was just one small window in the gable end of the house. That, if anywhere, was where the shriek came from. Well, I don't know what I'd have done. I might have been standing there yet wondering what to do, only this big hand slapped hard on my shoulder. I nearly shit myself! Then this voice said, 'What's to do, Constable Dalziel?' and when I looked round there was my sergeant, doing his rounds.

'I could hardly speak for a moment, he'd given me such a fright. But I didn't need to explain. For just then came another shriek and voices, a man's and a woman's, shouting at each other. 'You hang on here,' said the sergeant. 'I'll see what this is all about.' Off he went, leaving me still shaking. And as I looked down that gloomy passageway, I began to remember some local stories about this mill. I hadn't paid much heed to them before. Everywhere that's more than fifty years old had a ghost in them parts. They say Yorkshiremen are hardheaded, but I reckon they've got more superstition to the square inch than a tribe of pygmies. Well, this particular tale was about a mill-girl back in the 1870s. The owner's son had put her in the family way which I dare say was common enough. The owner acted decently enough by his lights. He packed his son off to the other end of the country, gave the girl and her family a bit of cash and said she could have her job back when the confinement was over.'

'Almost a social reformer,' said Pascoe, growing interested despite himself.

'Better than a lot of buggers still in business round here,' said Dalziel sourly. 'To cut a long story short, this lass had her kid premature and it soon died. As soon as she was fit enough to get out of bed, she came back to the mill, climbed through a skylight onto the roof and jumped off. Now all that I could believe. Probably happened all the time.'

'Yes,' said Pascoe. 'I've no doubt that a hundred years ago the air round here was full of falling girls. While in America they were fighting a war to stop the plantation owners screwing their slaves!'

'You'll have to watch that indignation, Peter,' said Dalziel. 'It can give you wind. And no one pays much heed to a preacher when you can't hear his sermons for farts. Where was I, now? Oh yes. This lass. Since that day there'd been a lot of stories about people seeing a girl falling from the roof of this old mill. Tumbling over and over in the air right slowly, most of 'em said. Her clothes filling with air, her hair streaming behind her like a comet's tail. Oh aye, lovely descriptions some of them were. Like the ones we get whenever there's an accident. One for every pair of eyes, and all of 'em perfectly detailed and perfectly different.'

'So you didn't reckon much to these tales?' said Pascoe.

'Not by daylight,' said Dalziel. 'But standing there in the mouth of that dark passageway at midnight, that was different.'

Pascoe glanced at his watch.

'It's nearly midnight now,' he said in a sepulchral tone.

Dalziel ignored him.

'I was glad when the sergeant stuck his head through that little window and bellowed my name. Though even that gave me a hell of a scare. "Dalziel!" he said. "Take a look up this alleyway. If you can't see anything, come in here." So I had a look. There wasn't anything, just sheer brick walls on three sides with only this one little window. I didn't hang about but got myself round to the front of the house pretty sharply and went in. There were two people there besides the sergeant. Albert Pocklington, whose house it was, and his missus, Jenny. In those days a good bobby knew everyone on his beat. I said hello, but they didn't do much more than grunt. Mrs Pocklington was about forty. She must have been a bonny lass in her time and she still didn't look too bad. She'd got her blouse off, just draped around her shoulders, and I had a good squint at her big round tits. Well, I was only a lad! I didn't really look at her face till I'd had an eyeful lower down and then I noticed that one side was all splotchy red as though someone had given her a clout. There were no prizes for guessing who. Bert Pocklington was a big solid fellow. He looked like a chimpanzee, only he had a lot less gumption.'

'Hold on,' said Pascoe.

'What is it now?' said Dalziel, annoyed that his story had been interrupted.

'I thought I heard something. No, I mean really heard something this time.'

They listened together. The only sound Pascoe could hear was the noise of his own breathing mixed with the pulsing of his own blood, like the distant sough of a receding tide.

'I'm sorry,' he said. 'I really did think . . .'

'That's all right, lad,' said Dalziel with surprising sympathy, 'I know the feeling. Where'd I got to? Albert Pocklington. My sergeant took me aside and put me in the picture. It seems that Pocklington had got a notion in his mind that someone was banging his missus while he was on the night shift. So he'd slipped away from his work at midnight and come home, ready to do a bit of banging on his own account. He wasn't a man to move quietly, so he'd tried for speed instead, flinging open the front door and rushing up the stairs. When he opened the bedroom door, his wife had been standing by the open window naked to the waist, shrieking. Naturally he thought the worst. Who wouldn't? Her story was that she was getting ready for bed when she had this feeling of the room suddenly becoming very hot and airless and pressing in on her. She'd gone to the window and opened it, and it was like taking a cork out of a bottle, she said. She felt as if she was being sucked out of the window, she said. (With tits like you and a window that small, there wasn't much likelihood of that! I thought.) And at the same time she had seen a shape like a human figure tumbling slowly by the window. Naturally she shrieked. Pocklington came in. She threw herself into his arms. All the welcome she got was a thump on the ear, and that brought on the second bout of shrieking. She was hysterical, trying to tell him what she'd seen, while he just raged around, yelling about what he was going to do to her fancy man.'

He paused for a drink. Pascoe stirred the fire with his foot. Then froze. There it was again! A distant scratching. He had no sense of direction.

The hairs on the back of his neck prickled in the traditional fashion. Clearly Dalziel heard nothing and Pascoe was not yet certain enough to interrupt the fat man again.

'The sergeant was a good copper. He didn't want a man beating up his wife for no reason and he didn't want a hysterical woman starting a ghost scare. They can cause a lot of bother, ghost scares,' added Dalziel, filling his glass once more with the long-suffering expression of a man who is being caused a lot of bother.

'He sorted out Pocklington's suspicions about his wife having a lover first of all. He pushed his shoulders through the window till they got stuck to show how small it was. Then he asked me if anyone could have come out of that passageway without me spotting them. Out of the question, I told him.

'Next he chatted to the wife and got her to admit she'd been feeling a bit under the weather that day, like the 'flu was coming on, and she'd taken a cup of tea heavily spiked with gin as a nightcap. Ten minutes later we left them more or less happy. But as we stood on the pavement outside, the sergeant asked me the question I'd hoped he wouldn't. Why had I stepped into that alley in the first place? I suppose I could have told him I wanted a pee or a smoke, something like that. But he was a hard man to lie to, that sergeant. Not like the wet-nurses we get nowadays. So after a bit of humming and hawing, I told him I'd seen something, just out of the corner of my eye, as I was walking past. "What sort of thing?" he asked. Like something falling, I said. Something fluttering and falling through the air between the mill wall and the house end.

'He gave me a queer look, that sergeant did. "I tell you what, Dalziel," he said. "When you make out your report, I shouldn't say anything of that. No, I should keep quiet about that. Leave ghosts to them that understands them. You stick to crime." And that's advice I've followed ever since, till this very night, that is!'

He yawned and stretched. There was a distant rather cracked chime. It was, Pascoe realized, the clock in Eliot's study striking midnight.

But it wasn't the only sound.

'*There!* Listen,' urged Pascoe, rising slowly to his feet. 'I *can* hear it. A scratching. Do *you* hear it, sir?'

Dalziel cupped one cauliflower ear in his hand.

'By Christ, I think you're right, lad!' he said as if this were the most remote possibility in the world. 'Come on! Let's take a look.'

Pascoe led the way. Once out of the living-room they could hear the noise quite clearly and it took only a moment to locate it in the kitchen.

'Rats?' wondered Pascoe.

Dalziel shook his head.

'Rats gnaw,' he whispered. 'That sounds like something bigger. It's at the back door. It sounds a bit keen to get in.'

Indeed it did, thought Pascoe. There was a desperate insistency about the sound. Sometimes it rose to a crescendo, then tailed away as though from exhaustion, only to renew itself with greater fury.

It was as though someone or something was caught in a trap too fast for hope, too horrible for resignation. Pascoe had renewed his acquaintance with Poe after the strange business at Wear End and now he recalled the story in which the coffin was opened to reveal a contorted skeleton and the lid scarred on the inside by the desperate scraping of fingernails.

'Shall I open it?' he whispered to Dalziel.

'No,' said the fat man. 'Best one of us goes out the front door and comes round behind. I'll open when you shout. OK?'

'OK,' said Pascoe with less enthusiasm than he had ever OK'd even Dalziel before.

Picking up one of the heavy rubber-encased torches they had brought with them, he retreated to the front door and slipped out into the dark night.

The frost had come down fiercely since their arrival and the cold caught at his throat like an invisible predator. He thought of returning for his coat, but decided this would be just an excuse for postponing whatever confrontation awaited him. Instead, making a mental note that when he was a superintendent he, too, would make sure he got the inside jobs, he set off round the house.

When he reached the second corner, he could hear the scratching quite clearly. It cut through the still and freezing air like the sound of a steel blade against a grinding-stone.

Pascoe paused, took a deep breath, let out a yell of

warning and leapt out from the angle of the house with his torch flashing.

The scratching ceased instantly, there was nothing to be seen by the rear door of the house, but a terrible shriek died away across the lawn as though an exorcized spirit was wailing its way to Hades.

At the same time the kitchen door was flung open and Dalziel strode majestically forward; then his foot skidded on the frosty ground and, swearing horribly, he crashed down on his huge behind.

'Are you all right, sir?' asked Pascoe breathlessly.

'There's only one part of my body that feels any sensitivity still,' said Dalziel. 'Give us a hand up.'

He dusted himself down, saying, 'Well, that's ghost number one laid.'

'Sir?'

'Look.'

His stubby finger pointed to a line of paw prints across the powder frost of the lawn.

'Cat,' he said. 'This was a farmhouse, remember? Every farm has its cats. They live in the barn, keep the rats down. Where's the barn?'

'Gone,' said Pascoe. 'George had it pulled down and used some of the stones for an extension to the house.'

'There you are then,' said Dalziel. 'Poor bloody animal wakes up one morning with no roof, no rats. It's all right living rough in the summer, but comes the cold weather and it starts fancying getting inside again. Perhaps the farmer's wife used to give it scraps at the kitchen door.'

'It'll get precious little encouragement from Giselle,' said Pascoe.

'It's better than Count Dracula anyway,' said Dalziel.

Pascoe, who was now very cold indeed, began to move towards the kitchen, but to his surprise Dalziel stopped him.

'It's a hell of a night even for a cat,' he said. 'Just have a look, Peter, see if you can spot the poor beast. In case it's hurt.'

Rather surprised by his boss's manifestation of kindness to animals (though not in the least at his display of cruelty to junior officers), Pascoe shivered along the line of paw prints across the grass. They disappeared into a small orchard, whose trees seemed to crowd together to repel intruders, or perhaps just for warmth. Pascoe peered between the italic trunks and made cat-attracting noises but nothing stirred.

'All right,' he said. 'I know you're in there. We've got the place surrounded. Better come quietly. I'll leave the door open, so just come in and give a yell when you want to give yourself up.'

Back in the kitchen, he left the door ajar and put a bowl of milk on the floor. His teeth were chattering and he headed to the living-room, keen to do full justice to both the log fire and the whisky decanter. The telephone rang as he entered. For once Dalziel picked it up and Pascoe poured himself a stiff drink.

From the half conversation he could hear, he gathered it was the duty sergeant at the station who was ringing. Suddenly, irrationally, he felt very worried in case Dalziel was going to announce he had to go out on a case, leaving Pascoe alone.

The reality turned out almost as bad.

'Go easy on that stuff,' said Dalziel. 'You don't want to be done for driving under the influence.'

'What?'

Dalziel passed him the phone.

The sergeant told him someone had just rung the

station asking urgently for Pascoe and refusing to speak to anyone else. He'd claimed what he had to say was important. 'It's big and it's tonight' were his words. And he'd rung off saying he'd ring back in an hour's time. After that it'd be too late.

'Oh shit,' said Pascoe. 'It sounds like Benny.'

Benny was one of his snouts, erratic and melodramatic, but often bringing really hot information.

'I suppose I'll have to go in,' said Pascoe reluctantly. 'Or I could get the Sarge to pass this number on.'

'If it's urgent, you'll need to be on the spot,' said Dalziel. 'Let me know what's happening, won't you? Best get your skates on.'

'Skates is right,' muttered Pascoe. 'It's like the Arctic out there.'

He downed his whisky defiantly, then went to put his overcoat on.

'You'll be all right by yourself, will you, sir?' he said maliciously. 'Able to cope with ghosts, ghouls, werewolves and falling mill-girls?'

'Never you mind about me, lad,' said Dalziel jovially. 'Any road, if it's visitors from an old stone circle we've got to worry about, dawn's the time, isn't it? When the first rays of the sun touch the victim's breast. And with luck you'll be back by then. Keep me posted.'

Pascoe opened the front door and groaned as the icy air attacked his face once more.

'I am just going outside,' he said. 'And I may be some time.'

To which Dalziel replied, as perhaps Captain Scott and his companions had, 'Shut that bloody door!'

It took several attempts before he could persuade the frozen engine to start and he knew from experience that it would be a good twenty minutes before the heater began to pump even lukewarm air into the car. Swearing softly to himself, he set the vehicle bumping gently over the frozen contours of the long driveway up to the road.

The drive curved round the orchard and the comforting silhouette of the house soon disappeared from his mirror. The frost-laced trees seemed to lean menacingly across his path and he told himself that if any apparition suddenly rose before the car, he'd test its substance by driving straight through it.

But when the headlights reflected a pair of bright eyes directly ahead, he slammed on the brake instantly.

The cat looked as if it had been waiting for him. It was a skinny black creature with a mangled ear and a wary expression. Its response to Pascoe's soothing noises was to turn and plunge into the orchard once more.

'Oh no!' groaned Pascoe. And he yelled after it, 'You stupid bloody animal! I'm not going to chase you through the trees all bloody night. Not if you were a naked naiad, I'm not!'

As though recognizing the authentic tone of a Yorkshire farmer, the cat howled in reply and Pascoe glimpsed its shadowy shape only a few yards ahead. He followed, hurling abuse to which the beast responded with indignant miaows. Finally it disappeared under a bramble bush.

'That does it,' said Pascoe. 'Not a step further.'

Leaning down he flashed his torch beneath the bush to take his farewell of the stupid animal.

Not one pair of eyes but three stared unblinkingly back at him, and a chorus of howls split the frosty air.

The newcomers were young kittens who met him

with delight that made up for their mother's wariness. They were distressingly thin and nearby Pascoe's torch picked out the stiff bodies of another two, rather smaller, who hadn't survived.

'Oh shit,' said Pascoe, more touched than his anti-sentimental attitudes would have permitted him to admit.

When he scooped up the kittens, their mother snarled in protest and tried to sink her teeth into his gloved hand. But he was in no mood for argument and after he'd bellowed, 'Shut up!' she allowed herself to be lifted and settled down comfortably in the crook of his arm with her offspring.

It was quicker to continue through the orchard than to return to the car. As he walked across the lawn towards the kitchen door he smiled to himself at the prospect of leaving Dalziel in charge of this little family. That would really test the Fat Man's love of animals.

The thought of ghosts and hauntings was completely removed from his mind.

And that made the sight of the face at the upstairs window even more terrifying.

For a moment his throat constricted so much that he could hardly breathe. It was a pale face, a woman's he thought, shadowy, insubstantial behind the leaded panes of the old casement. And as he looked the room behind seemed to be touched by a dim unearthly glow through which shadows moved like weed on a slow stream's bed. In his arms the kittens squeaked in protest and he realized that he had involuntarily tightened his grip.

'Sorry,' he said, and the momentary distraction unlocked the paralysing fear and replaced it by an equally instinctive resolve to confront its source.

There's nothing makes a man angrier than the aware-ness of having been made afraid.

He went through the open kitchen door and dropped the cats by the bowl of milk which they as-saulted with silent delight. The wise thing would have been to summon Dalziel from his warmth and whisky, but Pascoe had no mind to be wise. He went up the stairs as swiftly and as quietly as he could.

He had calculated that the window from which the 'phantom' peered belonged to the study and when he saw the door was open he didn't know whether he was pleased or not. Ghosts didn't need doors. On the other hand it meant that *something* was in there. But the glow had gone.

Holding his torch like a truncheon, he stepped in-side. As his free hand groped for the light switch he was aware of something silhouetted against the paler darkness of the window and at the same time of movement elsewhere in the room. His left hand couldn't find the switch, his right thumb couldn't find the button on the torch, it was as if the darkness of the room was liquid, slowing down all movement and washing over his mouth and nose and eyes in wave after stifling wave.

Then a single cone of light grew above Eliot's desk and Dalziel's voice said, 'Why're you waving your arms like that, lad? Semaphore, is it?'

At which moment his fingers found the main light switch.

Dalziel was standing by the desk. Against the win-dow leaned the long painting of the pre-Raphaelite girl, face to the glass. Where it had hung on the wall was a safe, wide open and empty. On the desk under the sharply focused rays of the desk lamp lay what Pascoe took to be its contents.

'What the hell's going on?' demanded Pascoe, half relieved, half bewildered.

'Tell you in a minute,' said Dalziel, resuming his examination of the papers.

'No, sir,' said Pascoe with growing anger. 'You'll tell me now. You'll tell me exactly what you're doing going through private papers without a warrant! And how the hell did you get into that safe?'

'I've got you to thank for that, Peter,' said Dalziel without looking up.

'*What?*'

'It was you who put Eliot in touch with our crime prevention officer, wasn't it? I did an efficiency check the other morning, went through all the files. There it was. Eliot, George. He really wanted the works, didn't he? What's he got out there? I thought. The family jewels? I checked with the firm who did the fitting. I know the manager, as it happens. He's a good lad; bit of a ladies' man, but clever with it.'

'Oh God!' groaned Pascoe. 'You mean you got details of the alarm system and a spare set of keys!'

'No, I didn't!' said Dalziel indignantly. 'I had to work it out for myself mainly.'

He had put on his wire-rimmed National Health spectacles to read the documents from the safe and now he glared owlishly at Pascoe over them.

'Do you understand figures?' he asked. 'It's all bloody Welsh to me.'

Pascoe consciously resisted the conspiratorial invitation.

'I've heard nothing so far to explain why you're breaking the law, sir,' he said coldly. 'What's George Eliot supposed to have done?'

'What? Oh, I see. It's the laws of hospitality and friendship you're worried about! Nothing, nothing.

Set your mind at rest, lad. It's nowt to do with your mate. Only indirectly. Look, this wasn't planned, you know. I mean, how could I plan all that daft ghost business? No, it was just that the Fletcher business was getting nowhere . . .'

'Fletcher?'

'Hey, here's your income tax file. Christ! Is that what your missus gets just for chatting to students? It's more than you!'

Pascoe angrily snatched the file from Dalziel's hands. The fat man put on his sympathetic, sincere look.

'Never fret, lad. I won't spread it around. Where was I? Oh yes, Fletcher. I've got a feeling about that fellow. The tip-off sounded good. Not really my line, though. I got Inspector Marwood on the Fraud Squad interested, though. All he could come up with was that a lot of Fletcher's business interests had a faint smell about them, but that was all. Oh yes, and Fletcher's accountants were the firm your mate Eliot's a partner in.'

'That's hardly a startling revelation,' sneered Pascoe.

'Did you know?'

'No. Why should I?'

'Fair point,' said Dalziel. 'Hello, hello.'

He had found an envelope among the files. It contained a single sheet of paper which he examined with growing interest. Then he carefully refolded it, replaced it in the envelope and began to put all the documents read or unread back into the safe.

'Marwood told me as well, though, that Fletcher and Eliot seemed to be pretty thick at a personal level. And he also said the Fraud Squad would love to go over Fletcher's accounts with a fine-tooth comb.'

'Why doesn't he get himself a warrant then?'

'Useless, unless he knows what he's looking for. My tipster was too vague. Often happens with first-timers. They want it to be quick and they overestimate our abilities.'

'Is that possible?' marvelled Pascoe.

'Oh aye. Just. Are you going to take that file home?'

Reluctantly, Pascoe handed his tax file back to Dalziel, who thrust it in with the others, slammed the safe, then did some complicated fiddling with a bunch of keys.

'There,' he said triumphantly, 'all locked up and the alarm set once more. No harm to anyone. Peter, do me a favour. Put that tart's picture back up on the wall. I nearly did my back getting it down. I'll go and mend the fire and pour us a drink.'

'I am not involved in this!' proclaimed Pascoe. But the Fat Man had gone.

When Pascoe came downstairs after replacing the picture, Dalziel was not to be found in the living-room. Pascoe tracked him to the kitchen, where he found him on his hands and knees, feeding pressed calves-tongue to the kittens.

'So you found 'em,' said Dalziel. 'That's what brought you back. Soft bugger.'

'Yes. And I take it I needn't go out again. There's no snout'll be ringing at one o'clock. That was you while I was freezing outside, wasn't it?'

'I'm afraid so. I thought it best to get you out of the way. Sorry, lad, but I mean, this fellow Eliot is a mate of yours and I didn't want you getting upset.'

'I *am* upset,' said Pascoe. 'Bloody upset.'

'There!' said Dalziel triumphantly. 'I was right,

wasn't I? Let's get that drink. These buggers can look after themselves.'

He dumped the rest of the tongue onto the kitchen floor and rose to his feet with much wheezing.

'There it is then, Peter,' said Dalziel as they returned to the living-room. 'It was all on the spur of the moment. When Mrs Eliot suggested we spend a night here to look for her ghosts, I just went along to be sociable. I mean, you can't be rude to a woman like that, can you? A sudden shock, and that dress might have fallen off her nipples. I'd no more intention of really coming out here than of going teetotal! But next morning I got to thinking. If we could just get a bit of a pointer where to look at Fletcher . . . And I remembered you saying about Eliot doing your accounts at home.'

'Income tax!' snorted Pascoe. 'Does that make me a crook? Or him either?'

'No. It was just a thought, that's all. And after I'd talked to Crime Prevention, well, it seemed worth a peek. So come down off your high horse. No harm done. Your mate's not in trouble, OK? And I saw nowt in his safe to take action on. So relax, enjoy your drink. I poured you brandy, the scotch is getting a bit low. That all right?'

Pascoe didn't answer but sat down in the deep old armchair and sipped his drink reflectively. Spur of the moment, Dalziel had said. Bloody long moment, he thought. And what spur? There was still something here that hadn't been said.

'It won't do,' he said suddenly.

'What's that?'

'There's got to be something else,' insisted Pascoe. 'I mean, I know you, sir. You're not going to do all this *just* on the off-chance of finding something to incriminate Fletcher in George's safe. There *has* to be something else. What did you expect to find, anyway? A signed confession? Come to that, what *did* you find?'

Dalziel looked at him, his eyes moist with sincerity.

'Nowt, lad. Nowt. I've told you. There'll be no action taken as a result of anything I saw tonight. None. There's my reassurance. It was an error of judgement on my part. I admit it. Now does that satisfy you?'

'No, sir, to be quite frank it doesn't. Look, I've got to know. These people are my friends. You say that they're not mixed up in anything criminal, but I still need to know exactly what is going on. Or else I'll start asking for myself.'

He banged his glass down on the arm of his chair so vehemently that the liquor slopped out.

'It'll burn a hole, yon stuff,' said Dalziel, slandering the five-star cognac which Pascoe was drinking.

'I mean it, sir,' said Pascoe quietly. 'You'd better understand that.'

'All right, lad,' said Dalziel. 'I believe you. You might not like it though. *You'd* better understand *that.*'

'I'll chance it,' replied Pascoe.

Dalziel regarded him closely, then relaxed with a sigh.

'Here it is then. The woman Giselle is having a bit on the side with Fletcher.'

Pascoe managed an indifferent shrug.

'It happens,' he said, trying to appear unsurprised. In fact, why was he surprised? Lively, sociable, physical Giselle and staid, self-contained, inward-looking George. It was always on the cards.

'So what?' he added in his best man-of-the-world voice.

'So if by any chance, Eliot did have anything which might point us in the right direction about Fletcher . . .'

Pascoe sat very still for a moment.

'Well, you old bastard!' he said. 'You mean you'd give him good reason to do the pointing! You'd let him know about Giselle . . . Jesus wept! How low can you get?'

'I could have just let him know in any case without checking first to see if it was worthwhile,' suggested Dalziel, unabashed.

'So you could!' said Pascoe in mock astonishment. 'But you held back, waiting for a chance to check it out! Big of you! You get invited to spend the night alone in complete strangers' houses all the time! And now you've looked and found nothing, what are you going to do? Tell him just on the off-chance?'

'I didn't say I'd found *nothing*,' said Dalziel.

Pascoe stared at him.

'But you said there'd be no action!' he said.

'Right,' said Dalziel. 'I mean it. I think we've just got to sit back and wait for Fletcher to fall into our laps. Or be pushed. What I did find was a little anonymous letter telling Eliot what his wife was up to. Your mate *knows*, Peter. From the postmark he's known for a few weeks. He's a careful man, accountants usually are. And I'm sure he'd do a bit of checking first before taking action. It was just a week later that my telephone rang and that awful disguised voice told me to check on Fletcher. Asked for me personally. I dare say you've mentioned my name to Eliot, haven't you, Peter?'

He looked at the carpet modestly.

'Everyone's heard of you, sir,' said Pascoe. 'So what happens now?'

'Like I say. Nothing. We sit and wait for the next call. It should be a bit more detailed this time, I reckon. I mean, Eliot must have realized that his first tip-off isn't getting results and now his wife's moved back into town to be on Fletcher's doorstep again, he's got every incentive.'

Pascoe looked at him in surprise.

'You mean the ghosts . . .'

'Nice imaginative girl, that Giselle! Not only does she invent a haunting to save herself a two hours' drive for her kicks, but she cons a pair of thick bobbies into losing their sleep over it. I bet Fletcher fell about laughing! Well I'm losing no more! It'll take all the hounds of hell to keep me awake.'

He yawned and stretched. In mid-stretch there came a terrible scratching noise and the fat man froze like a woodcut of Lethargy on an allegorical frieze.

Then he laughed and opened the door.

The black cat looked up at him warily but her kittens had no such inhibitions and tumbled in, heading towards the fire with cries of delight.

'I think your mates have got more trouble than they know,' said Dalziel.

Next morning Pascoe rose early and stiffly after a night spent on a sofa before the fire. Dalziel had disappeared upstairs to find himself a bed and Pascoe assumed he would still be stretched out on it. But when he looked out of the living-room window he saw he was wrong.

The sun was just beginning to rise behind the orchard and the Fat Man was standing in front of the house watching the dawn.

A romantic at heart, thought Pascoe sourly.

A glint of light flickered between the trunks of the

orchard trees, flamed into a ray and began to move across the frosty lawn towards the waiting man. He watched its progress, striking sparks off the ice-hard grass. And when it reached his feet he stepped aside.

Pascoe joined him a few minutes later.

'Morning, sir,' he said. 'I've made some coffee. You're up bright and early.'

'Yes,' said Dalziel, scratching his gut vigorously. 'I think I've picked up a flea from those bloody cats.'

'Oh,' said Pascoe. 'I thought you'd come to check on the human sacrifice at dawn. I saw you getting out of the way of the sun's first ray.'

'Bollocks!' said Dalziel, looking towards the house, which the sun was now staining the gentle pink of blood in a basin of water.

'Why bollocks?' wondered Pascoe. 'You've seen one ghost. Why not another?'

'One ghost?'

'Yes. The mill-girl. That story you told me last night. Your first case.'

Dalziel looked at him closely.

'I told you that, did I? I must have been supping well.'

Pascoe, who knew that drink had never made Dalziel forget a thing in his life, nodded vigorously.

'Yes, sir. You told me that. You and your ghost.'

Dalziel shook his head as though at a memory of ancient foolishness and began to laugh.

'Aye, lad. My ghost! It really is my ghost in a way. The ghost of what I am now, any road! That Jenny Pocklington, she were a right grand lass! She had an imagination like your Giselle!'

'I don't follow,' said Pascoe. But he was beginning to.

'Believe it or not, lad,' said Dalziel. 'In them days I

was pretty slim. Slim and supple. Even then I had to be like a ghost to get through that bloody window! But if Bert Pocklington had caught me, I really would have been one! Aye, that's right. When I heard that scream, I was coming out of the alley, not going into it!'

And shaking with laughter the Fat Man headed across the lacy grass towards the old stone farmhouse where the hungry kittens were crying imperiously for their breakfast.

ONE SMALL STEP

FOREWORD

TO THE ORIGINAL EDITION,
PUBLISHED IN 1990

WE'VE BEEN TOGETHER NOW for twenty years. That's a lot of blood under the bridge. Sometimes 1970 seems like last weekend, sometimes it seems like ancient history. Famous men died—Forster who we thought already had, and de Gaulle who we imagined never would; Heath toppled Wilson, Solzhenitsyn won the Nobel Prize for Literature, Tony Jacklin won the US Open, and in September, Collins published *A Clubbable Woman*.

All right, so it wasn't the year's most earth-shaking event, but it meant a lot to me. And it must have meant a little to that hard core of loyal readers who kept on asking for more.

And of course to Andy Dalziel and Peter Pascoe, it meant the difference between life and death!

If time moves so erratically for me, how must it seem to that intermittently synchronous being, the series character? I mused on this the other day as I walked in the fells near my home. I'm not one of those writers who explain the creative process by saying, 'Then the characters take over.' On the page I'm a tyrant, but in my mind I let them run free, and as I walked I imagined I heard the dull thunder of Dalziel's voice, like a beer keg rolling down a cellar ramp.

'It's all right for him, poncing around up here, feeling all poetic about time and stuff. But what about us, eh? Just how old are we supposed to be anyway? I mean, if I were as old as it felt twenty years back when this lot started, how come I'm not getting meals-on-wheels and a free bus pass?'

'You're right,' answered Peter Pascoe's voice, higher, lighter, but just as querulous. 'Look at me. When *A Clubbable Woman* came out, I was a whizzkid sergeant, graduate entrant, potential high-flier. Twenty years on, I've just made chief inspector. That's not what I call whizzing, that's a long way from stratospheric!'

It was time to remind them what they were, figments of my imagination, paper and printers' ink not flesh and blood, and I started to formulate a few elegant phrases about the creative artist's use of a dual chronology.

'You mean,' interrupted Peter Pascoe, 'that we should regard historical time, i.e. your time, and fictive time, i.e. our time, as passenger trains running on parallel lines but at different speeds?'

'I couldn't have put it better myself,' I said. 'A perfect analogy to express the chronic dualism of serial literature.'

'Chronic's the bloody word,' growled Dalziel.

'Oh, do be quiet,' said Pascoe, with more courage

than I ever gave him. 'Look, this is all very well, but analogies must be consistent. Parallel lines cannot converge in time, can they?'

'No, but they can pass through the same station, can't they?' I replied.

'You mean, as in *Under World,* where the references to the recent miners' strike clearly set the book in 1985?'

'Or 1986. I think I avoided that kind of specificity,' I said.

'You think so? Then what about *Bones and Silence* in which I return to work the February after I got injured in *Under World,* making it '87 at the latest, yet that book's full of specific dates, like Trinity Sunday falling on May 29th, which set it quite clearly in 1988?'

'You tell him, lad,' said Dalziel. 'Bugger thinks just because he's moved from Yorkshire into this sodding wilderness, he can get away scot-free with stunting our growth.'

'Think of your readers,' appealed Pascoe. 'Don't you have a duty to offer them some kind of explanation?'

'Bugger his readers!' roared Dalziel. 'What about us? Do you realize, if he dropped down dead now, which wouldn't surprise me, he'd leave you and me stuck where we are now, working forever? Is that fair, I ask you? Is that just?'

Lear-like, I was beginning to feel that handing over control wasn't perhaps such a clever idea, but I knew how to deal with such imaginative insurrection. I headed home and poured myself a long Scotch, and then another. After a while I let out an appreciative burp, followed by a more genteel hiccup.

Now I could ponder in peace the implications of what I had heard.

There's no getting away from it—in twenty years, Dalziel and Pascoe have aged barely ten. But the readers for whom Pascoe expressed such concern don't seem to find it a problem. At least, none of them has mentioned it in their usually very welcome letters.

On the other hand a flattering and familiar coda to these letters on whatever topic is a pleasurable anticipation of further records of this ever-diverse pair. But if we are all ageing at twice their rate, there must come a time when . . .

But suddenly I jumped off this melancholy train of thought. Time can be speeded up as well as slowed down. I write, therefore they are! And what better birthday gift can I give my loyal readers than a quick trip into the future, nothing too conclusive, nothing to do with exit lines and bones and silence, but a reassuring glimpse of Pascoe when time has set a bit of a grizzle on his case, and of Dalziel still far from going gentle into that good night?

So here it is, my birthday gift. 'Bloody funny gift,' I hear Andy Dalziel mutter deep within. 'Have you clocked the price? And look at the length of it! There's more reading round a bag of chips.'

To which Peter Pascoe thoughtfully replies, 'Half-bottles cost more than fifty per cent of the full-bottle price because production costs stay constant. Besides, if this book deletes one tiny item from those endless lists of things unknown and deeds undone which trouble our sleeping and our dying, then it will be priceless.'

Dalziel's reply is unprintable. But, pricey or priceless, unless you've got the brass nerve to be reading this on a bookshop shelf, someone's paid for it. Accept my thanks. Next time, we'll be back to the present. Meanwhile, a very Happy Twentieth Birthday to us all!

Ravenglass
Cumbria

January 1990

ONE SMALL STEP

1

THE FIRST MAN TO land on the moon was Neil Armstrong on July 20th, 1969. As he stepped off the module ladder, he said, 'One small step for a man, one giant leap for mankind.'

The first man to be murdered on the moon was Emile Lemarque on May 14th, 2010. As he fell off the module ladder, he said, '*Oh mer—*'

There were two hundred and twenty-seven million witnesses.

One of these was ex-Detective-Superintendent Andrew Dalziel who was only watching because the battery of his TV remote control had failed. What he really wanted to see was his favourite episode of *Star Trek* on the Nostalgia Channel. By comparison, Michelin-men bouncing dustily over lunar slag heaps made very dull viewing, particularly with the Yanks and Russkis leapfrogging each other to the edge of the

solar system. But the Federated States of Europe had
waited a long time for their share of space glory and
the Euro Channel had been ordered to give blanket
coverage.

In the UK this met with a mixed response, and not
just from those who preferred *Star Trek*. Britain's decision to opt out of the Federal Space Programme had
always been controversial. During the years when it
appeared the Programme's best hope of reaching the
moon was via a ladder of wrecked rockets, the antis
had smiled complacently and counted the money they
were saving. But now the deed was done, the patriotic
tabloids were demanding to know how come these
inferior foreigners were prancing around in the Great-
est Show Off Earth with no UK involvement whatever, unless you counted the use of English as the
expedition's *lingua franca*? Even this was regarded by
some as a slight, reducing the tongue of Shakespeare
and Thatcher to a mere tool, like Esperanto.

But all most True Brits felt when they realized their
choice of channels had been reduced from
ninety-seven to ninety-six was a vague irritation which
Andy Dalziel would probably have shared had he
been able to switch over manually. Unfortunately he
was confined to bed by an attack of gout, and irritation rapidly boiled into rage, especially as his visiting
nurse, who had retired to the kitchen for a recupera-
tive smoke, ignored all his cries for help. It took a
violent splintering explosion to bring her running,
white-faced, into the bedroom.

Dalziel was sinking back into his pillows, flushed
with the effort and the triumph of having hurled his
useless remote control through the telly screen.

'Now look what you've made me do,' he said.

'Don't just stand there. Fetch me another set. I'm missing *Star Trek*.'

It took three days for it to emerge that what the two hundred and twenty-seven million witnesses had seen wasn't just an unhappy accident but murder.

Till then, most of the UK press coverage had been concerned with interpreting the dead man's possibly unfinished last words. The favourite theory was that *Oh mer . . .* was simply *oh mère*, a dying man's appeal to his mother, though the Catholic *Lozenge* stretched this piously to *Oh mère de Dieu*. When it was suggested that a life member of the *Société Athéiste et Humaniste de France* (Lourdes branch) would be unlikely to trouble the Virgin with his dying breath, the *Lozenge* tartly retorted that history was crammed with deathbed conversions. The *Jupiter*, whose aged owner ascribed his continued survival to just such a conversion during his last heart attack, showed its sympathy for this argument by adopting Camden's couplet in its leader headline—BETWIXT THE MODULE AND THE GROUND, MERCY HE ASKED, MERCY HE FOUND. The *Defender*, taking this literally, suggested that if indeed Lemarque had been going to say *Oh merci*, this was less likely to be a plea for divine grace than an expression of ironic gratitude, as in, 'Well, thanks a bunch for bringing me so far, then chopping me off at the knees!' The *Planet* meanwhile had torpedoed the *oh mère* theory to its own satisfaction by the discovery that Lemarque's mother was an Algerian migrant worker who had sold her unwanted child to a baby farm with many evil results, not the least of which was the *Planet*'s headline—WOG DOG FLOGGED FROG SPROG. Ultimately the child had come into the hands of a Lourdes couple who treated him badly and *never took him to the seaside* (the *Planet's* italics), persuading the editor that this poor deprived foreigner had reverted to infancy in the face of annihilation and was once again pleading to be taken *au mer*. Chortling with glee, the *Intransigent* pointed out that *mer* was feminine and congratulated the *Planet* on now being illiterate in two languages. Then it rather surrendered its superior position by speculating that, coming from Lourdes, Lemarque might have fantasized that he was falling into the famous healing pool and started to cry, *Eau merveilleux!*

It took the staid *Autograph* to say what all the French papers had agreed from the start—that Lemarque was merely exclaiming, like any civilized Gaul in a moment of stress, *Oh merde!*

But it was the *Spheroid* who scooped them all by revealing under the banner CASE OF THE EXPIRING FROG! that the Eurofed Department of Justice was treating Lemarque's death as murder.

Even Dalziel's attention was engaged by this news. For weeks the Current Affairs Channel had been stagnant with speculation about the forthcoming Eurofed Summit Conference in Bologna. The key areas of debate were Trade and Defence, and the big question was, had the Federation at last become homogeneous enough to stand on its own two feet as a Superpower or, at the first sign of crisis, would there still be the old clatter of clogs, sabots, espadrilles and sturdy brogues rushing off in all directions?

All this Dalziel found rather less enthralling than nonalcoholic lager. But a murder on the moon had a touch of originality which set his nerve ends tingling, particularly when it emerged that the man most likely to be in charge of the case was the UK Commissioner in the Eurofed Justice Department, none other than his old friend and former colleague, Peter Pascoe.

'I taught that lad everything he knows,' he boasted as he watched Pascoe's televised press conference from Strasbourg.

'Lad?' snorted Miss Montague, his new nurse, who could snatch and press her own considerable weight and whose rippling muscles filled Dalziel with nostalgic lust. 'He looks almost as decrepit as you!'

Dalziel grunted a promise of revenge as extreme, and as impotent, as Lear's, and turned up the sound on his new set.

Pascoe was saying, 'In effect, what was at first thought to be a simple though tragic systems failure resulting in a short circuit in the residual products unit of his TEC, that is Total Environment Costume, sometimes called lunar suit, appears after more detailed examination by American scientists working in the US lunar village, for the use of whose facilities may I take this chance to say we are truly thankful, to have been deliberately induced.'

For a moment all the reporters were united in deep incomprehension. The man from the *Onlooker* raised his eyebrows and the woman from the *Defender* lowered her glasses; some scribbled earnestly as if they understood everything, others yawned ostentatiously as if there were nothing to understand. Dalziel chortled and said, 'The bugger doesn't get any better.' But it took the man from the *Spheroid* to put the necessary probing question—'You wha'?'

Patiently Pascoe resumed. 'Not to put too fine a point on it, and using layman's language, the micro-circuitry of the residual products unit of his TEC had been deliberately cross-linked with both the main and the reserve power systems in such a manner that it needed only the addition of a conductive element, in this case liquescent, to complete the circuit with unfortunate, that is, fatal, consequences.'

Now the reporters were united in a wild surmise. The *Onlooking* eyebrows were lowered, the *Defending* spectacles raised. But once again it was the earnest seeker of enlightenment from the *Spheroid* who so well expressed what everyone was thinking. 'You mean he pissed himself to death?'

Dalziel laughed so much he almost fell out of bed, though the nurse noted with interest that some internal gyroscope kept his brimming glass of Lucozade steady in his hand. Recovering, he downed the drink in a single gulp and, still chuckling, listened once more to his erstwhile underling.

Pascoe was explaining, 'While there would certainly be a severe shock, this was not of itself sufficient to be fatal. But the short circuit was induced in such a way as to drain completely and immediately all power from the TEC, cutting dead all systems, including the respiratory unit. It was the shock that made him fall. But it was the lack of oxygen that killed him, before the dust had started to settle.'

This sobered the gathering a little. But newsmen's heartstrings vibrate less plangently than their deadlines and soon Pascoe was being bombarded with questions about the investigation, which he fielded so blandly and adroitly that finally Dalziel switched off in disgust.

'What's up?' asked Miss Montague. 'I thought you taught him everything he knows.'

'So I did,' said Dalziel. 'But one thing I could never teach the bugger was how to tell reporters to sod off!'

He poured himself another glass of Lucozade. The nurse seized the bottle and raised it to her nostrils.

'I think this has gone off,' she said.

'Tastes all right to me,' said Dalziel. 'Try a nip.'

Miss Montague poured herself a glass, raised it, sipped it delicately.

'You know,' she said thoughtfully, 'you could be right.'

'I usually am,' said Dalziel. 'Cheers!'

At nine that night the telephone rang.

'This is a recording,' said Dalziel. 'If you want to leave a message, stick it in a bottle.'

'You sound very jolly,' said Pascoe.

'Well, I've supped a lot of Lucozade,' said Dalziel, looking at the gently snoring figure of Nurse Montague on the sofa opposite. 'What's up?'

'Just a social call. Did you see me on the box?'

'I've got better things to do than listen to civil bloody servants being civil and servile,' growled Dalziel.

'Oh, you did see it, then. That's what we call diplomatic language out here in the real world,' said Pascoe.

'Oh aye. Up here it's called soft soap and it's very good for enemas.'

Pascoe laughed and said, 'All right, Andy. I never could fool you, could I? Yes, this whole thing has got a great crap potential. To start with, we reckon the Yanks deliberately leaked their suspicion of foul play to bounce us into letting them take full control of the investigation. Now, we're not terribly keen on that idea.'

'Oh aye? Don't they have jurisdiction anyway?'

'Certainly not. Space is international by UN treaty. But they're established up there with all the facilities, so on the surface it's a generous, neighbourly offer, only . . . Look, it's a bit complicated . . .'

'Come on, lad, I'm not quite gaga and I do read the papers still,' snarled Dalziel. 'This is all about the Eurofed Summit, isn't it?'

'Is it?' murmured Pascoe. 'Do expound.'

'All right, clevercuts. There's a lot of Euros reckon all them trade agreements they signed in the nineties have worked out a lot better for the Yanks than anyone else. Plus some of the soldier boys would like to give NATO the elbow and concentrate on a pure Eurofed force, dumping America, and buying nowt but made-in-Europe hardware. As usual it's the French stirring up most trouble. If they can get the Germans to go along, the rest will follow, no problem. So anything that gets the Krauts and the Frogs at each other's goolies just now will be very good news in Washington.

'Conclusion. The Americans have elected the German crew member number one suspect, and you reckon any investigation they mount will make bloody sure that's where the finger points. How's that for a bit of close political analysis?'

'Marvellous,' breathed Pascoe admiringly. 'Who speaks so well should never speak in vain.'

'I don't know about in vain, but I do prefer in plain English. So what have they got on this German, then?'

There was a long pause.

'Come on, lad,' said Dalziel. 'They must have a pretty good case against him, else you'd not be so worried.'

'Yes, they do. But it's not . . . Look, Andy. I'm sorry, but the thing is, security. You're not cleared for this. It's a need-to-know classification and the only people who need to know outside of government are the investigating officers. So I really can't tell you any more. Not unless I appointed you an investigating officer!'

He said this with a light dismissive laugh, but Dalziel had had many years' experience of interpreting Pascoe's light laughs.

'All right, lad,' he said softly. 'What's going off? Spit it out and make it quick, else this phone goes back down so hard it'll need a jemmy to prise it back up.'

'There's no fooling you, is there, Andy?' said Pascoe. 'OK. Straight it is. I've been asked to take charge of the case, not because I'm the best, but because I'm not French, German, Spanish, Italian, Dutch, Danish or Irish. Meaning none of the countries actually involved in the *Europa*'s mission will trust any of the others to give them a fair deal! They've given me a free hand. They've also given me four days to get a result.'

'*Any* result?'

'The truth, Andy,' said Pascoe heavily. 'That's the result I'm looking for.'

'Only asking,' said Dalziel. 'So how come you're wasting time talking to a clapped-out candidate for the boneyard?'

'Andy, I need eyes and I need a nose. All right, I know I could have any of the Yard's top men for the asking. Only, nowadays they get to the top by being on top of the technology and that's no use to me here. Technology's a two-way ticket. If you live by it, you can be fooled by it. Also the Yard's best will still be on the way up. Europe's wide open to an ambitious man nowadays. But ambitious men need to tread carefully, else when their names come up for advancement there can be more vetoes in the air than flies round a dustbin. So what I need is a seat-of-the-pants copper with a bloodhound's nose, who's got nothing to lose or to gain, and who doesn't give a tuppenny toss about any bugger. I fed this data into my computer and it let out a huge burp. So I picked up the phone and I rang you, Andy. What do you say?'

'You cheeky sod!' exclaimed Dalziel. 'I say you must be off your trolley! My nose is so out of practice I can hardly tell Orkney from Islay. As for seat-of-the-pants, I've been stuck in bed with gout for nigh on a fortnight, and I don't want no jokes either.'

'Who's laughing? Andy, what you clearly need is a place where you won't have to worry about putting pressure on your foot, and I can help you there.'

'Hold on,' said Dalziel. 'I didn't quite get that. This must be a bad line. You *are* talking about bringing the *Europa*'s crew back to Earth for investigation, aren't you? Well, *aren't you?*'

'Andy!' said Pascoe reprovingly. 'First thing you taught me was, good investigation starts at the scene of the crime. And anyway, you always expected the moon from me. So how can you turn me down now that I'm finally offering it to you?'

2

Space travel weren't so bad after all, thought Andy Dalziel. It put him in mind of an occasion half a century ago when he'd supped about twenty pints and ended up on his back in a rowing boat drifting slowly down the cut, looking up at a midnight sky, heavy and dark as a nautch-girl's tits, all studded with a thousand stars.

He should have realized how easy it must be when Pascoe told him the Yanks had dumped a minority party senator and his wife to make room for them on their state-of-the-art lunar shuttle which had been ferrying distinguished visitors to the moon for half a decade. But he'd still been protesting even as Pascoe urged him into the soft yielding couch.

'What's going off?' he demanded in alarm. 'This thing's trying to feel me up!'

'It's all right,' assured Pascoe. 'It's just a wrap-around fabric to hold you in place when we achieve weightlessness. Honestly, it'll just be like riding in a limo, without any traffic jams.'

'If it's so bloody easy, why's the Federation making such a big thing about it?'

'It's like going up Mont Blanc,' explained Pascoe patiently. 'You can either book a table at the summit restaurant and take the scenic railway or you can pack your sarnies into your rucksack and climb. That way it's harder, but you get a lot more Brownie points. More important in the long run, it establishes the Federation's right to be there. Space is international now, but there may come a time when the carving up starts, and we don't want to be scavenging for crumbs under the Americans' chair.'

'Bloody hell,' said Dalziel. 'I'll leave the politicking to you, lad. I'll stick to nicking villains. If I survive the trip, that is.'

In fact, he was feeling better than he'd done for some time. The doctor had confirmed that his heart was in good order for a man of his age. He'd been more concerned about the high blood pressure related to Dalziel's gout, but the drugs Dalziel was taking seemed to have this under control, and reluctantly he'd given the go-ahead. Now as the shuttle came swooping in over the moon's surface, the Fat Man was delighted to find that his gout symptoms had almost completely vanished.

'You were right, lad,' he admitted. 'There's nowt to this astronaut business.'

'Not this way,' agreed Pascoe. 'Mind you, *Europa's* not so luxurious.'

'Can't be, if they're still crapping in their breeks,' said Dalziel.

'Andy, I thought I'd explained,' said Pascoe long-sufferingly. 'They only need their TECs for moving around the moon's surface. In the mother ship they just wear light tunics. The TECs were kept in the hold. Each crew member has his or her own locker and each suit is individually tailored and has a name tag stuck to it, so it's quite clear that whoever tampered with Lemarque's was aiming at him and no one else. Now, have you got it?'

'All right, I'm with you,' said Dalziel. 'No need to go on about things. Christ, have you looked down there? It's like the M1 on a Bank Holiday. All dug up and no bugger working. Where's this village at?'

'Let's see. Yes, there it is, down there, in the Sea of Tranquillity.'

'Those pimples? Looks like an outbreak of chicken pox.'

Dalziel wasn't altogether wrong. The Village, a complex of sealed domes linked by corridors, covering about five acres, did indeed resemble a patch of blisters on the lunar skin till their third braking orbit brought out the scale of the thing. Next time round, one of the domes loomed large before them, threatening collision, and then they were slipping smoothly into a docking bay, and suddenly the stars were out of sight.

The Commander of the Lunar Village was waiting to greet them. He was a small balding astrophysicist with a nervous manner who reminded Dalziel of a snout who'd been foolish enough to feed him duff information twenty years earlier. With good behaviour the man should be getting out shortly.

The Commander passed them over with speed and unconcealable relief to his Head of Security, Colonel Ed Druson, who was a lean and wiry black man with the stretched look of an athlete who has carried his twenties training schedules into his forties.

'Welcome to the moon,' he said, offering his hand. 'Hope you had a good trip.'

'Aye, it were grand,' said Dalziel, bouncing gently up and down to test the effect of low gravity on his gouty foot. Delighted to feel no pain, he went on, 'Only thing is, that space ship of thine didn't seem to have a bar, and it's thirsty work travelling.'

'Andy,' said Pascoe warningly. 'Should you, with your gout?'

'Bugger the gout,' said Dalziel. 'I've got a throat like a spinster's tit. I could even thole bourbon if you've not got the real stuff.'

'I'll see what we can do,' said Druson, clearly wondering what the hell the Brits were up to, filling valuable shuttle space with an overweight, geriatric alcoholic who had gout.

He went on, 'Like we told your people, *Europa*'s in a parking orbit with one of our guys acting nightwatch. We've got the crew in our new accommodation dome. We're expanding our technical staff and they don't start arriving till the weekend.'

'We should be finished well before then,' said Pascoe confidently.

'Yeah? Well, you sure ought to be,' said Druson.

'Looks like an open and shut case. Could have saved yourselves the bother of a trip, I reckon. You've seen our file on the German? Jesus, you Euros surely know how to pick 'em!'

To Dalziel it sounded like a just rebuke. Pascoe had provided him with copies of all the astronauts' files plus the American incident report. This contained statements from the *Europa* crew, setting out where they were and what they were doing at the time of the fatality, plus Druson's own analysis and conclusions. He saw little reason to look further than Kaufmann as culprit, and offered two pieces of concrete evidence and a motive.

The first pointer was an entry in Lemarque's private journal, removed from his locker in a search of doubtful legality. Several of the astronauts kept such journals with an eye to a literary future after their flying days were over. Lemarque's consisted mainly of fluorescently purple prose about the beauties of space with mention of his colleagues kept down to a dismissive minimum. Then at the end of a much polished speech in which he told the world of his sense of honour at being the first Euro, and more importantly, the first Frenchman, to step out on to the moon's surface, he had scribbled almost indecipherably, *Ka s'en fâche. Gardes-toi!*

Ka is getting angry. Watch out!

Was *Ka* Kaufmann? Druson had asked. And the discovery during the same illegal search of a microprobe in the German's locker had deepened his suspicions. A gloss for the non-technical pointed out that a microprobe was a kind of electronic screwdriver which would have been necessary in the readjustment of the TEC circuits.

But there was still the question of motive. And why was Ka getting angry?

'Blackmail,' Druson replied promptly. 'You've read the file. It's obvious.'

It certainly appeared so. The major part of the American report was a digest of a CIA investigation which concluded that Captain Dieter Kaufmann of the Eurofed Air Corps had been acting as an agent for the Arab Union and passing them secret NATO technology for a decade at least.

It was detailed and unanswerable. And it hadn't been compiled overnight.

'It would have been neighbourly to pass this information on a little earlier,' suggested Pascoe mildly. 'Say three years earlier.'

It was three years since Kaufmann had joined the *Europa* crew.

'We like to be sure of our facts in such a serious matter,' said Druson.

Also, thought Pascoe, Kaufmann's full-time transfer into the Eurospace programme had removed him from access to NATO information and left him with nothing to pass on but European astro-technology which in American terms was yesterday's news. With no threat to themselves, the Americans had decided to keep their information under their hat till they could make maximum profit from it.

Now that moment had come.

'Can we look at the body?' said Pascoe. 'Just for the record.'

'Sure. But it ain't very pretty.'

Dalziel had seen a lot worse.

'Not very big, is he?' said Pascoe.

'Depends where you're looking,' said Dalziel.

He turned away from the body and picked up the Frenchman's TEC which was also on display.

'I bet he fancied himself too,' he said. 'These little fellows often do.'

'Why do you say that, Andy?' asked Pascoe.

'His name tag for a start.'

Instead of following a horizontal line, the adhesive name strip had been adjusted to a jaunty thirty degree angle echoing the shoulder seam.

'Used to get buggers in the Force who tried to tart up their uniforms like that,' said Dalziel, sniffing at the headpiece. 'And they usually wore aftershave that'd kill mosquitoes too.'

'Seems he did have a reputation for being a cocky little bastard,' said Druson, looking at Dalziel with a new respect.

Pascoe said, 'And the circuitry was definitely interfered with?'

'Oh yeah. Clear as a fox among chickens. Rush job by the look of it. Well, it would have to be, in the *Europa*'s hold. No time for finesse.'

'No,' agreed Pascoe. 'Seen enough, Andy?'

'More than enough. I'd got to thinking the next dead 'un I saw would be me.'

'Good Lord,' said Pascoe. 'When did you start believing in an afterlife?'

'Man who lets himself be talked into flying to the moon to stare at a dead Frog's got no right to disbelieve *anything*,' said Dalziel. 'Did someone say something about a room with a bed in it?'

'Let's go,' said Druson.

He led them to their quarters, two small bedrooms with a shared living-room. When the door had shut behind him, Dalziel said, 'OK, lad. What do you reckon? Still a fit-up by the Yanks?'

'Open mind,' said Pascoe. 'They've certainly put a reasonable case together. Maybe Kaufmann did do it.'

'Mebbe. I'd trust 'em a lot more if yon black bugger hadn't managed to forget that Glenmorangie he promised me!'

Pascoe grinned and said, 'A good night's sleep will do you more good, Andy. Nothing more to be done till the morning or whatever they call it up here. Then it'll be straight down to the interrogations.'

'Hold on,' said Dalziel. 'Scene of the crime, remember? That's why you said we had to come here, and you were dead right. Only this isn't the scene, is it? The Frog dropped dead somewhere out there. And the actual scene of the real crime is floating around somewhere up there. Shouldn't we fix up to visit the *Europa* before we do owt else?'

'Don't worry,' said Pascoe. 'I'll be arranging a trip as soon as possible. But time's too short to waste, so in the morning let's get on with talking to the crew, shall we? Now I thought we'd work individually. I'll take three and you take three, then we'll swap over like a sort of reverse singles . . .'

'It's not bloody tennis!' said Dalziel obstinately. 'I'll need to ask what these sods got up to on *Europa* and unless I've seen *Europa,* what they say won't make bloody sense, will it?'

There was a tap at the door. Pascoe didn't move. Dalziel scowled at him and went to answer it.

A smiling young man handed him two litre-sized bottles saying, 'There you go, pops.'

'Pops!' said Pascoe as Dalziel closed the door. 'You must be mellowing, Andy. Time was when you'd have nutted anyone who spoke to you like that.'

'That was when I was young and daft,' said Dalziel, removing the seal from one of the bottles. 'At my age, anyone who gives me two litres of Glenmorangie can call me Mavis if he likes. You want a splash?'

'Only water,' said Pascoe. 'I'll have a shower. Then I'll work out a schedule for the interrogations before I go to bed. OK?'

He spoke defiantly. Dalziel stared at him for a moment, then shrugged.

'Fine,' he said. 'You're the boss now.'

'So I am,' smiled Pascoe as he left. 'So I am.'

'And I'm to be Queen of the May, Mother,' murmured Dalziel raising the bottle to his lips. 'I'm to be Queen of the May!'

3

Dalziel had a bad night. He dreamt he challenged Nurse Montague to the best of three falls and lost by a straight submission. It wouldn't have been so bad if the dream had been erotic but it was merely humiliating and he woke up dry and droopy as a camel's tail. Whisky only washed his black thoughts blacker and when finally there came a tap on the door and Pascoe's voice invited him to go to breakfast, he snarled, 'Sod off!' He was still not washed or dressed half an hour later when Pascoe returned with a cup of coffee and a chocolate doughnut, and, even worse, the kind of sympathetic smile usually reserved for tedious old relatives in twilight homes.

Only the younger man's offer to call the Village medics and have someone check him out got Dalziel out of bed. He was still running his portable electric razor over the shadowy planet of his face as they made their way to the *Europa* crew's dome, and this at last provoked an honestly irritated response from Pascoe.

'For heaven's sake, Andy, put that thing away. We *are* representing the Federal Justice Department, after all!'

With his first twinge of pleasure of the day, Dalziel slipped the slim plastic razor case into his breast pocket and followed Pascoe into the dome.

The six survivors of the *Europa* crew were an interesting assortment. It was almost possible to identify them by racial characteristics alone.

The two women were easiest. The Dane, Marte Schierbeck, was pure Viking, long-bodied, long-faced, and grey-eyed, with hair so fair it was almost silver. By contrast the Spaniard, Silvia Rabal, was compact and curvaceous, with huge dark eyes, full pouting lips, and a rather prominent, slightly hooked nose. Her jet black hair was razored back above her ears and sculpted into a rose-tipped crest. The total effect was arrestingly beautiful, like some colourful exotic bird.

Of the men, a rather spidery figure with a face crumpled like an old banknote and eyes blue as the lakes of Killarney had to be the Irishman, Kevin O'Meara, while a Rembrandt burgher, solid of frame and stolid of feature, was typecast as the Dutchman, Adriaan van der Heyde. Only the German and the Italian ran counter to type with the six-foot, blue-eyed blond turning out to be Marco Albertosi, which meant the black-haired, volatile-faced, lean-figured gondolier was Dieter Kaufmann.

Pascoe introduced himself formally, explaining Dalziel simply as his assistant. He made heavy weather of insisting on the serious nature of the affair and the absoluteness of his own authority, and by the time he finished by saying, 'The investigation will be carried on in English since, perhaps regrettably, neither Mr Dalziel nor myself are fluent in any of your languages,' he had succeeded in relaxing the crew into a union of mocking anglophobia, which was precisely what he intended. In his own case the linguistic disclaimer was a downright lie. He was fluent in French, German and Italian, and could get by in the rest. In Dalziel's case . . . well, he'd learned a long time ago that it was dangerous to assume his ignorance about *anything*!

'We will start with individual interviews,' said Pascoe. 'Herr Kaufmann, would you come with me? Mr Dalziel . . .'

Pascoe had already decreed the order of interview, but Dalziel let his eyes slowly traverse the group with the speculative gaze of a sailor in a brothel. Then, with a macho aggression which should have sat ill on a man of his age, but didn't, he stabbed a huge forefinger at Silvia Rabal and said, 'I'll have *her*!'

Space was short for special interview facilities so the interrogations took place in the newcomers' rooms. Rabal sat on the bed without being asked. Dalziel eased himself carefully onto a frail-looking chair and began to open the second bottle of malt.

'Drink?' he said.

'No. Why have you picked me first?' she asked in a rather harsh voice.

'Well, I said to myself, if she's the one who killed the Frog, mebbe she'll try to seduce me to keep me quiet.'

The woman's huge eyes opened even wider as she ran this through her mental translator to make sure she'd got it right. Then she drew back her head and laughed, no avian screech but a full-throated Carmen laugh, sensual, husky, sending tremors down her body like the inviting ripples on a jungle pool.

'Perhaps I will have that drink, Dalziel,' she said.

'Thought you might,' he said, handing her a glass.

She held it close to her breast so he had to lean over her to pour. She looked up at him and breathed, 'Enough.' Her breath was honeyed, or more precisely spiced as if she had been eating cinnamon and coriander. Such perfumes from a restaurant kitchen would have alarmed Dalziel, who liked his food plain dressed, but from the warm oven of this woman's mouth, they were disturbingly appetitive, setting juices running he thought had long since dried to a trickle.

He sat down heavily and the frail chair spread its legs, but held.

'Cheers,' she said, lifting her glass to her lips.

'Cheers,' he answered. It was time to grasp the initiative.

'Look, love,' he said. 'Cards on the table, that's the way I work. That Pascoe, now, he's different, a right sly bugger, you'll need to keep an eye on him. Me, though, I'm not clever enough to be cunning. But God gave me a fair share of good Yorkshire common sense, and that tells me you're about the least likely suspect of the lot, and *that's* the real reason I picked you first. So I can get some answers I can be sure are honest.'

She said, 'Thank you. I am flattered. But how do you work this out?'

'For a start, you weren't on the module, were you? You stayed on *Europa* to look after the shop, you and the Eyetie. So while the module party all had plenty of reason to be mucking about with their TECs in the hold, you didn't.'

'And this is when this interference was done, you think?'

'Has to be, hasn't it?'

'I suppose. This fault in Emile's suit, could it not be just a fault? That American tells us nothing, just makes hints.'

'No. It were deliberate interference, no doubt,' said Dalziel with the technological certainty of a man who used to repair police radios with his truncheon. 'Must've been done in a hurry. I mean, given time, I expect you lot are all clued up enough to have covered your tracks.'

'Oh yes, I think so.' She regarded him thoughtfully. 'So I am in the clear because I stay on the ship? Then Marco who stayed with me must be clear too?'

'That depends if his legs are as pretty as yours,' leered Dalziel. 'But why do you ask? Would it surprise you if Marco was innocent?'

'No. I do not say that.'

'But he didn't get on with Lemarque, is that it?'

'They were not good friends, no. But not so bad that he would kill!'

'How bad does that have to be for an Italian?' wondered Dalziel. 'Why'd they not like each other? Rivals, were they? Or maybe they had a lovers' tiff?'

'I'm sorry?'

'You know. If they had something going between 'em, and they fell out . . .'

He made a limp-wristed rocking gesture.

'What do you say?' she cried indignantly. 'That is not possible!'

'No? Well, there's things in these files as'd amaze you,' he said, patting the pile of folders on the floor next to him. 'Do you not have fairy tales in Spain, then? Kiss a frog and you get yourself a princess, that sort of thing?'

Puzzlement, irritation, and something else besides were chasing each other across that expressive face.

'You are mistaken, I think,' she said, recovering her poise. 'They were rivals, yes. Each wanting to be the most macho, that is all.'

'You reckon? Mebbe they didn't bother you much. I'll be interested to hear what that Danish lass made of them. She's a lot more boyish than you, might have turned them on a bit more . . .'

She looked ready to explode, recovered again and said, 'Yes, if you are interested in low-temperature physics, go to her.'

'No, thanks. Me, I prefer the high-temperature Latin type,' he said lecherously.

She gave him a thin smile and said, 'You talk a lot, Dalziel. Can you, I wonder—what is the phrase?—put your money where your mouth is?'

'Depends where you want me to put my mouth,' said Dalziel negligently. 'Thanks for the offer, but. Mebbe later when I've a minute to spare, eh?' Or a week, he thought ruefully. Though there had been a time . . . At least his diversionary tactics had worked.

'Offer? What offer? You do not think . . .' Suddenly she broke into indignant Spanish.

Dalziel yawned and said, 'Stick to English, luv. If a man's worth swearing at, he's worth swearing at in his own language. Now, I've read all the statements but I'm not much good at technical stuff, so mebbe you can give us a hand. First, these TECs, once they were activated in the module, you could monitor their circuits on *Europa,* is that right?'

'Yes.'

'And from *Europa* this info would go back to Earth Control?'

'Yes. There is non-stop transmission of pictures and technical data from *Europa* to Earth.'

'Aye,' scowled Dalziel. 'Made me miss *Star Trek.* But weren't there a transmission blackout from *Europa* as the module went down?'

'That is right. There was an electrical storm.'

He whistled and said, 'That must have been scary.'

'No,' she said with professional indifference. 'It happens often. Fortunately it did not last long and we got pictures back in time for the big event. Emile stepping on to the moon, I mean, not . . .'

She shuddered. A sympathetic smile lit Dalziel's face like a wrecker's lantern and he said, 'Don't take on, lass. Now, let's see. It were just *Europa*'s Earth transmissions that were affected? You still kept your contact with the module?'

'There was a little interference but we still got pictures.'

'And technical data on the TEC circuits?'

'Yes,' she snapped with the growing exasperation of the expert at being made to repeat the obvious. Dalziel scratched his nose. To him, such exasperation was the reddening skin above a boxer's eye. You pounded at it till it split.

'And there was no sign of owt wrong with Lemarque's suit? No hint that his circuits had been mucked around?'

'I have said so in my statement!' she cried. 'There was nothing till the moment when he made water. Then pouf! it is finished. No one can say it was my fault! There were two of us watching. It was a systems malfunction I think, no one to blame. Who has been blaming me . . . ?'

'Calm down, woman!' bellowed Dalziel. 'You'll be gabbling away in Spanish again just now, and then where will we be? Have another drink. That's it, straight down. If you buggers drank more of this stuff and less of that gangria, you'd mebbe not need to run around screaming like banshees and slaughtering bulls. Now, get it into your noddle, nobody's blaming you, least of all me. So, just a couple more questions . . .'

4

Pascoe and Dalziel had agreed to confer between interviews.

'Anything?' asked Pascoe.

'She's been bonking either the Italian or the Frog or mebbe both, and she doesn't much care for the Dane, so mebbe she got in on the act too. And she says that Albertosi and Lemarque didn't much hit it off.'

'She volunteered all this?'

'I prodded a bit. Told her I suspected they were a couple of poofters.'

'Oh Andy. Any more disinformation I should know about?'

'I told her you were a right bastard, and I said she weren't on my list of suspects.'

'And isn't she?'

'You know me, lad. *You*'re on my list till I get the evidence to cross you off. She certainly had less chance than the others of fiddling with Lemarque's suit. Mind you, she got very agitated when she thought I was hinting she were to blame for not monitoring the TEC transmissions properly. That electrical storm checked out, did it?'

'Happens all the time, evidently. And there were two of them doing the monitoring.'

'Aye. I take it, from what you're saying, you haven't clamped the Kraut in irons? Not even for spying? He is a spy, I take it?'

'Oh yes, no question. He doesn't deny it.'

Dalziel considered, then said gently, 'Now that should be a great big plus for the Yanks' theory that he knocked the Frog off. So why do I get the feeling it's nowt of the sort?'

Pascoe regarded him blankly. Time was when Dalziel reckoned he could have followed most of his old colleague's thought-processes along a broad spoor of telltale signs, but not anymore. Perhaps time had dulled his perception. Or perhaps it had honed Pascoe's control.

Then the younger man smiled and was his old self again.

'I'm glad to see the nose is getting back into shape, Andy,' he said. 'The truth is, I knew all about Kaufmann's relations with the Arabs long before Druson told me. As usual, the CIA have only managed to get half a story. The more important half is that Kaufmann's a double, always has been. Oddly enough, that's partly the reason he got into the Fed's space programme in the first place. He's a high flier in every sense and was due a promotion. The Arabs were licking their lips as the logical career step would have taken him into a very sensitive area of missile guidance. His own people recognized how hard it would be to keep up his act with duff info at this level, so someone came up with the bright idea of nominating

him for the moon shot. That way, he kept his cred
with the Arabs by passing them what is in their terms
a lot of relatively antiquated space technology. The
Yanks were right about that at least!'

He laughed, inviting Dalziel to join in his amusement. But the Fat Man was not to be manipulated so
easily.

'Fuck me rigid!' he said angrily. 'Why the hell
didn't you tell me this before?'

'*Need-to-know*, remember, Andy? Look, for all I
knew, the Americans had got it right, Kaufmann was
the killer, and I was into damage-limitation. I didn't
see a need to load you down with classified stuff that
wasn't necessary.'

Dalziel swallowed his irritation with difficulty and
said, 'Meaning, now you've talked, he's definitely off
your list?'

'Ninety per cent, I'd say. But I'd still like your opinion, Andy, and it'll be a better opinion now you know
this spy business didn't really figure as motive.'

'Because if Lemarque *had* threatened to tell the
Fed that Kaufmann was an agent, it wouldn't be
much of a threat, as they know already?'

'Right.'

'But suppose he was threatening to tell the Arabs
that Kaufmann was a double?'

'In that case,' said Pascoe quietly, 'Kaufmann
would have told us and Lemarque would have been
taken care of much more discreetly.'

Dalziel digested this, then shook his head unhap-
pily and said, 'Oh, Pete, Pete. Listen, lad, I'm far too
old a dog to be learning new tricks. If this is a good
old-fashioned killing because some bugger's been dip-
ping his hand or his wick where he shouldn't, that's

fine. But if it's spies and politics and that kind of crap, better beam me down to the twilight zone.'

Pascoe smiled and said in a kindly tone, 'I think you're mixing your programmes, Andy. And if you're going to try for pathos, better lose a bit of weight. Look, why do you think I brought you along? I've learnt enough new tricks to deal with the politics, but some of the old tricks may have gone a bit rusty. If it *is* just a good old-fashioned killing, and it could be, I'm relying on you to sort it out. You're my failsafe, Andy. OK? Now let's get on. I've got the Irishman and you've got the Dane. And try to hold back on the Hamlet jokes, won't you?'

Marte Schierbeck was a very different proposition from Silvia Rabal. The atmosphere had changed from Mediterranean heat to Nordic coldness, but a native Yorkshireman knows better than to trust in mere weather. A fragment of hymn from his distant Sunday School days drifted through Dalziel's mind as he met the woman's cool grey eyes.

> *A man who looks on glass*
> *On it may stay his eye,*
> *Or if he pleases through it pass . . .*

He said, 'Was Emile more jealous of Marco than the other way round, do you think?'

She expressed no surprise but simply asked, 'What has Silvia said?'

'Does it matter?'

'The truth matters. We must tell the truth, mustn't we? Especially to policemen.' She spoke with no apparent irony.

'That's how it works in Denmark, is it? Do you do lecture tours?'

'Sorry?'

'Just my little joke. So what about Marco, then? Was he very jealous of Emile?'

'All men are jealous of their successors. That is why they hate their sons.'

'Jesus,' said Dalziel.

'There too,' said the woman.

A man who looks on glass . . . Dalziel made a determined effort to refocus.

'Was it you who broke off the affair, then?' he asked.

'*Affair*,' she echoed.

Not even his gout had made Dalziel feel older than the delicate way in which she savoured the old-worldliness of the word.

'Yes,' she went on. 'I broke it off. That is perhaps why Marco was jealous, not because he cared about having me, but because I let him see I did not care about having him. But I think what you are really asking is, "Was he jealous enough to kill?" Perhaps. He is Italian, and their self-image permits crimes of passion.'

'Not much passion in fixing a man's space suit so that first time he passes water he drops down dead,' sneered Dalziel, suddenly keen to pierce this icy carapace.

It was like spitting on a glacier.

She said, 'To the Latin mind, it might seem . . . apt.'

Dalziel didn't reply at once and the woman, mistaking his silence, tried to help him over his repression.

'Because the electrical connection which killed him would be through his sex organ,' she explained.

'Aye, lass,' he said irritably. 'First thing they taught me at Oxford was to know when a tart's talking dirty. What I'm trying to work out is, how come you're so keen to fit this randy Eyetie up for murder?'

'Please?'

'Forget it. You're not about to tell me, are you? I see from your file that you were the module pilot?'

'Yes. That surprises you?'

'I stopped being surprised by lady drivers a long time back,' he said. 'And you landed safely? No bumps?'

'No bumps.' She almost smiled.

'Then what?'

'I extended the outside arm to set up the external camera to record this historic moment for posterity. Then Emile activated his TEC and entered the airlock. I opened the exit door and he began to descend. The rest you have seen.'

'Why was he the first out?' asked Dalziel. 'Did you draw lots, or what?'

Now she definitely smiled.

'Certainly we drew lots,' she said. 'Being first is important. Everyone remembers Armstrong, but who can remember the others? Can you, Mr Dalziel?'

'Nowadays I can't remember to zip me flies till I feel a draught,' said Dalziel. 'Lemarque won when you drew lots, then?'

'Oh no. He did not even bother to take part. He knew it was pointless. Next day the decision came from above. He was chosen. No arguments.'

'Oh aye? How'd they work that out, then?'

She said, 'Who knows? But perhaps you remember from your schooldays, in the playground there was always one little boy or girl who had to have first turn at everything. In Europe that child is France.'

'Was anything said in the module before he left?'

'Only trivial things, I think.'

'My favourites,' said Dalziel.

'Emile said something like, I hope the Yankees have built a McDonald's. Even American coffee must be better than the dishwater we have to drink. Something like that.'

'What do you think he was trying to say before he died?'

She shrugged and said, 'Who can know?'

'*Oh mer* . . . How about, *Oh Marte*?' said Dalziel.

'The vowel sound is not right,' she observed indifferently.

'Dying Frenchman pronouncing a Danish name,' he said. 'What do you want? Professor Higgins?'

She took the reference in her stride and said, 'It would be touching to believe his thoughts turned to me at such a time.'

Touching, thought Dalziel. Aye, mebbe. A hand on the shoulder in an identity parade, *that's* touching!

But he didn't bother to say it. *Or if he pleases through it pass* . . . Silly bugger who wrote the hymn can't have heard of frosted glass, he thought.

5

'You don't look happy,' said Pascoe.

'You do. Found the Paddy amusing, did you?'

'Oh, he's a broth of a boy, sure enough. More froth than a pint of Guinness.'

'Get you anywhere?'

Pascoe said uncertainly, 'I'm not sure, I got a feeling he was trying to manipulate me . . . but you know how Irishmen love to wind up the English. We'll see what you think in the reverse singles. Who do you fancy now. Van der Heyde or Albertosi?'

Dalziel said, 'How come I suddenly get a choice? You made out the list and I'm down for first stab at the Eyetie.'

'Sorry. I got worried in case you thought I was being a bit rigid, pulling rank, that sort of thing.'

'Oh aye? Word of advice,' said Dalziel gravely. 'Pulling rank's like pulling bollocks; once you start, you'd best not let go.'

'Oh aye?' mocked Pascoe. 'You've been at your Rochefoucauld again, I see. Well, one good maxim deserves another. Look before you leap on top of a touchy Italian. Albertosi's psych report says he's got a short fuse. He probably wouldn't have made the trip if the other Italian nominee hadn't fallen off his scooter and cracked his skull. So tread carefully.'

'No need to warn me, lad,' said Dalziel. 'I'm a changed man these days. No more clog dancing. It's all tights and tippie-toe now, believe me!'

'Here's something that'll make you laugh, Marco,' said Dalziel. 'From what's been said so far, you're looking the man most likely to have knocked off Emile Lemarque!'

The Italian's English was nowhere near as good as the two women's, but he had no difficulty with the idiom.

'Who has said this? What have they said?' he demanded angrily.

'General notion seems to be you and him were

bonking rivals. You know, jealous of each other's success with the ladies.'

'What? Me jealous of Lemarque? More chance I am jealous of a flea because he bites the woman I love!'

'Flea, you say? You want to watch where you get your women,' said Dalziel kindly. 'But you were both after Silvia Rabal, weren't you?'

'What? Oh yes, he bothers her. Is always flapping round her, calling her his little cockatoo, making jokes. But is all words like with all these Frenchman, talk, talk, talk, so much talk, so little action. Women like men who act, real men, big men. He is no bigger than she is, a midget almost! When a true man comes along, his little cockatoo soon jerks him off the nest!'

Dalziel hid a grin and said, 'So what you're saying is, Lemarque wasn't worth bothering about, right? But he did bother you, didn't he? So why was that?'

Albertosi grimaced and said, 'You are right. I will not lie. I did not like the Frenchman. But not because of Silvia.'

'Why, then?'

'Because he has a poison tongue! Because he makes slander about me.'

'They're like that, these Frogs,' said Dalziel sympathetically. 'Think yourself lucky you've still got the Alps between you. We've let the buggers build a tunnel so they can come hopping across any time on a day return. What was it he said about you?'

'He said that I have injured my comrade, Giuseppe.'

'Eh?'

'Giuseppe Serena. We are Italy's team for the moon shot, but only one of us will go, it is not yet decided which. Then my friend is riding back to the base on his scooter when a car forces him off the road. He is not badly injured but bad enough to put him out of the running, you understand. Then this pig, this Frenchman, he says it is I who drive the car, I who hurt my friend so that I will be selected!'

It came out in a volcanic rush, flaring (as with Silvia Rabal) into a violent spout of his own language which did not need a dictionary to translate.

'So you wouldn't be too unhappy about Lemarque's death?' said Dalziel.

'What do you say? I am not happy that a colleague dies, does not matter how I feel personally. But, how is it in English?—pride comes, then a fall. He was so boasting he was to be the first to step on the moon. Only he doesn't step, he falls!'

The idea clearly amused him.

'It bothered you, did it? Him getting the prima donna's job?'

'*Prima donna!* That's it! That is how he acts, like he is more important than the others. But what important is it, stepping on the moon? It is more than forty years since Armstrong did it. Since then many more Americans and Russians too. No, this is not a first, not a *real* first.'

'No? What would you reckon is a real first, then?' asked Dalziel.

The Italian smirked knowingly but did not reply.

'All right. Let's stick to facts. You and Silvia Rabal stopped on *Europa* and watched the monitors. Did you see anything unusual?'

This seemed to amuse Albertosi. First he internalized his laughter till his whole body was shaking. Then finally it burst out in a full-throated roar as Dalziel watched, stony-faced.

'Please, I am sorry,' gasped the Italian. 'Go on. Ask

your questions. It is reaction, you understand. Much tension, then it comes out in laughter or in anger, makes no matter which.'

'Depends what you're laughing at,' said Dalziel.

'Nothing. Only my foolishness. Go on.'

'All right. Silvia Rabal says that she noticed nothing unusual on the monitor.'

But he was off again, turning red in his effort to suppress his amusement.

For a moment Dalziel felt nothing but a schoolteacher's exasperation in the face of a giggling adolescent. Then it began to dawn on him what this was all about.

'Oh, you dirty sod!' he said slowly. 'That's it, isn't it? That was *your* first! While Lemarque and the others were in the module heading for the surface, you and Silvia were bonking in space. You dirty sod!'

He began to chuckle and a few seconds later his laughter mingled with Albertosi's in a saloon bar chorus. It took the pouring of a couple of large Scotches to calm things down.

'So neither of you was watching the monitor?' said Dalziel.

'When Albertosi makes love, who watches television?' said the Italian complacently.

'And this electrical storm that knackered the transmissions to Earth was just a happy coincidence?'

'A slight adjustment of the controls,' smirked Albertosi. 'A man must protect a lady's modesty, hey? Down there these bureaucrats watch us all the time but this they were not going to watch.'

He sipped his drink with a look of ineffable self-congratulation. Dalziel regarded him with an admiring envy which was mainly, though not entirely, assumed. It would be nice to puncture this inflated self-esteem, he thought, but that wasn't the name of the game. The way to a man's mind was through his pleasures.

He leaned forward and said confidentially, 'Just a couple more questions, Marco. First: floating around up there, what was it like?'

6

'Break for lunch now,' said Pascoe. 'Then we'll have the reverse singles.'

'Fine. How was the Dutchman?'

'Phlegmatic. And the Italian?'

'A bit up in the air,' said Dalziel. And laughed.

The *Europa* crew ate together in their dome, segregated partly by choice, partly by command. Druson had invited Pascoe and Dalziel to join him in the central mess. Conversation stilled for a moment as they entered but quickly resumed.

'So how's it going?' asked Druson.

'Early days,' said Pascoe. 'The crew are naturally eager to get this over and get back to work. Would you have any objection to a limited resumption of duties? It would ease a lot of tension.'

'You mean turn them loose on the surface?' said Druson doubtfully.

'Why not? It's not Jack the Ripper we're dealing with. And there's a hell of a lot of money invested in this programme.'

This appeal to the Great American Motivator just made Druson laugh.

'Hell, they're not going to find anything out there they couldn't read about in our college manuals!'

'Perhaps not,' said Pascoe equably. 'Think about it,

anyway. Meanwhile I think at least we ought to have one of our people back on *Europa*. We've tied up your man long enough.'

Again Druson looked doubtful.

Dalziel, who was carving a steak like a Sunday joint, said, 'What's up, Ed? Scared we'll pick the killer and he'll make a run for Mars?'

'Funny. Yeah, OK, why not? Anyone in mind?'

'Rabal, the Spaniard's the obvious choice. She's the pilot. Also, though I've not talked to her myself yet, Andy here reckons she's in the clear and I've never known him wrong.'

You lying bastard! thought Dalziel, chewing on his steak. He got the feeling that Druson for all his street-wisdom was being edged into doing exactly what Pascoe wanted.

'OK,' said the American after a pause for thought. 'Why not? I'll arrange for one of our pods to make the transfer. No need to fuck around with that steam-powered module of yours!'

Dalziel noted the transfer of irritation. You've got the feeling you've been stitched up as well, my lad, he thought. And you've no idea how or why!

Pascoe pushed aside his almost untouched omelette and stood up.

'If you'll excuse me,' he said. 'Couple of things to do. Back to work in, say, fifteen minutes, Andy?'

He just about got the interrogative lift in, dulling the imperative edge of the sentence.

'Whatever you say,' said Dalziel.

They watched him walk away, a slim, upright figure, from behind very little changed from the young detective-constable Dalziel had spotted signs of promise in so many years ago.

'Hard man, your boss,' opined Druson. 'And in a hurry. Man in a hurry can make mistakes.'

'Whoever fixed the Frog's suit must have been in a hurry and he didn't make mistakes,' said Dalziel. 'Apart from leaving yon microprobe thing in his locker.'

'Could be even that wasn't a mistake,' said Druson. 'Could be he got instructions to put himself under suspicion and stir things up between the Germans and the French.'

'Oh aye. From which of his masters?' wondered Dalziel.

'From whichever wanted it most,' said Druson. 'I'm just a plain security jock. I don't mess with politics. Now if you'll excuse me, Andy. Anything you want, just ask, OK?'

He's getting worried about the lad wandering around free, thought Dalziel.

He said, 'Aye, there's one thing you could tell me, Ed. What do you lot do about sex up here?'

Back in their dome after lunch Dalziel said, 'Nice guy, Druson. Quite bright too, for a Yank.'

'Indeed,' said Pascoe. 'This afternoon, Andy, let's whip them through at a fair old pace. Don't give them time to think. How does that sound to you as a strategy?'

It was the old Peter Pascoe's voice, easy, friendly, slightly diffident. But running through it now like a filament of high-tensile steel was the unmistakable tone of a man used to giving orders and having them obeyed.

'Sounds fine,' said Dalziel.

* * *

He followed Pascoe's instructions to the letter with Kaufmann, hitting him with rapid-fire questions all of which the German handled with the assurance of a man well grounded in the interrogative arts.

'Did you like Lemarque?' he asked finally.

'He knew his job, he did his work,' answered the German.

'Aye, but did you like him?'

Kaufmann considered, then said, 'As a man, no. He was like many small men, too aggressive. Always compensating for his lack of height.'

'Give me an example.'

'Well, I recall during training, he found out that O'Meara had been a boxer in his youth, an amateur, you understand. All the time after that, he made jokes about it, pretended to fight with him, challenged him to a bout in the gym.'

'And did O'Meara take up the challenge?'

'Naturally not. Such things would not be allowed. We were training for the mission. Physical injury would have been disastrous for any one of us.'

'So what happened?'

'Nothing,' said Kaufmann. 'O'Meara kept his temper, though I think it was difficult for him sometimes. Eventually Lemarque found a new target.'

'Which was?'

'Me, I think. The Germans in the wars of the last century, something like that.'

'And you kept your temper too?'

'Oh yes. Sometimes I imagined what I would like to do to the troublesome little creature, but it stayed in my imagination.'

'Oh aye. And can you prove that?'

The answer came unhesitatingly.

'All I can say is, if I had decided to kill him, one

thing is sure. Everyone would have been quite convinced it was an accident.'

'He had a point,' said Dalziel. 'But not just for him.
How come with all their electronic know-how, whoever did it made such a pig's arse of covering their
tracks?'

'We've been through this, Andy,' said Pascoe. 'It
must have been done in a hell of a hurry. I gather
there's only room for one person at a time in the *Europa*'s hold and the TV camera is blocked by the
body. So the opportunity's there. But if anyone spent
an unusually long time down there, it'd stick out in
the recordings at Control, and it doesn't.'

'Aye, well, mebbe I'll get the chance to see what
it's like up there for myself before we're done,'
growled Dalziel.

'Still thinking we're not following proper proce-
dure?' mocked Pascoe. 'You're such a stickler! It
wasn't always like that, I seem to recall. Incidentally, I
assume the new Andy Dalziel has been carefully
checking out the order they got themselves ready in?'

Dalziel looked uncomfortable and Pascoe allowed
himself a superior smile.

'Good news and bad news,' he said. 'The good
news is you haven't missed anything by not checking,
for the bad news is Lemarque was last into the hold,
so it could have been anyone who fixed his suit!'

'How does an Irishman get to be an astronaut?'
asked Dalziel.

Kevin O'Meara cocked his head on one side in best
leprechaun fashion and said, 'Is it an Irish joke you're
after telling?'

'Sorry?'

'Do I say, I don't know, and you say, he lights a rocket but doesn't retire till he's sixty-five? Or is it a real question?'

'That's the only sort I know.'

'All right, then. Here's the story of me fascinating life and hard times. I joined the Air Force at sixteen, not out of any sense of patriotism, you understand— *Nor law nor duty made me fight, Nor public men nor cheering crowds*—you'll know your Yeats? No, the only reason I had was to learn to fly so I could become a commercial airline pilot, and make a lot of money, and spend me spare time pleasuring hostesses in palatial hotels. Now isn't that a reasonable ambition for a randy young buck?'

'Sounds fair enough to me,' said Dalziel. 'What happened?'

'I grew up. Or at least I grew older. Young men should be given their heart's desires straight away. If you wait till you've earned them . . .'

He threw back his head and carolled, '*Oh, the youth of the heart and the dew in the morning, you wake and they've left you without any warning.*'

'Don't ring us,' said Dalziel. 'So you just more or less drifted into the space programme, is that what you're saying?'

'Isn't that the way of most things? You now, I dare say you just drifted into being a policeman.'

'No,' said Dalziel. 'It was what I wanted.'

'Was it now? OK, I'm sorry to hear that. I like my cops to be ordinary chaps like myself who can look at some poor devil in trouble and think: There but for the grace of God go I.'

'If I'd fancied the mercy business, I'd have trained as a nun,' said Dalziel. 'From your file, I see you had a longish period of sick leave about four years back.'

'Is it me file you've got there? Then you'll know more about meself than I'll ever want to know.'

'It was after your wife died, right?'

'Let me think. Yes now, you'll be right. Or was it after the budgie escaped? Drat this memory of mine!'

'Not much to choose between a wife and a budgie, I suppose,' said Dalziel. 'All bright feathers and non-stop twittering. Your missus flew away too, didn't she? Funny, that. You need to be a very cheeky sod to apply for sick leave 'cos the tart who dumped you's got herself killed.'

'That's me all over,' said O'Meara. 'More cheek than Sister Brenda's bum, as the saying is.'

'She'd run off with a Frog, hadn't she?' persisted Dalziel. 'Died with him in a car accident. Terrible bloody drivers, these foreigners.'

'Aha!' said O'Meara. 'At last I'm getting your drift! And here's me thinking you were just showing a friendly interest! Because me wife ran off with a Frog, as you call him, every time I see a Frenchman, I feel an irresistible desire to kill him, is that it? Sure now, it's a fair cop. Except it happens in this case, the Frog she ran off with was a Belgian!'

'Let's not split hairs,' said Dalziel.

'You're right. Many things I am, but not a hair-splitter. Do I get a choice of wearing the cuffs in front or behind? And what happens if I want to go to the little boys' room while I've got them on?'

'You pray no one's been mucking about with your wiring. This sick leave you had, exactly what was it that was supposed to be wrong with you?'

'Oh, women's trouble, you know the kind of thing.'

Dalziel slapped the file down on his knee with a crack that made the Irishman flinch.

'End of happy hour,' he snarled. 'Let's have some straight answers, right?'

'Oh God!' cried the Irishman, clenching his fists in a parody of a boxer's defences. 'You don't mean you're after fighting with the gloves off, is that it? I never could abide bare fists. Bare anything else you care to name, but not the bare fists!'

Dalziel looked at him thoughtfully and said, 'Yes, I'd heard summat about you being a boxer. And about the little Frog taking the piss.'

'Now that's what I call an unfortunate choice of phrase,' said O'Meara.

'I told you, lad. Cut the comedy! Let's just talk about you and Lemarque and the boxing ring, shall we?'

'I thought we agreed to whip this lot through double quick,' said Pascoe irritably.

'Sorry. He bothered me, that one. Something not right.'

'Ah, the famous nose again. What kind of not-rightness?'

'Too many jokey answers and I got the feeling he was trying to steer me around all the time.'

'So what did you end up not getting answers about that you asked questions about?'

Dalziel considered, then said, 'Hard to say exactly. One thing was why he got sick leave after his wife snuffed it, but that can't have owt to do with anything, can it?'

'Unlikely. What was wrong with him, anyway?'

'Don't know. That's the point I'm making,' said Dalziel heavily.

'There should have been a medical report in his file. Hang about, I've still got it here. Sorry. Let's see.

Emotional trauma, blah blah; physical symptoms, insomnia, slight hypertension blah blah; treatment, counselling and unpronounceable drugs; passed fit for duty, 7.10.06. Nothing there that's relevant, I'd say. Maybe he just doesn't like talking about that time. Stick this in his file, will you?'

Dalziel glanced at the medical report, shrugged and said, 'The bugger's still not right. How'd you do with Danish bacon? Fancy a slice?'

'I don't think so.'

'You don't fancy her or you don't think she's in the frame?'

'I don't think that Miss Schierbeck would judge any man worth killing,' said Pascoe. 'So. One each left. We're not doing too well, Andy.'

'Come on,' said Dalziel. 'You've scuppered the Yanks' motive for Kaufmann being the killer, haven't you?'

'Because he's a double? We knew that before I left Earth. It would still be very embarrassing to have to make that public in his defence. No, the only thing that's going to please my masters and cut the ground right from under the Americans' feet is for us to come up with the undeniably genuine perpetrator. There can't be any cover-up or fit-up. We need the real thing and we need it fast!'

After thirty minutes with Adriaan van der Heyde, Dalziel was convinced that either the Dutchman wasn't the real thing or if he was, it would take thumbscrews, rack and Iron Maiden to prise it out of him. He'd heard Pascoe's door open and shut after only ten minutes, signalling that the Commissioner was following his own precept of speed. It annoyed Dalziel to be accused of dragging his feet, annoyed him even more to suspect that perhaps it was age that was making him take so long.

'Look,' he said in desperation, 'let's say you're in the clear, right? Which of the others do you reckon most likely?'

The stolid Dutchman scratched his nose, then said very definitely, 'Albertosi.'

'What?' It occurred to Dalziel that, though it seemed unlikely, it would be nice to pin this on the Italian, not least because Pascoe obviously felt able to dismiss him so quickly.

'Why do you say that?' he asked. 'You reckon mebbe he was jealous of Lemarque?'

'Jealous? Sexually, you mean?' The Dutchman shook his head. 'That's all the British can think of. Sex!'

'Must be something to do with living above sea-level,' said Dalziel. 'All right, tulip. What do you say his motive was?'

'Revenge.'

There was an unnerving certainty about the man's manner and delivery.

Even Dalziel who was not easily impressed by the trappings of honesty couldn't help feeling he had better pay close attention here.

'You'd best explain,' he said.

The Dutchman nodded, took a deep breath and began to speak in a measured didactic tone which for a while disguised the incredible content of his allegations.

'Lemarque was approached by a consortium who wanted his help to take over the holy water bottling business in Lourdes. It is a multi-million-franc industry, you understand. He pretended to agree but went to the police. Unfortunately behind this consortium are people who decree that the price of betrayal of their confidence is death. Marco Albertosi was instructed to carry out the sentence.'

For a second Dalziel was reduced to a rare speechlessness. Then he burst out, 'For Christ's sake, are you telling me Albertosi is a Mafia hit man?'

'His family is Sicilian, did you know that?'

'No, I bloody didn't! Come on, lad, where's your hard evidence for all this? For *any* of it!'

'Lemarque's last words. They were incomplete.'

'*Oh mer* . . So?'

'He was trying to say *Omertà!*' said the Dutchman. 'The Mafia's code of silence.'

For a long moment Dalziel stared into van der Heyde's grave, unyielding face.

Finally he said, 'Are you taking the piss?'

Another long moment, then . . .

'Yes,' said van der Heyde. And his face crazed like an overfired Delft plate into myriad lines of laughter.

7

The pod spun round the moon in a climbing orbit and Earth swam into view like a schoolroom globe. It was easy for Dalziel to pick out Africa and India, but Yorkshire was invisible under a cloud. He felt a sharp pang of homesickness.

'Long way back, huh?' said Druson, observing him sympathetically.

'Long way to come just to hear a Dutchman crack a joke, right enough,' said Dalziel.

He had rewarded van der Heyde with a glass of Scotch. One glass led to another and he'd finally emerged from the interview with a feeling of childish self-satisfaction at having so blatantly ignored Pascoe's repeated instruction to hurry things along. Logically he had no cause to feel irritated when he found that Pascoe had joined Silvia Rabal in the pod taking her up to *Europa*, but he did. Even the return of Druson with the nightwatch and the message that his 'boss' wanted him up there too didn't mollify him.

'*Boss*'. He couldn't recall the last time he had acknowledged a boss, and he certainly wasn't about to start with a jumped-up detective-sergeant who'd struck lucky!

Mistaking his irritation, Druson said, 'Don't take it to heart, Andy. So the German still looks the man most likely, so what? Let the politicians work it out.'

'Eh? What makes you think I give a toss about politics?'

'You don't?' Druson looked at him shrewdly and said, 'I almost believe you, Andy. So what do you care about?'

'A fair measure in a clean glass,' said Dalziel. 'That'll do me.'

'And Commissioner Pascoe, is that how he feels too?'

'Peter? Straight as a donkey's shaft,' said Dalziel. 'Too honest for his own good sometimes.'

He spoke with a force he didn't quite understand the need for.

'He's done well for an honest man,' observed Druson neutrally. 'But at least he brought you along, so that's a point in his favour, I'd say.'

Dalziel tried to work out the drift of Druson's comments as they came in to dock with *Europa*, but once aboard he needed all his concentration to keep him from bouncing around like a ball in a bingo jar. On the US lunar shuttle he had been safe in the embrace of his wrap-around couch, so this was his first true experience of untrammelled weightlessness. Pascoe watched with open amusement, but Silvia Rabal showed a deal of concern which Dalziel found flattering till he realized she was more worried about her delicate instruments than his delicate body.

Finally, having discovered that the basic art was to reduce his energy output by ninety per cent, he gained sufficient control to follow Pascoe on a tour of the ship.

The fact that every dimension was usable made it feel surprisingly large. There were three main compartments: the bridge, which was the principal control area in the bow; the deck, which was the large central section housing most of the accommodation facilities; and the hold. This was basically a narrow cylinder walled by storage lockers, seven of which had the crew's names stencilled on them.

Dalziel almost filled the central space.

'You'd need to be a bloody contortionist to muck around with one of them TECs down here,' he said, pulling at the door marked *van der Heyde*. '*Locker*' proved a misnomer. It was held shut only by a magnetic catch and flew open. A framed photo came floating out and he grabbed it.

'These people are highly trained pros,' said Pascoe, behind, or above, or underneath him. 'Also they're very fit and fairly thin. What's that you've got?'

'Family snap,' said Dalziel, passing back a photo of two very plain girls and a scowling woman. 'You can see why he took to space. They're allowed personal stuff, then?'

'Within reason. Weight's not the problem it was.'

'Not for some,' said Dalziel. 'Let's have a shufti.'

He began opening other lockers. This felt more like

real police work! But he soon began to feel that these souvenirs of Earth were better material for a psychiatrist than a simple bobby.

Surprisingly, only the Dutchman had brought a family photo. Perhaps he didn't trust his memory and was insuring against the shock of reunion. Marco Albertosi obviously felt he could not live without a set of AC Milan's European Cup Programmes. Silvia Rabal's trust in technology did not extend to nourishment and her talisman was a soft leather bag containing sachets of camomile tea and various other pods, seeds, and dried herbs. Dalziel recalled her spicy breath and inhaled deeply. Marte Schierbeck's memento was more mysterious. An old tinder-box. Perhaps she was worried about being marooned? He opened it and found it contained a small tube of contraceptive pills. Perhaps it was who she was marooned with that bothered her! Kaufmann had brought with him a miniature score of Beethoven's *Emperor* concerto. Dalziel marvelled that these squidges could echo as music in some men's minds. Or perhaps it was just a spy's code book after all. The only other book he found was in O'Meara's locker, an ornately bound New Testament with a brass catch.

'Didn't strike me as religious,' observed Dalziel.

'What's that?' said Pascoe.

'New Testament in O'Meara's locker.'

'Oh, you know the priest-ridden Irish. Never shake it off. Bring it out anyway.'

'Hang on. Just one to go.'

It was Lemarque's and it was completely empty. Presumably it had contained nothing except the journal and that had been removed as evidence.

He gave a gentle push and floated backwards out of the hold into the deck area.

'So. One New Testament. Not quite the kind of testament I was hoping for,' said Pascoe glumly.

Dalziel undid the catch and opened the book. On the fly leaf, a book-plate had been stuck headed *Holy Cross Youth Club: Award for service.* Under this was a handwritten inscription *To Kevin (K. O.) O'Meara. Western District featherweight champion, 1993, 1994. Well done!* It was signed, *Father Powell (1 Tim vi, 12).*

'All his success since, and this is what still matters to him?' said Pascoe reflectively.

'You reckon?' said Dalziel, turning to the First Epistle to Timothy.

The page containing Chapter 6 verse 12 was folded in half and when he straightened it out he saw that either deliberately or by chance some flakes of white powder had been trapped there. Some of them floated free. Dalziel licked his finger and stabbed at them, then cautiously put it to his mouth.

'What are you after, Andy? Coke? Forget it. Druggies don't make it on to the space programme, believe me!'

'Why not? They let in spies and killers,' said Dalziel. 'It's not coke any road. But I know that taste . . .'

'Probably dandruff. Sorry. All right, pass it here and I'll take it back for analysis just to keep you quiet.'

Dalziel, who didn't think he'd been making any unusually loud fuss, folded the page back to retain the rest of the powder. As he did so he glanced at Verse 12. *Fight the good fight of faith.* No wonder young K. O. O'Meara had won his titles; he'd had the referee in his pocket. His eye strayed a few verses up the column. *For we brought nothing into this world and it is certain we can carry nothing out.* Now there's where Paul had got it wrong. He hadn't given God credit for space travel. Unless, as seemed not improbable, it wasn't a work of God after all.

He fastened the catch and gave Pascoe the book. The taste was still in his mouth, its source both figuratively and literally on the tip of his tongue.

Druson, who was reclining or hanging on the deck, depending how you looked at it, said, 'You guys gonna be much longer?'

'As long as it takes,' said Pascoe with an authoritative snap which made Dalziel smile and Druson look sour.

'What's in here?' asked Dalziel, examining a couple of doors in the bulkheads.

'Galley and the heads,' said Pascoe.

'Heads?'

'Loos.'

'Oh, the karzies. That's right. You said they just went normal here.'

'Not exactly normal,' said Pascoe, opening a door. 'With no gravity, you need a suction system, otherwise you could be in deep trouble.'

Dalziel examined the apparatus.

'Do yourself a nasty injury with that,' he opined.

He floated above the open door in silence for a while.

'Penny for them,' said Pascoe.

'Still charge a penny, do they,' said Dalziel. 'No, I was just thinking. The Frenchie was so chuffed at being the first to land, and he'd got his little speech ready and all; and he'd not been too long gone from *Europa* where he had summat like a proper bog . . .'

'So?'

'So how come he got so desperate he had to take a

leak on the ladder with the eyes of the universe on him?'

'No one would know,' pointed out Pascoe.

'*He*'d know,' said Dalziel grimly. 'And the data would register on the monitors up here, so they'd know. And then it would be transmitted back to Control on Earth so everyone there'd know. And you can bet your bottom dollar someone would leak the leak to the tabloids, so every bugger in the universe would know! So why'd he do it?'

'Stage fright? Or perhaps he drank something. Didn't someone mention something about coffee?'

'Aye. The Dane said he'd been moaning on about how bloody awful it was.'

'There you are, then,' said Pascoe dismissively. 'Coffee's supposed to be pretty diuretic, isn't it?'

And the word switched on a light in Dalziel's lingual memory.

'Bugger me!' he said.

'Why?' said Pascoe with unusual facetiousness.

'That powder in the Testament, I know what it is. It's ground-down Thiabon tablets!'

'You what?'

'*Thiabon*. Trade name for the latest thiazide drug. Quack put me on 'em last year for me blood pressure. They work by releasing sodium from the tissues and stimulating the kidneys to wash it out. In other words, they make you pee!'

'A lot?'

'Worse than draught lager,' said Dalziel. 'In coffee, I reckon they'd have most men going in half an hour. And the build-up's constant. No use crossing your legs. You've got to go!'

'What are you saying, Andy?' asked Pascoe with a frown of concentration.

'No use fixing Lemarque's suit unless you can be sure he's going to trigger the short circuit, is there? So you feed him a diuretic which you know about because you've been prescribed it yourself!'

'Hey,' interposed Druson. 'You're not confessing, are you, Andy? It'll take more than that to get Kaufmann off the hook.'

'No,' said Dalziel. 'But I know someone else who suffered from mild hypertension a while back and could have been put on these pills. Hey, lass. Got a minute?'

Silvia Rabal came down from the bridge. Hair piled up in its comb and wearing a silkily thin leotard in yellow and green, she hovered before them like some tropical bird.

Dalziel said, 'Before word came through that Lemarque was to be first out, who'd won when you drew lots?'

She thought, then said, 'Kevin. But I do not think anyone really believed they would let us decide ourselves . . .'

'Believing the impossible's never bothered the Irish,' said Dalziel. 'So in O'Meara's mind, he should have had the honour of being first out. And beside getting the Freedom of Dublin city and draught Guinness for life, it'd mean money in the bank when it came to writing his memoirs!'

Pascoe was shaking his head, unimpressed.

'It's a pretty feeble motive for killing a man,' he said. 'Now if you were saying it was a daft Irish joke . . .'

'Why not?' exclaimed Dalziel, now in full flow. 'Why not that too? There's nothing he can do about stopping Lemarque, but he can ruin his big moment. If the timing's right, there he'll be, standing on the ladder with all eyes on him, just about to launch into his big speech when suddenly he's got to pee. All right, he may have the nerve to carry *that* off, but not if his suit's been fixed to give him a short sharp shock along the dong? Man'd need to be Christian martyr material not to register that! In fact with a bit of luck, he might even fall off the ladder! Great gag, eh? Only without realizing, O'Meara had fixed it so that all the electronics in the TEC would jam, and the joke goes sour, and the poor bloody Frog is lying dead.'

Pascoe regarded him doubtfully, hopefully, longingly, like a pagan on the brink of conversion, and Dalziel's brain started working overtime, drawing fragile threads together in an effort to plait a cord that would bear the other's soul up to heaven.

'Someone, Kaufmann I think it was, said something about Lemarque twitting O'Meara about being a boxer. Suppose he knew that his nickname as a lad had been KO? Mebbe he'd taken a peek in yon Testament. And suppose what he scribbled in his journal wasn't *Ka is getting angry*, but *Ko is getting angry*. And if he was on the alert, mebbe when he felt his bladder filling up at a suspicious rate, he recalled the awful coffee he'd drunk and knew where to lay the blame. What he said just before he died, *Oh mer . . .* what he was trying to say was *O'Meara!*'

It wasn't much, but a man in search of salvation will make do with a candle if he doesn't get offered a blinding light.

Pascoe said with fervent gratitude, 'Andy, how have I managed without you all this time? I felt there was something about O'Meara when I talked to him. I mentioned it to you, didn't I? Like he was playing a game with me, almost like there was something he wanted me to know . . . Mr. Druson, I need to get back to the Village straightaway.'

Druson was looking as if his side's twenty-point lead had been clawed back in the fourth quarter and now in the dying seconds of the game he was watching the opposition shaping to kick a field goal.

'Come on, you guys!' he mocked, trying for time-out. 'I like baloney, but this is ridiculous! Let's just look at the facts here . . .'

'The only fact that need concern you, Colonel, is that we are getting into that pod and that during the flight there will be no talking with your base other than essential technical exchanges. I'm sure you understand me.'

Pascoe's tone was courteous, his voice quiet. But it was the quietness of deep space which can boil a man's blood in millisecs if he challenges it unprotected.

Druson clearly believed he had that protection for now he substituted belligerence for mockery.

'Now listen here. No limey cop gives me orders *anywhere* and especially not round the moon. Christ almighty, it's taken you guys half a century to get here in this junk heap. We've been *living* here for more than—'

Pascoe cut across him like Zorro's sword through a candle.

'Colonel Druson, you are presently on Federation territory and I would be quite within my rights to arrest you and fly the pod back myself with you under restraint. Oh yes, I could do it, believe me. Nor would my powers diminish on the moon's surface, which is by UN accord international territory where my authority is at least equal with that of your own Commander, who, incidentally, has received instructions from your President to extend me all facilities and full cooperation. I hardly think you want to be at the centre of a diplomatic incident which would wipe a mere accidental death right off our television screens. *Do you?*'

Now for the first time Dalziel admitted to himself how far beyond him Pascoe had gone. He'd always known that the sky was the limit for the lad, but somehow, somewhere, a step had been taken which he'd not noticed, a small step the mightiest of leaps could have taken Dalziel.

Druson too was taken by surprise, but like Dalziel he was a pragmatist.

'OK, OK, Commissioner,' he said, holding up his hands in mock surrender. 'I'm not taking on the UN, believe me. Down we go, and I'll button my lip all the way, I promise.'

'Thank you,' said Pascoe. 'Andy, perhaps you'd stay here till another pod fetches you. It would be a bit crowded for the three of us, I think.'

He smiled as he spoke, but his eyes flickered to Silvia Rabal and his finger touched his lips. The message was clear. Dalziel was to make sure the Spaniard too made no contact with the Village.

Dalziel had seen no particular evidence of the kind of group loyalty which might have her radioing a warning, but Pascoe was right to be cautious. All the same, Dalziel felt a little disgruntled that having done all the nose-work, he wasn't going to be in at the kill.

Still, as Druson had just acknowledged, it was no use kicking against a brick wall. Best to lean back against it and enjoy the sun on your face.

He watched the pod detach itself from *Europa,* then he turned to Silvia Rabal who was relaxing against a bulkhead with her legs tucked up beneath her, looking more like an exotic bird than ever.

'Right, luv,' he said, beaming broadly. 'Now what can an old vulture like me and a bright little cockatoo like you do to pass the time? With a bit of luck, mebbe we'll get an electrical storm, eh?'

8

It was the youngster who'd brought the whisky who piloted Dalziel back to the Village. He called Dalziel 'pops' a couple of times, but the Fat Man was not in the mood to respond and most of the journey passed in silence.

The first person he saw as he climbed from the pod was Druson whose face told him all.

'Seems the Shamrock folded like a zed-bed,' said the Colonel. 'Full admission, signed, sealed and delivered. Just the way you called it, Andy.'

'Oh aye? You might look more pleased,' said Dalziel.

'You too,' said Druson, regarding him shrewdly. 'Time for a snort?'

'Best not,' said Dalziel, to his own surprise as much as the American's. 'I'll need to find out what the lad's planning.'

Druson smiled and said, 'Last I saw of your *lad,* he was talking to the two congressmen and the Air Force general he'd just dumped off the next shuttle. I never heard a guy sound so polite as he says *up yours, fella*! So it looks like it's goodbye time, Andy. And I guess I'd better chuck in a congratulations. You two are a real class act. Though I'm still not sure if it's Laurel and Hardy or Svengali and Trilby.'

'Is that a compliment?' wondered Dalziel. 'It's about time you buggers learnt to speak plain English. Cheers anyway, Ed. And thanks for the Scotch.'

They shook hands and Dalziel returned to his quarters. Pascoe was already there with his suitcase open on the bed.

'You move quick,' said Dalziel. 'Not like way back when you'd take half a day to make sure a suspect was sitting comfortable.'

'It was like I said, Andy. He was longing to get it off his chest, but it seemed daft to confess when he didn't have to. All it needed was the realization that we had firm evidence. That was down almost entirely to you, Andy. You were brilliant! Fancy a job in the Justice Department?'

'No, thanks,' said Dalziel. 'Good beer doesn't travel. So all's well, eh? No aggro in the Federation after all.'

'The Irish will feel a mite embarrassed but they're used to that,' said Pascoe. 'Main thing is, whatever happens at the Summit, poor Lemarque's unfortunate death won't affect the outcome. It'll be down to honest political debate.'

'Oh aye? What was that thing they taught us about in grammar lessons, when two things are put together that don't make proper sense? Like *freezing fire*. Or *southern beer*.'

'An oxymoron, you mean.'

'Aye, yon's the bugger. Well, honest political debate sounds like one of them to me. And all them as claims they engage in it, I reckon they're oxy-bloody-morons too!'

Pascoe laughed and said, 'You don't change, Andy. Thank God! Come on. Don't hang about. I'm going to have a quick shower. All this frantic activity's made me sweat. You get yourself packed. We're on our way home in half an hour!'

They rose from the moon in a smooth accelerating orbit. As they slipped round for the second time, beneath them they glimpsed the heavy squat bulk of *Europa*, like some beautifully preserved steam engine on display outside a modern jet-station.

Then their flight path straightened out and they sped like a silver arrow towards the gold of Earth.

Dalziel raised himself on his couch. O'Meara was lying to his left, his eyes closed, his breath shallow, a childlike relaxation smoothing the crinkled face.

'Looks as innocent as a newborn baby, doesn't he?' said Pascoe, who occupied the couch to Dalziel's right.

'Aye, he does,' said Dalziel. 'Mebbe that's because he is.'

'I'm sorry?'

Dalziel turned to face the younger man and said in an exaggerated whisper, 'Safe to talk now, is it?'

Pascoe thought of looking puzzled, changed his mind, grinned and said, 'Quite safe. Clever of you to spot it.'

'They brought me Glenmorangie,' said Dalziel. 'I'd not mentioned any brand till we got to our rooms and I complained that Druson had forgotten. I checked it out again at lunch. Druson was listening all right. And you knew, but decided not to warn me.'

Pascoe didn't deny it.

'Sorry,' he said. 'Didn't see any point. We weren't going to be saying anything we cared about them hearing, were we?'

Dalziel considered, then said, 'No, lad. We weren't.

You because you're a clever bugger and knew they were listening. And me because . . .'

'Because what, Andy?' prompted Pascoe with lively interest.

'Because, not knowing, I'd just come across as a simple old copper doing his job the way he'd always done it.'

'I don't think I'm quite with you,' said Pascoe.

'Oh yes you are. You're only hoping you're not,' said Dalziel. 'Let me spell it out for you, lad. Here's what I think really happened back there. When the Frog snuffed it, the Yanks checked out his TEC. They found a malfunction but no definite sign of outside interference, so it looked like a bug had got into that particular circuit. Tragic accident. Trouble was, the suit was an American design and they don't like looking silly. So mebbe the first idea was to muck the circuits up a bit to make it look like a maintenance fault, not a design fault. Then someone, Ed Druson most likely, had a better idea. How about setting the French and the Germans at each other's throats by pinning this on Kaufmann? They'd know for some time he'd been spying for the Arabs and had been watching for the best chance to use this info to maximum advantage. A dead Frog blackmailer, a murdering Kraut spy; all they needed was a bit of evidence. So they mucked about with the suit to make the fault look deliberate, planted yon microprobe thing in Kaufmann's locker, leaked the news to the Press, and sat back.'

'And the entry in Lemarque's journal? They forged that too, I suppose?'

'Probably not. Too dangerous. That was just a stroke of luck. God knows what it really means.'

Pascoe leaned back on his couch, shaking his head in a parody of wonder.

'Andy, this is fascinating! Have you been doing a lot of reading in your retirement? Fantasy fiction perhaps?'

'Don't get comic with me, lad,' snarled Dalziel. 'And don't think you can pull that rank crap you got away with on Druson either. You may be a Federal bloody Commissioner, but me, I'm a private citizen, and I can recollect you telling me more than once in that preachy tone of thine that in England at least being a private citizen outranks any level of public service you care to mention. Or have you changed your mind about that too?'

'No,' said Pascoe quietly. 'I'm sorry. Go on.'

'I was going to, with or without your permission,' observed Dalziel. 'Now your lot, being clever college-educated buggers like yourself, soon sussed out what had really happened, only there was no way to prove it. So someone *really* clever came up with the solution—let's accept what the Yanks say about Lemarque's death being deliberate, but let's fit somebody else up instead!'

'And how were we going to manage that, And?'

'Well, you had a head start, knowing that Kaufmann had been a double agent, which cut the ground from under the Yanks when it came to motive. But there was still a question of concrete evidence.'

'Concrete? Ah, I see. Like the good old days of slipping half a brick into a suspect's pocket?'

'Oh, you've come a long way from that, Peter,' said Dalziel. 'Anyone can plant a half-brick. Or a New Testament for that matter. But you needed more evidence. You needed an admission, and that requires a long, strong lever.'

'Which I just happened to have about my person?'

'That's where it would have to be, wouldn't it?' said Dalziel. 'I mean, if the Yanks had got us bugged, they'd not be shy about searching our luggage, would they? Though what they'd have made of a harmless list of names and addresses, I'm not sure.'

Pascoe's hand went involuntarily to his breast pocket and Dalziel laughed.

'It's all right, lad. I put it back after I'd taken a shufti while you were in the shower. I knew there had to be something, and it had to be in writing so you could slip it over to O'Meara while you were interrogating him. Then, after giving him time to take this list in, there'd likely be another piece of paper with his instructions on, like, *You're going to confess to killing Emile Lemarque, or else!*'

'Or else what, Andy?' inquired Pascoe. 'You're losing me.'

'Oh, I think I may have done that already,' said Dalziel coldly. 'I can make a stab at guessing what that list meant, but why should I bother when I can get it from the horse's mouth. So how about it, Paddy? I've never known an Irishman keep quiet for so long!'

He poked O'Meara savagely in the ribs and he opened his bright blue eyes and abandoned his pretence of sleep.

'Now there you are, Andy, me old love,' he said brightly. 'I should have known a man with a face like an old potato couldn't be as thick as he looks! No, no, that's enough of the punching. One thing I learned as a young boxer was not to fight outside me weight. And I got right out of me weight when I was a boy, believe me. Oh, the company I kept, you'd not believe it. Wild men, terrible men, men who drank Brit blood for breakfast and ate Proddy flesh for tea. I was just a messenger, a look-out, a tea-boy, nothing heavy, and I thought I'd put it all behind me when I joined up, and I was glad to be getting away from it all, believe me. But those boys don't forget so easily, and the top and the bottom of it is they came after me to do me old mates a few favours, like giving details of the guard routine at my training depot and looking the other way when I was on sentry so they could get into the arms store.

'Now I was young, but not so young I didn't know that once I started that road, I'd be on it for ever. So, I told our security officer. He was a real gem. He did a deal with the Brits, passing on all information on condition they did the cleaning-up job on their side of the border and pointed the finger a long way from me. A couple of days later, I don't know if it was a cock-up or policy, but the Brits laid an ambush and when the shooting stopped, all the wild men were dead, and me, I was both very guilt-ridden and very relieved, for this meant I was completely in the clear. Or so I thought. Only what I didn't reckon on was that full details of the affair would be carefully recorded in some great computer file where it would lie sleeping for all these years till Prince Charming here came along and woke it with a kiss!'

'He's good at that,' said Dalziel. 'And these names and addresses? They'd be relatives of the men who got killed? And members of your own family?'

'That's right. And if the first lot ever found out who bubbled their menfolk . . . they've got long memories back in Ireland, and they don't forgive. So now you know all about me, Mr Dalziel. And now you know too what nice company you've been keeping.'

Dalziel turned to Pascoe and said, 'Oh Peter, Peter, what have they done to you?'

'Come on, Andy!' protested Pascoe, looking uncomfortable. 'You've cut a hell of a lot of corners in your time, you can't deny it. And we've only got O'Meara's word for it that he turned his old chums in the first time they asked for his help. God knows what mayhem he contributed to before he got cold feet! And what'll happen to him now? He was planning to get out after this mission, we know that. He already has a deal tied up with a publisher, and this will do him no harm at all. An Irish jape that went tragically wrong. End of a promising career with full pension rights guaranteed. Punishment enough from his own conscience, sentence suspended. Advance sales astronomical, serialized in the *Spheroid,* he buys a castle in Killarney and he and his family live happily ever after. I'm practically doing him a favour!'

Dalziel had started shaking his huge head halfway through Pascoe's plaintive self-justification, but he didn't speak till it had run its course.

'Oh Pete, Pete,' he said now. 'Christ, but you've started running slow since you've not had me to wind you up! You don't really imagine I'm bothered about this poor Paddy and his tribal troubles, do you? I never met a Mick yet who didn't deserve ten times worse than he got!'

'So why the shaken head, the plummeting sigh, the heartfelt reproach?' asked Pascoe, trying unsuccessfully for lightness.

'Because in all my years of cutting corners, as you put it,' said Dalziel heavily, 'I did a lot of chancy things, but I never screwed up a mate. I badgered you, and I bullied you, and I buggered you about something rotten. But I never took advantage of you, or made a dickhead out of you, or fobbed you off with a load of lies. Did I?'

'Well,' said Pascoe uncertainly, 'there were a couple of . . .'

'*Did I?*'

'OK, no. In principle, in essence, at the end of the day, no, you didn't.'

'So why've you done it to me, lad? Why've I spent the last few days with your hand up my arse working my jaw-hinges like Charlie McCarthy? Don't answer that. I'll tell you. It wasn't my sodding expertise and independence you wanted. With your clout, you could have had any bright young thing in the game at your service, spouting your script with a will. But why risk an act when for no extra cost you can have the real thing? That would shut the Americans up, eh? Not a Euro whizzkid out to please daddy, but a genuine geriatric, out to please no bugger but himself, who would trip over the truth with his walking frame and leave the Yanks too bothered and bewildered to cry, "Foul!" Was it all your plan, Pete? Every bit of it? Or did some other genius set it off and you just threw me in as a makeweight to make sure you got your share of the glory?'

His voice never rose above a murmur, but its pace increased and its timbre changed, as waters that start soft and slow become harsh with menace when the meadows give way to rock and the stream starts accelerating towards the cataract.

O'Meara said, 'Oh dear. If you two girls are going to quarrel, I really am going to sleep.'

And sinking back, he closed his eyes once more.

Pascoe too had slumped back into his couch. He did not speak for a long time, then said simply, 'Andy, you're absolutely right. What I did was unforgivable. I don't know how . . .'

His voice failed.

Dalziel said, 'It's a tightrope, lad. The higher you go, the more dangerous it gets. Me, I got as far as I could safely. Beyond that, I didn't fancy the trip. One small step in the wrong direction and you can end up bent, or you can end up using people. People that matter, I mean. Your mates. The other buggers are there to be used, aren't they? Everyone thought I got stuck because them above me didn't care for the colour of my eyes. Bollocks! I could make 'em and I could break 'em. And if I'd wanted . . . but I didn't. Where I was was right for me. Anything more would have been giving a face-lift to a cuddy's backside. But I always thought: There's one bugger I know that I'll trust to go all the way; who'll be able to look up without getting delusions and down without getting giddy; who'll not change to fit changes; who'll not let new honours get more important than old mates . . .'

Now it was his voice that died away.

When Pascoe finally spoke, his voice was tight with restraint.

'Andy, I'm sorry. More sorry than ever I've been about anything. I've let you down and I know it. God knows if I can hope to put things right with you, but I'll try, I promise I'll try. But there's a more pressing problem even than that. I've got to ask you something, not as a friend or even an ex-friend, but as a Federal Justice Commissioner. Andy, you've got knowledge, possibly dangerous knowledge, about O'Meara, about Kaufmann, about the fit-up, about everything.

'Andy, what are you going to do about it?'

* * *

What are you going to do about it?

Dalziel rubbed a hand like an eclipse across his face.

This was the second time that day he'd been asked this question.

Then as now he had not given an immediate answer, though he doubted if the delay would have the same result now as then.

His doubts had started long before their arrival on the moon; as soon as Pascoe had telephoned him, in fact. He was no Holmes or Poirot to be hauled out of retirement to solve one last all-baffling case. He was a pensioned-off bobby, suffering from gout, flatulence, distiller's droop, and the monstrous regiment of visiting nurses.

So what the hell was the lad playing at?

He hadn't worked it out straightaway but he'd soon worked out the role Pascoe wanted him to play. The old steam-age detective puffing his way to the pre-ordained terminus! And to start with, he'd really enjoyed playing it. Of course in the old days he'd have done things his way. They'd have visited *Europa* to get the feel of the ship before interrogating the suspects. But his resistance to Pascoe had been token. It was the lad's game, so play to his rules. And the lad had been right. It was pointless planting his clues till he was sure the victim of the fit-up was going to play ball. Mind you, it had been rather offensive the way he'd shovelled them at Dalziel thereafter, as if he really did think his old taskmaster was past it! Best thing that could be said for him was he was working to a timetable. If they hadn't caught this shuttle, they'd have had to wait forty-eight hours for the next, and that would have given the Yanks time to re-group and counter-attack O'Meara with a better offer.

Once Pascoe had got the famous stubby finger to point at the Irishman, all he had to do was get back to the Village as quickly as possible and go through the pre-arranged charade of accusation and confession, with the Yanks listening in helplessly. And preferably without a fat old steam-age cop sitting in the corner, nebbing in with awkward questions.

So the cunning bastard had left him on *Europa*, with the alleged task of making sure Silvia Rabal didn't broadcast anything of what had taken place, this from a ship which was pumping out sound and pictures twenty-four hours of the day!

At this stage he still wasn't sure what was going off. Mebbe Pascoe genuinely believed O'Meara was the perpetrator and had at last learned a lesson Dalziel had once despaired of teaching him, that like faith without works, belief without evidence got you nowhere, so where was the harm in giving God a helping hand?

But it rankled not to be admitted to the plan, if that *was* the plan.

And also, like a stuffed owl, the case against O'Meara *looked* right, but it didn't fly.

With these thoughts in his mind he had watched the pod depart, then turned to look at Silvia Rabal, no stuffed owl this but a living and exotic creature of the air, and matters forensic were flushed from his mind.

'Right, luv,' he said. 'Now what can an old vulture like me and a bright little cockatoo like you do to pass the time? With a bit of luck, mebbe we'll get an electrical storm, eh?'

Even though his tone was nostalgically playful rather than lewdly insinuating, it was not the most gallant of things to say, and had her reaction been scornful abuse, mocking indifference, or even righ-

teous indignation, he would have accepted it as his
due. But what rounded those huge dark eyes was surprise; more than surprise, shock; in fact more than
shock—fear!

And suddenly, in a flash—but not at all sudden in
truth, for this was where the subtle independent
micro-circuits of his mind had been directing him
while Pascoe was busy with spanner and wrench at
the pistons and cogs of his consciousness—he saw the
stuffed owl topple off its perch to be replaced by a
warm, living, tremulous . . .

'Tell me, luv,' he said. 'What's French for cockatoo?'

She went floating away up into the bridge, fluttering her supple hands over the bank of control
lights, and for a moment both terrifying and exhilarat-
ing he thought she might be going to send them blast-
ing off into the depths of space.

But then she turned and floated back to face him.

She said, '*Katatoès*. He called me Ka when we
were . . . in private. But you know this, and more.
Not everything perhaps. But enough to guess everything. From the start I saw you were the dangerous
one.'

She spoke almost flatteringly. She was also speaking unnecessarily freely considering all those TV cameras.

He said warningly, 'Mebbe we should . . .' What?
There was nowhere private to go! But she took his
meaning and laughed, making a flapping gesture with
her hands.

'It is all right. No witnesses. These electrical storms
are sometimes convenient, hey?'

'You mean you've fixed it?' A light dawned. 'Of

course, it was you who fixed it last time, not Marco. It was *your* idea.'

'Of course. I guessed Marco might boast, but he's too macho to tell it was not his initiative!'

'Why'd you need to do it?'

'I often imagined how it might be in zero gravity,' she said mischievously.

'I meant the blackout.' He frowned.

'Oh, that. If Control had spotted a fault in Emile's TEC circuits during the module descent, they might have aborted the landing and spoilt my plan.'

She was bloody cool, thought Dalziel. Another thought occurred to him and he said, 'But weren't the suits tested earlier in the voyage out?'

'Of those involved in the landing, yes.'

She regarded him expectantly. It was as if she wanted him to justify her decision to black out the cameras and confront him directly. Though what she hoped to gain by that . . .

As often happens with sight, taking his eye off a sought-after object brought it into view.

He said, 'I saw the files. You and Lemarque are the same height, so your suits would be much the same. You fixed your suit at your leisure, didn't you? You had time to do a real job on it, not this botched-up job the Yanks claimed. Then all you had to do was swap the suits. And the name strips. That's why his was out of line. You had to do that in a hurry down in the hold. I should have remembered the smell.'

'Smell?'

'In Lemarque's suit. That spicy smell. I thought it were a funny kind of aftershave . . .'

And now the memory of her spiced breath and the contents of the leather pouch in her locker came together and he said, 'What was it you put in his coffee to make him pee? Dandelion juice? Used to call them piss-the-beds when I were a lad.'

'Dandelion, pansy, burdock, black briony—just a very little of the briony, it is very poisonous, very dangerous to those who do not know how to use it. When I hear he is dead, at first I thought: My God, I have used too much and killed him!'

Her face paled with the memory of shock. Dalziel scratched his nose reflectively and said, 'Aye, but you *did* kill him, lass.'

'No!' she protested indignantly. 'He dies by accident! All I do is give him a shock, make him ridiculous in front of the whole world! You must believe me, Dalziel. You must!'

She looked at him beseechingly and he said, 'Must I? I'll need to know a lot more before I can go along with that. First thing I need to know is why you wanted to electrify his goolies anyway.'

She scowled and said, 'He was a rat! He turned from me to that Danish icicle. Well, that was his right. I grow tired of men too. But this rat wanted us both, he is insatiable. Even that I don't mind. But he hid it from me and he did not hide it from her, and that I mind very much! She knew I was being tricked and found it amusing. They screw with their minds, these Scands. But it was his fault, so I decided he must be punished and this idea came. It seemed to me—what is your phrase? Poetical justice! That's it. To pain him in the places he valued most. His vanity and his sex! But pain only, not death. You cannot laugh at a dead man, can you?'

This sounded like a clinching argument to Dalziel.

'So you're saying it was a fault in the TEC design that killed him? But if you hadn't interfered with it, that fault would never have shown up.'

'My interference was a possible fault, therefore it could occur, so this other fault was the real fault,' she flashed.

'Mebbe that makes sense in Spanish,' he said. 'So you definitely left it looking like an accidental fault?'

'Of course! You think I am stupid?' she cried. 'So what has happened? How is it you are looking for a killer? And why is Kevin accused? How can that idiot who comes with you believe such a stupidity? Kevin will prove his innocence, won't he?'

He missed the implication of this for the moment as his mind tried to rearrange everything he knew into something he could understand. And as the picture emerged like a negative in developing fluid, his slab-like face grew cold and hard as a rock on a wintry fell.

'I'd not put money on it, luv,' he said. 'In fact, I'd bet that yon idiot who comes with me has probably got O'Meara's full and frank confession in his pocket already.'

'Confession? Why should he confess?'

'I don't know yet. But one thing's for sure. Somehow it'll seem a better option for him than not confessing.'

She digested this.

'You think so? Then in fact, I will be helping Kevin by keeping quiet, is that not so?'

He grinned at her ingenuity, and also at her naïvety.

'Bit late to be thinking of keeping quiet when you've just coughed your guts out to me, luv,' he said cheerfully.

'Coughed? Oh yes. I understand.' She smiled at him with wide-eyed innocence. 'But I do not understand why you say I have coughed? There is no one here. Just you and me and the electrical storm. No witnesses.'

She gestured at the useless TV eyes.

Dalziel shook his head and showed his gums in a chimpanzee's smile.

'Good try, luv,' he said. 'But they don't like us using a notebook and a stubby pencil anymore.'

From his breast pocket he took a flat black plastic case with a silver grille along one edge, held it up to his ear, pressed a button and listened to the resulting faint hiss with every appearance of satisfaction.

'That's grand,' he said switching off. 'I was a bit worried in case the electrical storm had affected the recording quality.'

She stared at him, baffled, unsure, as he replaced the instrument in his pocket. He met her stare full on, raised his eyebrows as if to invite her comment. She moistened her lips nervously. At least it started as nervousness, but the tiny pink tongue flickering round the full red lips carried a sensual jolt like an electric shock, and when she saw his reaction, she smiled and let the tongue slowly repeat the soft moist orbit.

And then it was he heard that question for the first time.

'So, tell me, Dalziel,' she said. 'What are you going to do about it?'

They were facing each other across the desk, resting against the bulkheads. If there was an *up* and a *down* on the *Europa,* this configuration came closest to what Dalziel thought of as 'standing up'. Perhaps that's what made him take the step.

One small step.

Indeed, hardly that. On Earth it would have been a mere shuffling of the feet, a rather nervous adjustment of a man's weight as he wondered what the hell to do next.

Only here there was no weight to adjust, and the small forward movement of the left foot provoked a counterbalancing backward movement of the right; and as this was against the bulkhead, it caused an equal and opposite reaction, thus doubling his forward movement; and now his arms swung back to grab for support, but, finding nothing to get hold of, merely struck hard against the surface, and this energy too was translated into forward momentum.

And so it was that one small step for Dalziel became in a split second a mighty leap.

She came to meet him. In her eyes a deal had been offered and enthusiastically accepted, and she was no niggard in a bargain. There was perhaps a moment when she became aware that the thin black plastic device spinning in the asteroid belt of clothing that soon surrounded them was not a recorder but an electric razor, but by then it was far too late to abort the blast-off. Far too late . . . far, far too late . . .

'Andy? *Andy!* Are you OK?'

'What? Oh aye. Sorry. What was it you said?'

'I thought we'd lost you there,' said Pascoe. 'I asked you: What are you going to do about it?'

Dalziel regarded Pascoe with the exasperated affection he had bestowed on him ever since their first almost disastrous encounter. He'd thought then that mebbe the bugger was too clever for his own good, and now he'd got the firm evidence. The lad had sat down and worked out everything, method, motive, the lot. Jealous resentment, a jape that went wrong, the use of a diuretic in the coffee, everything had been there in his theoretical model. Only, that was all it had been to Pascoe. A model theatre into which he could dangle his puppets and watch them dance as he pulled their strings. He hadn't been able to take the next small step and see that if a model works, then mebbe the reality works too, and perhaps there was no need of puppets, because there was a real culprit out there, waiting to be caught.

And because he was so obsessed by clever trickery, he had thought to authenticate it all by dropping fat old Andy Dalziel into the play, a figure so obviously real that not even the suspicious and distrustful Druson could believe he was anyone's puppet.

So what *was* he going to do? In a way, the ultimate disappointment was that the lad needed to ask. Dalziel didn't believe in practising everything he preached, but the golden rule he'd recently re-proached Pascoe with was twenty-two carat. You don't drop your mates in it.

And anyway, whether he'd intended it or not, a deal had been struck back there on *Europa*.

'Do?' he growled. 'What can I do? You're in with the dirty tricks mob now, lad, and I don't want to end my days with a poisoned umbrella up my gunga!'

'Andy, you don't really believe that?' protested Pascoe. 'No threats. It's what you think right that matters.'

'I think it right to go on living as long as I can,' said Dalziel. 'All right, all right. For Christ's sake, take that hang-dog look off your face before the RSPCA puts you down. I'll keep stumm. And I'll forgive you. It's my own fault, I suppose. Teach a fledgling to fly and you've got to expect he'll crap on you some day. But I'm not going to kiss and make up, if that's what you're after!'

Pascoe's face split in a smile of undisguised, uncontrived relief.

'I should have known better than to mess around with you, Andy,' he said. 'I thought . . . well, to tell the truth, I thought you'd be so rusty, I wouldn't have any bother. And I wanted to see you again, and to work with you. Honestly, that was part of it. But I underestimated that nose of yours. It must be the weightlessness that got it back working at full power.'

'Not just the nose,' muttered Dalziel.

'Sorry?'

'Nowt. Summat I meant to ask. *Europa*, it doesn't just mean Europe, does it?'

'No. It's the name of a Phoenician princess who got ravished by Zeus in the form of a bull.'

'Oh aye. I thought I recollected something like that,' said Dalziel with a certain complacency.

Pascoe turned his head to look back to the moon. They were far too distant now to see the orbiting spaceship, and the moon itself had declined from a world to a silver apple hanging in space.

'I can't believe I've really been there,' he said dreamily. 'I used to look up at it when I was a kid and have these fantasies. Now I'll be able to look up and remember . . . but I doubt if I'll believe what I remember. What about you, Andy?'

'Oh, I'll believe right enough,' said Dalziel, who was lying back with his eyes shut, thinking of Nurse Montague and a nice little surprise he might be bringing home for her. 'Like yon Yank said, one small step for a man, one mighty jump for an old copper.'

'Leap.'

'Eh?'

'*Leap,*' repeated Pascoe with that stern pedantry which neither age nor advancement had been able to rid him of. 'I think you'll find it was *one giant leap*, not *one mighty jump*.'

'You speak for yourself, lad,' said Andrew Dalziel.

THE END

REGINALD
HILL

"The master of form and sorcerer of style."

—*The New York Times Book Review*

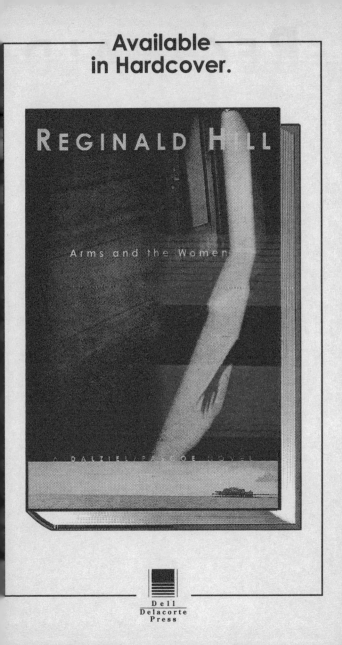